Magick Broom Publishers

Regal House, 30 Woodbank Drive Nottingham NG8 2QU

Prefix: 978-0-9934178

ISBN: 978-0-9934178-6-3

www.dragonstonebook.com

Book 1: Dragonstone - The Legend of the Half Prophecy

Book 2: Dragonstone - The Alchemists' Riddle

THIRD EDITION

I want to honour the memory of my beloved
father and express my deepest gratitude to my mother for
her unwavering support.

Strive, no matter what!

CHAPTER ONE

REVELATION

'Are you certain, Astrophos?'

'I'm afraid so, Cosmolos.'

'How in the Magicklands could this have happened? Surely, we should have spotted the scroll mapping their magick potential?' said Astrophos worriedly.

Cosmolos stood across from Astrophos in the back chamber. They had just finished testing the latest astrological equipment: the two-way astroscope.

'Well, they aren't the first magickal family to be missed,' said Cosmolos. 'At least they have been found so that they can begin training,' he said.

'Very true, but none of the scrolls has been purposely tampered with like this! Surely they would have been lost if we hadn't received their letter by chance?' replied Astrophos, sounding very concerned.

'Fortune indeed,' said Cosmolos. 'However, you know the will of the universe. When someone is truly destined to be somewhere, no matter what happens, you will always end up where you are supposed to be,' he explained as they walked under the large archway back into the main room. 'Nevertheless, I agree, someone has made considerable efforts to disguise their scroll chart—the likes of which I've never seen before. I have no idea why the dark charm broke when the letter arrived; it is a point for meditation.'

Cosmolos proceeded to set up the room. He added frankincense to the burner on one of the smaller altars on the left side of the chamber, and the sweet fragrance spread throughout the air. Instantaneously, a mist filled the room, creating a serene atmosphere perfect for meditation.

There was a moment of silence before Cosmolos spoke again.

'My dear friend, I'm afraid this raises other questions: Why would someone do such a thing? Who would do such a thing? How did they get access to our room? And what do they know that we don't or, at the very least, suspect?' he snarled that someone had forced their way into their sacred domain, tampered with their equipment, and left without a trace.

'Furthermore, how on earth was the house disguised against the Trackers?' Astrophos interjected. 'OK, some scrolls are lost or damaged; families move on before their time, but the Trackers always find their man—or family, for that matter! It is frustrating that magick cannot work properly in the Plainlands; we could do our work much more efficiently if it did.'

Astrophos held his hand to his head and rubbed it to remove the tension that had suddenly formed there.

'Yes, what a sad day,' said Cosmolos solemnly. 'I don't know how they live without magick in their lives. Life seems so much more complicated. As for the house, there is a possible answer for why the Trackers couldn't find them. However, I will have to go and investigate,' he continued, revealing nothing more, furthering the frustration of his close friend Astrophos.

Astrophos and Cosmolos began to pace around the beautiful, circular, wooden coned room. It was intricately designed with beautifully crafted patterning and a rich tapestry of golden symbols that were bold and powerful and had meanings intended to protect, enhance, and energise the room.

Cosmolos' embroidered dark blue robes flowed lightly behind him. In his profoundly focused state, he avoided the centre altar table well. He stopped. His deep blue eyes cast a gaze as if to look beyond the confines of the room, twisting his beard as he did so.

'Just... just look at this chart. It's incredible!' The excitement began to rise from the pit of his stomach.

Astrophos raised his hand and muttered, 'Venio.' Immediately, the scroll rolled up and swiftly flew over, landing gently in his hand.

He opened it and carefully analysed the astrological correspondences; his eyes widened gleefully at what he saw, and then a shudder went down his spine. Simultaneously, goose pimples crawled along his skin like some great ancestor had walked through him from beyond the grave.

'Could he be the one mentioned in the Half Prophecy?' Astrophos added.

I'm not sure, my dear friend. Others have similarly exciting astrological information, so it isn't easy to tell. If I remember rightly, the Half Prophecy mentions the "man born of dragon," though sadly, we cannot decipher this. The other half of the Prophecy mysteriously disappeared.'

'What does the pendulum say?' asked Astrophos.

'It hasn't said anything in a while.' Guilt suddenly masked itself over Cosmolos' face, tinged with regret. 'I think it is annoyed by its last divining mission and refuses to talk. I suppose winding him up like that wasn't the brightest idea,' he confessed. 'Well, I should apologise, I suppose - alcohol never really agreed with me, although I do like mead or a drop of sherry.' They laughed.

Fresh colours started to appear on their faces. Cosmolos and Astrophos looked kindly upon each other and smiled.

The tension previously formed on Astrophos' brow began dissipating as he relaxed.

The Mages sat down whilst the firedrakes zipped around the room, dimming the flaming torches and allowing meditation.

Astrophos closed his eyes and began to meditate whilst Cosmolos searched the room for answers. He hoped the answer was hiding somewhere, like a book off a shelf, so that he could summon it quickly.

His blue eyes scanned the room, admiring the solid oak struts curving upwards to form a dome-like country cottage.

The altar table was positioned behind him. His gaze took him to the adjacent stained glass window encircled the top half of the room. The colours in the window changed intuitively, depending on their thoughts.

The colours become more intense during times of deep reflection. An interchange of purple and violet light emanated from the window, indicating they were in deep, magickal thought.

Momentarily, Cosmolos noticed a bit of dirt that had somehow attached itself to his night-blue robes. With a waft of his hand, the dust vanished.

He pushed back his white hair and took some deep breaths.

Cosmolos was very particular about everything: how he appeared, how the room looked, and how everything was organised. Astrophos wasn't as meticulous. He was untidy and often eccentric, like a mad scientist when he was working. Therefore, it was strange for him to be the one meditating.

An hour had passed, and it seemed that no solution would come. Cosmolos then spoke.

'Astrophos!!' he said suddenly, startling his friend. We must consult with Artuk Ra. He might be able to interpret some of these complex alignments in this chart. After all, the Egyptians are masters of this kind of phenomenon.'

'Agreed,' said Astrophos. 'We must also consult the Head of School, the Head of the Elemental Houses and the Governing Council of Elders.'

'Yes, but let's see what Artuk has to say first. We wouldn't want to appear overzealous or, even worse, idiotic, like a couple of over-enthused teenage magicians with their first fire element experiment. Previous Astro-Mages have made wild claims about various charts and paid for it dearly with their jobs. If there is any truth to the alignment, we must proceed cautiously. Let events unfold, naturally,' he said, as the stained glass window suddenly turned into a vibrant yellow to indicate that logic had entered his thinking.

'Agreed,' said Astrophos, realising that over-reacting could have severe consequences. 'In the meantime, we must move forward and introduce the family to our world,' he said excitedly. 'I have to admit; I like to see the confused look on their faces when they realise they have magickal abilities. Not to mention the shock when they see our world in all its glory,' said Astrophos teasingly.

'Yes,' said Cosmolos with youthful enthusiasm. It brings me joy to my heart to see folk realise there's something better than the mundane realms of the Plainlands,' he said. His eyes glistened like the birth of two new suns, and the stained glass window shone a glowing red and bright gold, showing enthusiasm and power.

'Oh, yes! I nearly forgot. I will investigate my theory into why the Trackers couldn't find them. If I am correct, it will be a clever form of hoodwinking—devious, though brilliant!'

'What is it? Tell me,' he said excitedly.

'Ah, my friend, in time—in time....'

Astrophos didn't look impressed. Instead, his face seemed to contort like a teenager being grounded.

'Do you know something, Astrophos?' Cosmolos asked, clearly distracted. 'You know, the most impressive thing about the Astroscope?'

'You mean that it can display and project the star positioning as if we were back at that moment in history?' I did come up with the idea,' he said proudly.

'Yes, my apologies, my dear friend. But this should help me finally prove the link between past and present events. However, there is much work to be done,' said Cosmolos, taking over with excitable emotion.

'First things first,' blurted Astrophos, taking on the role of an organised thinker. 'We need to contact the communication department to deliver the acceptance letter. Also, the relevant details about the city tour and visit have to be sent. And, oh, yes! Don't forget the letter to the apothecary; they must prepare the potion so the transition can occur.'

'I'll prepare and send the scroll,' Cosmolos enthused. Quickly, he went to the parchment table, picked out a sheet, and said, 'Annoto, imprimo invitatium.'

The parchment flew over to the writing mangle, and it casually began to print the invitation.

'And the scroll to Artuk,' said Astrophos.

'Artuk, annoto, imprimo, decidio,' said Cosmolos; another parchment was printed.

Cosmolos picked up the neatly sealed scrolls and took them to the scroll porter. He slid one of the scrolls upright into the bracket and said, 'Incedo Artuk Ra.' The scroll dematerialised into light blue sparks with specks of orange and vanished downwards towards its destination. He then sent the second scroll.

'The job is done. All we can do now is wait—and Astrophos, my dear friend.'

'Yes.'

'I think this year will be very interesting!'

Chapter Two

CONCERN

The sun had already begun to rise in the Great City, though its rays hadn't quite reached the Political Quarter.

The air was crisp and fresh, and the sky started to glow its usual vivid blue colour. The smell of flowers from the lavender fields caught the easterly wind, imbuing the area with a sense of peace and tranquillity.

Markus Rome, a political officer to the English Quarter, had just reached the Great Gate, where Sedrick, the Viking guard, kept watch.

Sedrick came out of his security box, standing very tall and broad.

'Good Morning, Markus,' Sedrick chirped.

'Morning,' said Markus with a distracted tone.

'Are you—OK, Markus?' he said, concerned.

'Yeah, I suppose. I've had a bad night's sleep and a very early appointment with the Governor.'

'Oh dear,' he said sympathetically.

'I have a new batch of *Percy Pick-Up Juice*,' he said, pointing to the bottle with purple and turquoise liquid. The colours circulated in the bottle, mixed, and separated again.

'Go on, have it. It's the new brand formula. It works; look at me,' he said, beaming as the sun had already reached him.

He stood up, revealing his massive frame. His silver chainmail was spotless, and his helmet, sword, axe and spears sat comfortably beside him.

'Wait a moment,' he continued, 'It's a bit early to be having a meeting—it's not even 6 a.m.! So what does he want with you at this time?'

'Not sure,' said Markus shiftily. 'Though I must be hurrying along,' he said, wanting to get away before any more questions could be asked.

'OK, I understand,' he winked. 'Magick business, I presume.'

Markus momentarily said nothing.

'Thanks for the drink,' he said, changing the subject.

'That's OK, I have three crates at home. You know the routine, Markus,' he continued.

Markus walked over to the centre of the Great Gate and muttered something, but what he said was not recognisable to Sedrick's ears. Finally, the Iron Gate, as it is more commonly known, opened, and Markus walked in.

'I'll be seeing you later then,' Sedrick shouted.

'OK, though I might need something more than a *Percy Pick-Up* when I've finished,' he bellowed.

He gulped down the drink Sedrick gave him, accurate to the Viking's word. He felt a warm, tingly sensation rising from his feet and finishing at his head. Even the smell of Lavender seemed more intense.

He smiled. The gate closed, and the city symbol separated in the middle united. The emblem was a massive red dragon. Its claws grasped half a scroll, which represented the Half Prophecy.

Markus walked down a dusty pathway, separating Sedrick from himself. The track now turned into a large, smooth, stone road.

The Political Quarter was located in the middle of the city. Each quarter was linked to the other city quarters by a separate gateway.

The sun had risen sufficiently, and its rays had passed Markus, covering the city.

Alert after taking his *Percy Pick-Up Juice*, Markus noticed the grandeur of his surroundings.

He walked down the Parthenon Main Street. It was tranquil as most people were asleep. A gust of wind caught his wavy, blond hair, which covered his eyes, so he brushed it back with his hands.

The road was long. At its centre was an enormous Parthenon building, which stood on a massive marble clifftop that seemed impossible to climb.

On either side of the main street, entrances to other avenues were perfectly straight, branching out to smaller ones.

Merchants, bankers, tradesmen, and women conducted business in different buildings on each road. These buildings resembled miniature versions of the Parthenon, each with a unique design and signage.

Markus paused to adjust his clothing, styled after early 1800s fashion reminiscent of a Jane Austen novel, as he caught his reflection in a window.

He turned around and gazed at the Parthenon in the distance. It was constructed from polished white marble, but its size made it seem threatening. It resembled the impregnable castles of ancient times. In comparison, its Athenian counterpart appeared like a small-scale replica.

The Parthenon was where the Magickal Peace Alliance was signed to ensure magickal cooperation amongst magickal nations; it was also the parliament of the entire Great City.

Suddenly, a voice startled Markus, which increased his heart rate and made him more flustered.

'Allo Markus,' spoke Napoleon as the statue's malleable stone-like substance suddenly took form.

'Hello, Napoleon. Your turn, is it then?'

'Oui Monsieur... I couldn't rest; the uthers were sleeping. So what are you doing before zee shops open?' asked a surprised Napoleon.

'Meeting with the Governor,' Markus said, feeling déjà vu after his conversation with Sedrick.

'Mon Dieu! What—at ziss time!' his surprise clearly showed. 'It must be important. Be on your guard—take no prisoners,' he said, reminiscing about his French imperial days. 'I'll be 'ere for you, Monsieur, if you need me.'

'Thank you, Napoleon... I'll bear that in mind,' he said courteously. The concrete formed back into a solid state.

Markus hoped he wouldn't encounter anybody else on his journey, so he hurried along, hoping no one could distract him.

He arrived at the next statue, though no one came through. He turned left and walked down one of the smaller side streets. Finally, Markus arrived at another gate and whispered the exact words he did at the main entrance to the city.

When it opened, Marcus walked in. He was now in the Political Government-Building Sector, where prominent governors and staff handled the city's day-to-day operations.

The Governors' offices were much more prominent and grander than their staffing counterparts and were located some distance apart.

Markus' pulse and temperature rose again, but they didn't recede. His heartbeat got stronger and louder, and a vein on the side of his head began to throb.

He approached the gate, and his hands and brow became clammy as he approached the Governor's house. The house guard came out.

'Ah, Markus, the Governor informed me you will arrive early. I have to say he doesn't seem too happy. You'd better come in,' said the guard. 'I suggest you hurry as he has to go away on business to the royal houses later this morning.'

Markus said nothing. His face suddenly went pale, and he wished Sedrick was handing him another *Percy Pick-Up Juice* or something stronger.

Markus walked up the marble steps past the main wooden gate into the hallway.

The wooden door suddenly closed as it was aware of his presence. However, despite the cooling temperature of the atmosphere, a chill persisted that failed to calm his nerves.

One of the two sleeping firedrakes opened a sleepy eye. It looked at the other drake and then at Markus. You could sense it wasn't impressed, as he knew it had to get up to tend to the torches.

The drake hovered casually over each torch that instantly lit as it passed. It stopped at the final torch and bathed in the glistening flames before returning to sleep. The air warmed slightly, though a chill remained.

'Come through,' said a commanding, echoing voice in the distance.

'You wanted to see me, Lord Balfour,' Markus said, pretending his invite was a surprise. The Governor said nothing.

Markus walked along a short corridor, where red and purple material hung down the walls, covering small sections on either side of the torches.

He walked into a massive rectangular room with no windows. Several pillars supported the roof surrounding the edge of the room, and four larger ones sat inside, forming the corners of a large square. A stone altar lay on the south side and was decorated with various magical implements.

Lord Balfour stood to set the table. Three black candles, a miniature cauldron, a dagger and an incense burner were placed perfectly towards the back.

Various gold symbols were strategically embedded into the walls and altar. Each character represented magickal significance that helped support and empower the magician in his work. Furthermore, triangular-marked giant banners indicated the directions of north, south, east, and west, further reinforcing the rituals.

'Follow me,' commanded Lord Balfour. Markus remained quiet and did as he was instructed. They walked beyond the south corner of the room and through another door—the corridor was divided into more passageways. They took the middle passage. It got colder as they walked along, despite the firedrakes floating in front of them, lighting the torches as they went.

A sign gave off orange and red sparks on the right-hand side, and a voice from nowhere announced, 'Welcome, Lord Balfour—12th Governor of the English Quarter—to your office,'

The door opened, and both of them entered.

The Governor walked behind his desk and sat down. After a moment of silence, Lord Balfour spoke.

'Please sit down,' Markus promptly did as he was told. 'I received your message scroll last night. Markus, are you sure?'

'Yes, my source is one hundred per cent accurate, my Lord,' said Markus confidently.

The Governor's calm tone settled his nerves, and he slowly relaxed.

'But how is this so? How was the invisibility enchantment hiding their Scroll Chart broken? The spellwork should have been beyond Astrophos and Cosmolos' knowledge—it is quite disturbing! Did you follow my instructions to the letter?' he asked accusingly. It took me years to find these old magickal documents.

'I'm not sure, my Lord, what happened, exactly. 'It had something to do with the letter of inquiry to the school they received from the mother. I am uncertain what the connection is!' Markus's heart rate returned to normal, knowing the Governor believed him.

'The child and the rest of the family will receive their invite for the usual tour before entering our world for magickal learning,' he concluded.

'You know it was for the protection of the child, don't you? I'm not sure what kind of protection I can offer him now. It was best for all concerned he stayed away from our world. A whole can of worms is about to be opened.' The Governor's usually assured demeanour was tainted by fear and sadness.

'But we are not a hundred per cent sure that it is him, my Lord. No one knows for sure.'

'True, but if it is, he will be in grave danger, and I won't be able to stop the others.' Markus became slightly agitated again.

'You must somehow keep watch. Stay out of sight until we know more,' Balfour instructed.

'Yes, my Lord, of course.'

'OK, Markus, you must return by Portal. Ensure you are not seen; the city must be bustling now.'

Balfour's mind was working away, planning the following stages.

'But I can't travel by Portal out of here. It is the Governor's privilege,' he said, reminding Balfour.

'Ah yes—well, you can use mine. 'Come with me,' he said, rediscovering his authoritative tone.

Both Markus and the Governor left the room. The door closed, and the voice from the door said: 'Take care—until your return, my Lord.'

Markus and Balfour moved quickly into the empty room opposite.

Balfour had fiery red hair like the firedrakes and was slightly stockier and taller than Markus.

Balfour raised his hand, pointed his index finger and said, 'Portus!' A black portal opened in the middle of the room.

'Home,' replied Markus.

At that moment, the back of the Portal became a dullish grey, and he could just about see the inside of a house.'

'Thank you, my Lord,' he said politely.

'I must consult the fires first, and then I will send you a secured scroll with your instructions.'

'Yes, my Lord,' he said as he raised his leg to put it into the hole, then vanished through the Portal.

With Marcus gone, Balfour hurried back along the corridor and into the main room.

He walked into the centre of the four main pillars, announcing: 'I wish to consult with the fires of Esrid.' Steps immediately formed in the middle of the square, and Balfour walked down into a separate chamber.

He wore some navy blue robes and a matching cloak covering his head.

He picked up a shoulder-length staff and said something inaudible as Markus did.

A stone wall submerged into the ground, and Balfour stepped into another chamber. It was as cold as the other rooms. As he entered, the torch flames automatically lit and dimmed.

A bright red carpet with a marble pit approximately waist-high appeared on the floor towards the back wall.

He stood in silence, closed his eyes and entered a meditative state.

Moments later, his eyelids moved rapidly. His jaw was firm, and his breathing was deep and purposeful. Then, with his energy focused, he raised his arms and said.

'By the fires of Esrid, I summon ye—come, COME TO ME!' The fires stirred, rose and *cracked*. *'BY THE POWER OF THE FLAME AND BY THE ALL-KNOWING FORCE—I BESEECH THEE—COME—COME AND GUIDE ME AS TO WHAT MUST BE DONE. SO MOTE IT BE!'*

The flames rose even higher with purpose and ferocity. They changed through a variety of colours and finished at a golden orange.

He knelt on the carpet, and a voice began to speak.

CHAPTER THREE
THE BULLY

It was a Friday, late June 1983. The bell rang for the final lesson in a small Derbyshire school called Little Middlings. Apart from a few, most of the children had gone to class.

'Hey, Tommy—get 'ere. Ya trying to run away again?' shouted Vinnie Sykes, the school bully.

'I-i-i-it wasn't me, V-V-Vinnie, I swear,' he quivered.

'Yeah—I believe ya,' he smiled. Tommy looked like he would get away with it when Vinnie laughingly concluded, 'NOT!' Vinnie went for poor Tommy.

Before he could grab him, the fear within Tommy sped him away, and he ran as fast as his legs could carry him.

The teachers' offices were behind Vinnie, so he could not reach their protection. He ran to the only place he could go, a small alleyway separating the junior school's two halves.

He turned left to run down the path—he was almost there. *I could reach the teachers from the front of the school.* He had covered three-quarters of the distance when Vinnie's three stooges, Baines, Smith, and Howard, stood in the middle, talking about football.

Poor Tommy's face was plain to see; it was as if someone had stabbed him and put salt in the wound.

'Stop him!' shouted Vinnie to his oversized friends.

'Going somewhere, Tommy?' Baines said with the smuggest look on his face.

'Yeah, yeah,' said Smith and Howard.

'Oh, poor little Tommy Thumb,' said Vinnie sarcastically as they surrounded and circled Tommy like a pack of wild hyenas ready for the kill.

He didn't know where to look, turning his head as best as possible to see what the bullies had in store for him.

Tommy's heart was beating so forcefully and rapidly that he was convinced it could pound the four if he took it out.

Vinnie started singing: 'Tommy Thumb, Tommy Thumb, where are you? Here he is...', but before he finished, Vinnie's fist flew out, catching him fully in his stomach. Tommy doubled up quickly; the pain was clear to see. Baines also lashed out with his foot straight into Tommy's side.

Tommy started crying and didn't know what to do. He couldn't run or hide. The only choice was deciding which side hurt the most to hold. Then Howard thrust his elbow straight into his back.

'Ahh!' Tommy screamed and cried as his captors showed no mercy. The evil twinkle in his eyes looked more menacing with each blow.

Smith was about to delegate further punishment when Vinnie raised his fist, ready to punch him in the face.

Tommy knew the punch was coming, but he steeled himself instead of cowering in fear. With self-assurance, he closed his eyes, ready to face the incoming attack confidently.

Suddenly, Vinnie went flying, tripping over Tommy as he passed, whilst scuffing his hands as he fell to the ground dazed. He turned around.

'Charlie?' he said, as his eyes began to focus.

'Get him!' Baines descended on Charlie like a grizzly bear about to maul its victim.

A swift uppercut came in, though Charlie was equal to it. Only the tiny gust of wind from the passing fist caught him in the face. Charlie raised his leg quickly toward Baines' nether regions, and he instantaneously doubled up in pain, just as little Tommy had moments earlier.

Immediately after, Smith launched himself to rugby tackle Charlie. Charlie, again too clever and quick for his thuggish friends, moved to the side, pushing Smith into the wall as he did so.

Howard adopted a defensive stance, his fists raised and ready for combat. With a sudden burst of energy, he launched a right punch aimed at Charlie's face, followed by a left aimed at his stomach. However, Charlie quickly anticipated Howard's moves and deftly sidestepped both punches.

As Howard tried to regain his footing, Charlie stepped forward with a swift right punch. In a surprising move, he lifted his leg and delivered a powerful kick to Howard's shin, causing him to wince in pain and grab his leg.

Seizing the moment, Charlie followed up with a left punch that landed squarely on Howard's jaw, sending him crashing to the floor.

As Howard lay on the ground, Charlie spun around with lightning speed, narrowly avoiding a punch from Vinnie, who had been waiting for his chance to attack. With a swift kick aimed at Vinnie's midsection, Charlie sent him tumbling backwards effectively.

'CHARLIE STUART!' shouted an authoritative voice at the top of the alleyway.

Charlie spun around to see the headmaster standing there.

Little Tommy picked himself up and ran towards the headmaster, shouting, 'Sir, sir, it was Vinnie and his friends—they got me and were beating me up.'

'You snitch, Tommy,' shouted Vinnie, his eyes burning ferociously.

'Cha...Cha, Charlie came to help me,' he stuttered, catching his breath.

'He was amazing, sir, and he took all four of 'em on—he stopped 'em.' Tommy's eye was beginning to darken, and the colour spread, touching the freckles on the upper part of his cheek.

'Is this true, Stuart?' the headmaster queried.

'Yes, sir, I was on my way to woodwork when I heard somebody shouting, so I went to help,' he said proudly.

'You got all four of them, you say,' said the headmaster, impressed.

'Yes, sir, he got 'em all, sir,' said Tommy, temporarily forgetting his pain while smiling at Charlie simultaneously. 'Thank you, Charlie! No one has ever stuck up for me before.'

'No problem,' said Charlie. 'It's a pity that they've never been caught before. You stick near me, Tommy, and it won't be long until our year leaves.'

Tommy was starting to feel refreshed despite his battered state.

'Vinnie...Baines, Smith, and Howard!' the headmaster said as if announcing a death sentence. 'To my office—NOW,' he said as his kindly old face crimpled, showing his anger and disapproval.

'Charlie, you follow too as I would like a word.'

Charlie knew he would get a talking-to for fighting despite his noblest efforts.

Vinnie and his band of thugs followed the headmaster, glaring at Tommy first and then at Charlie with an evil look.

Vinnie was about to mutter something to Tommy when Charlie leant forward quickly and purposefully, reminding Vinnie of what he had done to them. Vinnie looked defeated and didn't look as confident as he did at the beginning of the encounter.

They walked towards the headmaster's office, and little Tommy went to see one of the other teachers to tend to his wounds.

While Charlie stood outside, Vinnie and his gang were inside the headmaster's office.

The door was shut, and the headmaster was shouting, venting his anger at what they had done.

Charlie could hear him shouting, stating how he disliked bullies and would write to their parents. He also gave them playtime detention so they couldn't bully, and lines and litter-picking duty until the end of the year, which was only one week away.

'Charlie Stuart, you may enter!'

Charlie opened the door and walked in as Vinnie and his friends left.

'Close the door,' said the headmaster.

'Now, Charlie—that was a courageous thing that you did, though it is school policy that I inform your parents of what has happened here. Officially, we, the school, shouldn't condone the use of violence, though I admit I was quite impressed at how you handled yourself.' The headmaster's words were music to his ears.

'Kickboxing, sir—Mum sent me to classes since I was four.'

'Four?!' he said, nearly choking on the cup of tea he had made himself.

'Yes, sir, Mum said not to say I did it as it would cause others to come and want to fight you, so I stayed quiet about it.'

The headmaster looked at him with some surprise at the maturity of his statement.

'Well, well, Charlie. You will go far in your new school with an attitude. Which school are you going to again?'

'Compton Comprehensive, sir.'

'Ah yes, a good school, Charlie; you will do fine, I'm sure.'

The headmaster took out a pen and began to write. He said nothing as he scribbled for a few minutes.

Charlie examined the soft, white hair on the headmaster's head. He was amazed that it was all there. All the older people he knew looked like monks with shiny scalps and hair on either side or had a few strands combed diagonally in the hope that it would cover the head.

'Take this note to Mrs Harrington: this will explain briefly what has happened and that you were also with me. That is all, Charlie.'

'Thank you, sir.' The headmaster just smiled, and Charlie left the room.

'CHARLIE STUART!' said a voice in the main corridor.

'Where *have* you been?' *Not again,* Charlie thought. He looked up and saw Mrs Harrington. Charlie didn't like her because she prodded him when she told him off. He turned around, looked at the headmaster's door, and then at Mrs Harrington.

'Er, the headmaster's office, Miss,' he said sarcastically.

'Don't you cheek me, young man,' she said sharply. 'Been in trouble, have we?' raising her prodding finger like some viper about to strike its prey. 'Some of you lot won't get anywhere in life... You mark my words,' she barked.

How dare she? he thought.

'I have a letter from Mr Otterwell explaining what has happened!'

'Really,' she said in an equally sarcastic tone. 'Well—you have assignment work to catch up with.'

'Work?' he said, sounding confused. 'But we finish next week,' he said suddenly, feeling deflated.

'That is no excuse—and it has to be in on Monday.' Charlie groaned and muttered something under his breath.

Mrs Harrington threw out her arm, but Charlie instinctively moved out of the way.

'Here is your final coursework.'

Charlie picked up the paper and read it as Mrs Harrington walked off. *That's not good*, he thought, and he began visualising making martial arts moves on his teacher.

I will be away from that old bag one more week, thought Charlie.

Before thinking further on the subject, he heard the bell ringing outside.

He looked at his watch and noticed a crack on its screen he had from the fight, but he could still make out the time, and it was home time.

He ran towards the main gate, where his older brother Emmanuel and younger sister Lucy greeted him.

'Come on, Charlie—Mum's making dinner: egg, bacon, sausage, mushrooms, beans and toast.'

'Mmmm! Great! My favourite!'

His stomach began to rumble. After all, fighting was hungry work!

'Have I got a story for you, Brother!' said Charlie, smiling.

'What's that then, Brother?' asked Emmanuel. Charlie closed the gate behind him and told his brother what had happened.

'Nice one,' Emmanuel said upon hearing the story. High five that one,' he continued as their hands connected mid-air.

Lucy didn't seem too bothered, though she was pleased she had an older brother who could look after her.

'Good man, Mr Otterwell,' said Emmanuel.

'A good man, indeed. I'm not sure what Mum will make of it, though—ah well, it's happened now,' he said casually.

Fortunately, they didn't live far away and arrived home moments later.

CHAPTER FOUR

RECORDED DELIVERY

When they arrived at the front door, Charlie smelled the food escaping from under the door and an opened window. The enticing smell drew them towards the house.

Emmanuel searched his pockets for the house keys but couldn't find them.

'Hurry up, I am starving,' said Charlie.

'I bet fighting four people made you hungry,' said Emmanuel as they laughed.

He found the keys in his bag and opened the door. To the left was a tiny porch with a small front room. They walked through another door, and they were in the living room. An open staircase led to the bedrooms, visible from the living room.

'Hello, my lovelies—have you had a good day then?' their mother asked.'

'Charlie was fighting today,' said Lucy quickly.

'Did you have to tell her now?' Charlie said. 'You are a snitch sometimes, you know,' he said, sounding cross.

'WHAT?! YOU'VE BEEN FIGHTING? YOU ARE SO GROUNDED,' said Mrs Stuart angrily. 'Are you OK? What happened? Couldn't you have waited a week?' she said, concerned and frustrated.

'Mum, it was that bully Vinnie. He and his cronies were picking on little Tommy from down the road. They had him on the ground, kicking him and everything!'

'Oh, really!' said his mum, unconvinced. 'I knew kick-boxing would get you into trouble—if your father were here....' She stopped and seemed saddened by what she had said.

'Well, he's not here, is he, Mum?' said Emmanuel, getting angry.

'Well, it's the truth...' Charlie shouted. 'And Mr Otterwell was--' But before he could finish, the phone rang. She picked it up.

'Hello, can I help you?' she said. 'Yes, this is Victoria Stuart.' There was a pause. 'Ah, headmaster, I guess you are calling about Charlie's little incident today.' There was another pause whilst she listened to the headmaster. 'Yes... yes... yes,' she continued, 'Oh, I see—is the poor kid OK now?' Charlie's ears perked up as he knew the headmaster was explaining exactly what had happened. 'Oh, thank you, headmaster...I shall tell him—thanks again, bye!'

'Charlie, the headmaster is very pleased with you. Tommy's parents called the headmaster to thank you for saving him. Tommy was bullied throughout the year, but he never told his parents until now. Tommy's mother, Hilda, will write to Vinnie's parents to tell them what she thinks of their son. Also, Vinnie and friends got the cane for their actions, so it must have been bad,' she said.

'Well, then, Mum—do you believe me now? It wasn't my fault!'

'It seems you did play the hero, though be careful in...'

'Does this mean....' said Charlie, interrupting.

'Yes, you aren't grounded,' she interrupted him.

'YES!' said Charlie, scoring yet another victory.

'Charlie, Charlie,' he turned around. It was his youngest sister, Olivia.

'Awe, my baby,' said Charlie excitedly.

'She's not a baby,' said Lucy, who decided to join the conversation again.

Well, she was right. Olivia was three and a half, Lucy five, Charlie ten and Emmanuel the oldest at eleven. Olivia looked like Charlie, with lovely blonde hair and beautiful green eyes. However, Emmanuel and Lucy took after their mother with dark, mysterious brown eyes and hair.

It was 3:50 p.m., and they sat for dinner in the living room on a small table opposite the sofa.

They were all quiet as they tucked into their food, which smelled even more intense now that it was in front of them.

Emmanuel thought he was in paradise, and Charlie picked up some bacon and put it in his mouth. The fatty flavour tantalised his taste buds as he swallowed it, followed by sausage, egg, and toast.

Lucy dropped some of her toast on the brown flower-patterned carpet and went to pick it up off the floor.

'Leave it, sweetheart, and we'll pick it up at the end. We don't want to catch any germs now, do we?'

'Mmmmm, Mum, you're the greatest at cooking,' said Charlie, feeling rewarded for his hard work. His Mum smiled and started humming approvingly at what had just been announced.

Once they had finished, they started to take the pots into the kitchen, but Emmanuel began to go upstairs because he hated washing up. His mum's verbal summoning quickly brought him back to the kitchen.

As they were tidying up, the doorbell rang, followed by a knocking at the door.

'Charlie, is Lee coming round today?' she said, referring to his best friend.

'No, Mum, that's tomorrow as he's helping me with a project—I'll tell you about it later.'

'No problem,' she replied.

Victoria went through the first door, closed it, and opened the front door.

'Recorded delivery for Victoria Stuart,' said Jack, the postal worker.

'Oh—the post is late.' *I wonder who this is from*, she pondered.

'Sign here, Victoria,' said the postman. He passed her the form to sign.

She did so and then collected the round-tube parcel. She looked at the postage mark Nottingham, which had a stamped dragon coat of arms next to it.

'Thank you, Jack,' said Victoria, slightly confused. *What could it be?* she thought.

She closed the door behind her and headed for the kitchen cupboard. She opened the top drawer, picked a knife to break a small seal that kept the tube together, and pulled out the contents. Inside were a letter and some other documents.

She began to read. Victoria's jaw dropped as she couldn't fully absorb the information. The other children were utterly oblivious to what was happening whilst they were tidying up. Even Emmanuel got carried away with the cleaning, getting the vacuum cleaner and managing to vacuum the entire carpet.

'Come on, gang,' said Charlie, taking on the role of leader and coordinator. 'Working as a team, we'll soon get this done,' he said enthusiastically.

Victoria read and re-read the letter to ensure that she hadn't hallucinated. She even checked the packaging to *ensure that it wasn't a fake. But it was a recorded delivery*; it *couldn't be a joke,* she thought.

'Anything else?' said Emmanuel.

Victoria said nothing as she was still in deep thought.

'Earth, calling Mum,' laughed Charlie.

'Ooh, sorry, my lovelies. Just sit down, and I'll make us a cup of tea,' she said with a beaming smile.

'Can I put the TV on?' said Lucy, hoping to catch her favourite television programme.

'Of course, you can, sweetie,' she beamed again.

'Is Mum OK?' said Charlie to Emmanuel.

'I'm not sure, Charlie—she seems very happy, whatever it is! Leave her to it, that's what I say, ' laughed Emmanuel.

'Yes, we might get fish and chips tomorrow,' said Charlie. 'Thinking of your stomach again, Charlie.'

'Yes, I am. I love food,' he retorted. 'Mum always treats us more when she's in a good mood,' he concluded.

'Charlie—could you get Lucy and Olivia's juice out of the fridge, please— thank you!' she said, bouncing around the house and humming a cheerful tune.

'She's lost it,' said Emmanuel.

'Is everything OK, Mum?' asked Charlie.

'Oh, it certainly is,' she giggled, like a teenager just being asked out on a date for the first time. 'I have some great news,' Victoria said eagerly. 'I'll tell you all very soon,' she said, grinning like a Cheshire cat.

The suspense was now killing them all. They had not seen her in such a good mood for a long time.

'Go on, tell us—please!' they all implored.

'I'm afraid you will have to wait. I'm just about to put the kettle on.'

Lucy made a 'tut' noise, showing her disapproval and proceeded to watch the TV. Charlie desperately needed the toilet and hurried upstairs. Emmanuel found himself in the same predicament as his brother. He moved quickly to the downstairs bathroom whilst Olivia was delighted playing with her cuddly bears. She arranged them in a circle and then fed them pretend supper.

Fifteen minutes had passed, and the tension and anticipation had grown so much that it seemed like the house walls were about to burst.

They all gathered in the living room.

'Come on, tell us then,' said Charlie, his frustration had turned to annoyance.

'OK, now that we are all cleaned up and toileted, I can tell you the news I've just received,' she said.

'You mean in that tube that has just arrived,' Emmanuel observed.

'Yes, that is the one,' she confirmed. 'Well, here goes.' She took a deep breath, composed herself, and read the letter aloud.

Dear Victoria Stuart,

Thanks for inquiring about your son's possible attendance at Dragonstone School through our access programme for impoverished families. After careful consideration and consultation with the relevant department, we are delighted to accept your son's admission pending a provisional meeting at the school.

Furthermore, we will also allow your eldest son, Emmanuel, to attend. He must be placed on a fast-track program to catch up with specialist subjects attributed to our school. Your youngest daughter, Lucy, will attend the Junior Dragonstone School program, and our Crèche facilities are available for Olivia at Dragonstone Tots.

In addition, our Provision and Equality Department states that we will assist in providing housing and other financial provisions to ease your transition to the area for families who cannot afford the mandatory attendance fees.

Finally, it is customary for families who live outside the area to attend our two-day programme. The first day consists of a city tour, and proceedings are finalised at the school the following morning. See the attached sheet for details.

We promise an experience that no other school in the country can match.

We are looking forward to meeting you all.

School Headmistress and Principal, Hecate Winslow.

There was complete silence in the room, followed by synchronised jaw-dropping, except for Olivia, who was too young to understand. They all looked aghast, and the silence seemed to last an eternity until:

'Is this a joke?' Emmanuel asked, still not convinced by what he had just heard.

'It certainly isn't, my dear. Here is the letter! Look, read for yourselves,' she said calmly.

Emmanuel and Charlie dashed to get the letter, but their mum raised it before they could grab it.

'Hold your horses; you'll rip the thing if you're not careful. Just calm down, and you can read the letter together.'

She gave the letter to Emmanuel to hold, as he was the oldest. They sat down side-by-side on the sofa. Emmanuel positioned the message so Charlie could read it. It took them a few minutes, and then Charlie spoke.

'Crikey,' he said, taking in the magnitude of what he had just read.

'I know what you mean, Charlie,' said Emmanuel.

'Are we going to go then, Mum?' he asked.

'How can we not?' she exclaimed. It is our ticket to a better life. I have to admit that I was astonished to hear from the school. I just wrote a letter a long time ago explaining our situation. What I put in it must have convinced them. Well, what do you think about it, then?'

'This is amazing! I can't believe it,' said Emmanuel.

'Me too,' said Charlie. 'It's supposed to be the best school in England,' he continued.

'Wait a moment...' said Charlie. 'What about my friends? Will I ever see them again?' Emmanuel looked saddened at what Charlie said.

'Oh yeah, I never thought of that,' replied Emmanuel. The two brothers seemed upset about losing their friends, as they had grown up together.

'Well, we are only in the next county, so I'm sure you will see them at some point.' No one said anything.

Charlie was staring at the floor, replaying old memories of his fun times with his friends. Emmanuel seemed to be doing the same thing.

'I want to go,' said Lucy, already convinced.

'Listen, I tell you what. Let us go on this tour and see the school, and we can decide. I can't say fairer than that. If you both don't like it, we have lost nothing as you still have your schooling arranged for next year. What do you think?' asked Victoria.

'That sounds good to me, Mum. What do you think, Charlie?'

'It's not a good idea—it's a *great* idea!' said Charlie.

All seemed happier with this choice.

'When is the visit arranged for Mum?' said Emmanuel.

'Oh, an excellent point; let me look at the itinerary.'

Victoria pulled out the second item from the tube and studied the paper.

'Ooh, golly—it's Monday, the first of August,' she said excitedly. I suppose term starts again in September, which only leaves a month to prepare—goodness,' she exclaimed.

'Fantastic!' said Charlie, 'I can't wait to look at the school.'

'Me too!' said Emmanuel and Lucy, together.

'Oh, I mustn't forget that I must tell Mr Otterwell about the acceptance to Dragonstone School on Monday,' said Victoria.

It was getting close to six o'clock. Lucy was still hogging the TV, watching her cartoons, and Charlie had gone upstairs to start his project.

He walked into the small, cosy bedroom he shared with his brother. The wallpaper featured pictures of aeroplanes, but they had not changed it for years because they couldn't afford to redecorate.

'How am I supposed to make this when the school is closed?' he shouted, suddenly dawning that he had to create his project. 'Evil hag,' he said, punching the hanging boxing ball as he went red with rage.

It was a hot evening, so he opened the single-glazed windows to air into the room.

Charlie sat down to work on his project; Charlie always struggled with numbers and angles.

Emmanuel explained his predicament and realised he had completed the same task with his friend Jonny in his father's workshop the previous year.

After exploring his old trunk, he found it, giving it to a grateful Charlie.

'Brilliant, thanks, mate!' Charlie said with a look of victory on his face.

'Yeah, just redraw the diagrams, and you'll be fine.'

'Thanks so much! Once we finish our plans, we can relax for the rest of the weekend,' he said.

It didn't take long to copy his brother's plans, and he spent the rest of the evening watching a video before heading to bed.

Charlie, the younger brother, got the lower bunk bed, and Emmanuel lay on the top.

'What a day, hey, Brother?' said Emmanuel.

'Yeah, crazy indeed,' replied Charlie as he turned the light off.

'What do you think about going to Dragonstone?' asked Emmanuel.

'I think it's a brilliant idea! I can't believe they let us in! The more I think about it, the better it sounds to me. If we go, I'll miss my friends, that's for sure,' said Charlie.

'Yeah, I agree, though getting out of this place seems like a good idea,' said Emmanuel. 'Oh, I'm heading out with Jonny, Richie, Graeme and Craig to play five-a-side football, so I'm not coming to kickboxing.'

'Ah, OK, fair enough,' said Charlie.

An hour had passed, and they both lay there thinking about what had happened. Charlie's mind was working through the day's events. He hoped there would be a kickboxing school near where he lived: it was his favourite thing in the world.

Moments later, Charlie heard deeper breathing from above and knew his brother had fallen asleep.

After numerous yawns and stretches, Charlie's eyes became heavy and began to close.

Suddenly, Charlie thought he had spotted a small, shadowy figure and panicked. He quickly buried his head under the duvet.

After a moment, he slowly lowered the cover so that only his eyes were peering over the top. He remained in this position for several minutes, his eyes doing all the work. He was petrified and didn't get out of bed.

The shadow entity was moving around slowly, examining the room. Charlie's eyes widened with fear as the entity approached the bed, but it stopped a couple of feet away. The featureless creature stared at him, and he was so scared that he couldn't even call for help. It vanished a few seconds later.

Some time had passed. Charlie was drifting to sleep, and his eyes closed. With one last effort, he couldn't see anything and convinced himself it was a trick of the mind.

Having conceded defeat to tiredness, he finally closed his eyes and slept.

CHAPTER FIVE
FINAL WEEK

'Charlie, time to get up!' shouted his mother; his alarm went off moments later.

Charlie stretched, yawned and grunted as he opened his weary eyes. *Ah, one more week*, he thought to himself.

Charlie sat up, remembering what he had seen the night before. He then got up and checked under the bed and the cupboard. 'Nothing!' he said as he proceeded to the bathroom.

'One minute,' his brother said in a gargled tone as he brushed his teeth.

Charlie could hear him spitting the contents of his mouth into the sink. Moments later, he left, and Charlie went into the bathroom.

The bathroom was undoubtedly too small and desperately needed decoration. The dull yellow paint on the walls was peeling off, and the windows had spider-like cracks with green mildew growing from the bottom.

Charlie found the bathroom incredibly creepy, so he tried to avoid it as much as possible.

As he descended the stairs for breakfast, he saw his mother setting the table with a smile. Her weekend was filled with cheerful humming and grinning.

Charlie approached his mum, who was five feet tall. He was catching up to her fast despite Emmanuel being an inch taller than Charlie at his age.

'Mmmm, porridge,' he said as he sat down.

'It's the Best breakfast you can have,' she said, smiling again. By the way, Olivia will be going to her today, my lovelies—I have a lot to do.'

After breakfast, they tidied up together, collected their bags and left the house.

Charlie pondered the history of his home, where he and his mother, grandmother, and great-grandmother were all born. However, Charlie's arrival was complicated—his mother had been in labour for over 30 hours.

The day was pretty eventful for Charlie as the news of his acceptance spread like wildfire. The headmaster was especially ecstatic about the whole thing. Charlie's friends were, too, but a teary sadness lingered, knowing that this would be the last week they would be together. One of Charlie's other good friends, Michael, moved to London as his father had a new job, so only James and Lee would remain in the town.

At school, Mrs Harrington didn't seem too amused by Charlie's acceptance of Dragonstone and the fact that he and Lee had turned in their project on time.

Charlie was sure that the shadowy creature he saw in Mrs Harrington's lesson was the same one the previous night. It wasn't a mere figment of his imagination.

Charlie was immensely intrigued and amused when the shadow suddenly appeared. It caused Mrs Harrington to trip over whilst she was shouting and passing out lunchtime detentions to those who had not completed their projects. The entity also caused her chair to collapse in front of the whole school during assembly. Remarkably, most pupils held back from laughing, knowing she would get her own back sometime.

The family visited Arthur Stuart, Charlie's grandpa, at the hospital in the evening.

Arthur, who had collapsed two weeks ago, was initially suspected of having a heart attack, but it wasn't. He could be grumpy, and his stay in the hospital made him even more moody.

The doctors had spent some time finding out what had happened using all kinds of probes, needles, and scans to get to the root cause of his condition. They were mystified by what had happened to him, and he looked a lot paler than usual, losing some weight compared to his normal self.

'Hello, Dad,' said Victoria.

'Decided t' visit then' av ya?' he asked.

'We were only here last Wednesday,' Victoria reminded him.

'Two flippin' weeks I've been in 'ere, and them 'av no idea what the blinkin' 'ell is wrong wi' me,' he said in his distinct Yorkshire accent, sounding different from the rest of the family.

'Haven't they brought back the results yet?'

'The bloomin' idiots lost 'em or somthin'—I dunno.'

'I'm sure that they will get to the bottom of the problem soon, Dad,' said Victoria with a reassuring tone.

'I flippin' 'ope so,' he said, sounding fed up. 'Hey, Grandpa, guess what?'

'Wha', Charlie?'

'I, well, er, we've been accepted to go to Dragonstone School, and we're going to check it out next Monday,' he exclaimed, changing the conversation.

'Ooh, bloomin' 'eck; going all posh on me then?'

'I think so, Grandpa,' he smiled, quite like being considered posh, though the Stuarts were nicely spoken—that was down to Victoria.

'We aren't sure whether we're going to go to school. We're going on a visit before making our minds up.'

'I suppose you don't want t' look after me. I see; pack up 'nd leave me,' Grandpa said.

'Oh, Dad, don't be silly now. It is a marvellous opportunity to move and start up again. Especially since his, well, their father up and left. If I ever see him again, I'd...' she said threateningly.

They discussed the school and other life details when there was an interruption.

'OK, folks, visiting time is now finishing,' shouted a nurse.

'Thank goodness for that,' muttered Emmanuel.

'Oh, is that the time again?' said Victoria, 'It seems to go so quickly. Well, Dad, see you again next week.'

'I might be dead by then,' he said pessimistically.

'Oh, Dad, don't be silly,' she said, shaking her head disapprovingly.

'Bye, Grandpa,' said his grandchildren, who always remained quiet when they visited him, apart from Charlie, who was very fond of him.

'Sees ya later, then,' he said.

He closed his eyes to rest and immediately started to snore.

*

The rest of the week brought much laughter for Charlie in remembering the old times and more tears of sadness for the imminent parting of an eleven-year-old relationship of four close friends.

However, within these last few days, Charlie noticed another strange phenomenon: smartly dressed men in pinstripe suits with long umbrellas walking up and down the street. They stood out like a sore thumb, as you would never see such richly dressed men in the area where Charlie lived.

He observed them over the week to see what they were up to. Disappointingly for Charlie, nothing much happened.

What enthralled Charlie was that he could have sworn he saw the shadowy creature flying among them and away.

Charlie and Lee had attempted to learn more about the Dragonstone School, but sadly, they didn't have enough information.

The headmaster's announcement of Mrs Harrington's resignation from the school was met with thunderous cheers. However, the pupils were left utterly traumatised by the second announcement that she would be teaching in the secondary school they were heading to.

The biggest event of the week was a surprise disco that amazed everyone. Mrs Harrington, who briefly attended, scowled disapprovingly at the noise level and promptly left, much to the class's cheers.

Charlie, Lee, Michael and James danced away in the smoke-filled room, whilst James thought it humourous to crawl along the floor and grab some people's legs. Unfortunately for him, he got his head trodden on by Sarah Bennett.

That was to be the end. After shedding a few more tears, they said their goodbyes and wished each other luck. It was time for Charlie to experience something very different.

Chapter Six
THE BUS

'Charlie! Emmanuel, wake up!'

Charlie and Emmanuel could be heard making small groans and grunts from their bedroom during their mother's daily call, indicating they were still tired.

It was the morning of their trip to Nottingham, and the weekend had passed quickly and without incident. Victoria had been busy planning the trip, ensuring they were packed and ready the night before. The family was excited as they had never stayed in a hotel before.

'Are you two up yet?' she shouted again.

'Yes, Mum,' they both said at the same time.

'It's your turn to go into the bathroom first,' said Emmanuel, boasting he could have a few extra minutes in bed.

'Oh yeah,' grumbled Charlie as he slithered out between his bedsheets and walked zombie-like into the bathroom. He quickly got ready when he realised he was in the creepiest room of the house.

Victoria's continual nagging to get there on time sped them up in ten minutes. Once downstairs, they went to the breakfast table and swiftly ate their porridge.

Anticipation was building up in the room they created; it would be the fuel that would propel them onward towards the bus station.

'Walk quickly, you lot,' said Victoria in a frustrated tone. 'We're going to miss the bus,' she concluded whilst pushing Olivia's Pushchair.

'We're coming, we're coming,' Charlie said, holding Olivia's hand. As he picked up the pace, Olivia seemed to take off.

'Ouch,' shouted Olivia, 'you are hurting my arm!'

'Sorry, Olivia,' said Charlie as he loosened his grip and slowed slightly.

Moments later, they turned a corner, and the bus was in sight.

As they approached, the doors closed. Victoria, still slightly ahead, started banging on the side of the number 39 bus.

'Hold on!' she shouted.

'Hang on,' they all shouted. The driver glanced at his side mirror, considering whether to wait. 'Ha-ha,' the driver chuckled to himself as he was about to drive away. However, to his surprise, the doors suddenly flung open.

'Eh?' said the driver, sounding very confused.

'Ooh! Thank you, driver,' said Mrs Stuart as she put her foot on the bus' step. At that moment, Charlie saw the mysterious shadow creature leave the bus. He wisely said nothing, as he knew no one would believe him.

After they paid for their ticket, the driver closed the doors, bringing the smell of freshly baked bread from the nearby bakery to Charlie's nostrils. He enjoyed this, a far cry from the litter's usual stench.

After placing their baggage in the hold, they walked towards the back of the relatively empty bus and sat down.

Two old ladies sat discussing today's youth and how life differed from what it was in their time. 'No respect,' one of them shouted. Charlie knew they were right, thinking about the likes of Vinnie.

The morning was a little cooler than usual, so Charlie wore his red tracksuit top and black Star Wars T-shirt. Charlie loved fantasy adventures. His blue jeans sat nicely on top of his trainers. They were scuffed from all the running around he did at school.

Emmanuel wore clothes similar to Charlie's, though his jeans were darker and his trainers were newer than his brother's. He was wearing a black T-shirt with numbers and writing on it.

Victoria was dressed elegantly, as always, and her attire reflected her desire to make a good impression. She wore a knee-length summer dress in a shade of blue paired with fashionable sandals. Her love for beautiful clothing influenced both Emmanuel and Lucy.

Lucy wore a beautiful pink dress, matching tights and shoes with little stars on them. Her sister, Olivia, looked almost the same as her, except that she wore pink boots instead of shoes and had a slightly brighter shade of pink on her top.

Everyone sat in silence, their faces showing a range of emotions. Some were exhausted, others were full of anticipation, and some were lost in thought. Emmanuel's eyes drooped, opening and closing in a constant battle with sleep. Victoria was engrossed in a book while Olivia and Lucy were fast asleep.

Victoria cherished her children and went above and beyond for them. Coming to Nottingham was a dream come true.

Charlie stared outside, and his mind began to wander. He thought about the end-of-the-year party, smiling at the great send-off they received. He began to chuckle at James' head being trodden on after grabbing Sarah Bennett's leg to scare her.

Afterwards, his thoughts wandered about the dark shadowy figure that seemed to be following him around. *What is it? Where does it come from? Why is it following me? It hasn't hurt me so far, so he thought it couldn't be that bad.* Ultimately, he wasn't even scared by the strange apparition. Oddly, he felt something familiar but couldn't quite put his finger on it.

He then wondered about the school, subjects they would study, and sports he would participate in.

His thinking suddenly switched to his grandfather in the hospital. He was worried about him and hoped that he would be OK.

Charlie's thoughts were immediately interrupted by the repulsive reek of foul body odour that filled the bus, overpowering the pleasant aroma of fresh bread. Without hesitation, he turned his head to avoid the pungent stench.

Despite the smell, anticipation was sizzling in the air around them; they had never been to Nottingham.

Suddenly, the driver announced: 'OK, Friar Tuck Lane—final stop.'

Charlie jumped around joyously, anticipating what was to come.

CHAPTER SEVEN

FEAR, FOREST & THE UNEXPECTED

They all stood up and shuffled towards the front of the bus.

'Emmanuel, please get Olivia's pushchair out from the hold for me,' asked Victoria politely.

'OK, Mum, no problem!' he replied, and after the second attempt, he managed to lift the pushchair out.

They disembarked from the bus and were immediately greeted by the suffocating smell of exhaust fumes. Charlie was particularly displeased, having already been subjected to the foul stench of fellow passengers.

'Hello there,' a voice thundered from the entrance to an old pub called the Salvation Inn. 'You must be the Stuarts—pleased to meet you all. My name is Randle Fitwick, and I'll be your tour guide for the day. I'll also be taking you to school tomorrow.'

Randle was a tallish man of slight build, elegantly dressed and spoke with a posh accent. He was a caring, helpful, and knowledgeable man fond of architecture and history. He had a way of telling stories, which were quite engaging, and he could draw you in with the slightest adjustment to his voice; people found him captivating.

Charlie's eyes opened, realising Randle wore the same pinstriped suit as the men back in his village, but he said nothing.

He took them on a city centre tour, but Charlie never realised that Nottingham had such a strong history. He loved Nottingham Castle, and he was keen to learn more.

The day ended with a shopping trip to a large shopping centre, which the school amazingly paid for. Victoria was in her element, as she had never received such generosity.

After journeying across the city, they arrived back where they got off the bus. There, parked in front of them, was a significant bus coach.

'Terrific!' said Charlie. 'That's a nice coach,' he said, catching his breath.

The coach was bright red, with a massive golden dragon on its side. "Dragonstone School" was written in large, thick, swirling letters. The windows were tinted, so you couldn't see inside, which made it look important. The coach's belly was rounder than that of a regular coach.

From the roadside, another man appeared.

'Hello, Eric,' said Randle.

Eric moved to the side of the coach and opened a side panel.

'Just pop ya stuff in 'ere, then we can be off,' said Eric grumpily, so they all put their shopping onto the coach.

Eric was quite different from Randle: shorter, bolder, and prominent around the waistline. He wore a posh red blazer, but he looked scruffy.

He closed the luggage hold. Eric kept his head down and trundled towards the coach entrance.

'He looks happy,' said Emmanuel.

'Ha-ha,' laughed Charlie. 'I hope he doesn't go to sleep at the wheel.'

'Me too,' said Emmanuel, laughing.

'Oh, don't worry about him—that's Eric, the coach driver. He's been doing this for years. A good driver, though he can be a bit of a misery.'

'Well, come on then, we haven't got all day,' Eric's voice boomed from inside the coach.

They walked onto the coach one by one. Charlie was first, and he looked around. It was incredibly posh and the likes he had never seen before. It wasn't just full of seats. It was almost like a very comfortable mobile home, with a lounge area, TV, and a bookshelf with magazines and old-looking books. There was even a cosey bar-type area containing a variety of drinks, snacks and silver cutlery. The design was old and classy.

Charlie had seen something similar on a TV drama his mum liked. In it, men wore colourful clothing and strange-looking wigs. The windows had silk curtains that folded nicely inwards. As they walked on, they could see other people in the vehicle.

'Hello there,' said a man's deep voice. He was Scottish.

They all looked over, and another family sat towards the back. He stood tall and broad, with thick dark hair and a matching beard.

'You must be the Stuarts; a good Scottish name, aye! Och, sorry,' he said, 'how rude; my name is Andrew Campbell, and this is my wife, Victoria.'

'That's Mum's name,' shouted Emmanuel before Andrew could finish his sentence.

'Aye, and a grand name it is,' he concluded.

Charlie's mum blushed at his flattering comments.

'Always the charmer,' said Mrs Campbell.

'These are my children, Bruce, Amanda, Martha and Lottie.'

All were looking at the Stuarts eagerly.

'Lovely,' said Victoria, 'this is my eldest, Emmanuel, then Charlie, and these are my youngest, Olivia and Lucy.'

At that point, Randle climbed aboard.

'Ah, I see that you are already acquainted. That's good; we can now be on our way. Come now, Eric, *boot her up*, as they say in the films.

A grunting sound came from the front of the bus. He looked into the wing mirror to check for traffic. He indicated, waited, and then pulled out.

The Stuarts and the Campbells sat down, discovering that their seats could transform into comfortable recliners.

'Och aye—this is life,' said Andrew. After spending all those hours on that train, this is just what the doctor ordered. Have you travelled far, Victoria?' asked Andrew.

'We come from a small village called Eanor, only an hour away,' she replied.

'Oh, not too far away,' he said. 'We were supposed to go on this mini-tour of the City, though the train got delayed in Edinburgh...just for a change,' he said sarcastically. 'We arrived half an hour ago, so we decided to wait here. Did you go on the tour?' he asked curiously.

'Yes,' said Victoria. She began to explain everything they had done, which was greeted with nods, wide eyes and gasps, especially when she told me about the shopping excursion.

'I canna believe it,' he said, annoyed that they missed out.

'Not to worry,' blurted Randle interjecting. 'There will be plenty of time to catch up. Trust me—there are plenty more surprises for you all,' teased Randle.

Surely it can't be any better than this? Victoria thought.

At that moment, Randle came round with drinks for everybody as they were all thirsty.

'Hello, Charlie,' said Amanda. 'How old are you then?'

'Hi, Amanda,' replied Charlie. 'I am ten, and my brother, Emmanuel, is eleven. My birthday is in January.'

'Och! I'm the same age as you, and Bruce is the same as Emmanuel. I wonder if we will be in the same class?' she asked excitedly.

'Probably,' he replied. I wonder why it is just our two families on the bus. Don't you think this is a bit strange? I mean the tour, a visit to Sherwood Forest, and the fact that no one knows anything about the school?' said Charlie.

He took another sip of his drink and scratched a slight irritation on his nose.

'Aye,' said Amanda, 'very strange. Did you see those people wearing smart suits carrying those long umbrellas?'

'Yes. It all seems a bit creepy if you ask me.'

'Aye,' said Amanda, 'very!'

The conversation paused as they took another sip and munched on chocolate cookies.

I wonder if Amanda has seen any strange shadowy creatures following her, Charlie thought. How could he approach such a question to a stranger without looking completely deranged or, at the very least, insane? *OK, here goes...* 'Amanda, this might seem a bit bonkers, but have you seen anything strange, like a shadowy-type thing around?'

'Och no,' she said. 'Though I have seen ghosts,' she said casually.

'Really?!' he replied, sounding enthusiastic and curious.

'Aye, I was in a pub with my Dad, and there he was, an old man drinking beer. He looked at me, winked, and then vanished. I've seen him a few times and other ghosts, too,' she concluded.

Charlie relaxed as he met somebody who had seen something others hadn't. Charlie began to tell her all about his experience with the dark entity.

'That sounds *amazing*,' she said with a soft Scottish accent. 'I believe you, of course. Like me, no one would believe me when I explained what I'd seen. Everyone laughed and told me I had an overactive imagination and that ghosts don't exist.' They both laughed and took another sip of their drink.

Charlie looked around and saw Emmanuel laughing at what Bruce told him; they seemed fine.

'Och, my Brother,' she said. He's been in trouble recently, getting into all kinds of mischief. The other day, he got Martha's teddies and hid in front of her bed. He held them up as if floating and then made spooky noises at Martha—she started to cry. Dad got furious, and it took Martha a week to sleep properly.'

'Oh dear,' said Charlie. However, Amanda said something that hit Charlie like a tonne of bricks: the 'D-word.' Charlie dearly loved his mother, though he also missed his dad. Charlie didn't fully know his father, but he remembered having a good time with him when he was around. He always seemed to be disappearing on business, and, of course, eventually, he went altogether.

If his thoughts had not been enough to cope, Amanda came up with the dreaded question.

'Where's your father?' asked Amanda. Charlie suddenly felt angry at the intrusion of this question.

'Er—Mum and Dad separated a few years ago,' he replied.

Charlie gazed at the floor, his anger shifting to sadness. He didn't confess he had left abruptly.

'I'm sorry, Charlie. I shouldn't have said anything,' she said, her cheer turning into remorse.

'Oh, it's not your fault,' said Charlie, understanding it was a question he might have to get used to. 'Anyway,' he responded, feeling more upbeat, '... we've still got Mum, and I have my Brother and Sisters. My Dad left when Mum got pregnant with Olivia; I'm not sure he knows about her. Lucy was too young to remember him.'

'Oh, dear,' said Amanda. She looked at her father, laughing and joking with Charlie's mum and her mother. *She thought I canna imagine what it would be like without my Papa.*

'Good, good,' said Randle, 'great to see everyone getting along wonderfully. We're not far away now, so start to gather your things together, and I'll collect the rubbish.'

Whilst everyone was getting organised, the coach turned a sharp left into a road at the start of the forest. Everyone was falling all over the place, apart from Amanda, who was still sitting down, hanging on for dear life.

'Eric, my dear boy, not so fast,' Randle said disapprovingly. 'Just think of our guests.'

Eric quietly chuckled like a child who knew he had done something wrong but enjoyed it.

The families on the coach were growing anxious, and their eyes were transfixed by the trees on either side of the road.

The coach travelled a little further, and there were signs of more life as it arrived.

Suddenly, the flames breathed out from the fire-eaters, standing on either side of the coach, and greeted them. You could see the sweat dripping off their foreheads as they had the daytime heat and the fire to contend with.

'Wow,' said Bruce, 'that's fantastic. I love the fire.'

'Me too,' said Emmanuel.

'That is cool!' said Charlie, transfixed by the flames.

At that moment, the coach stopped, and the doors opened.

Sword jugglers and acrobats interlinked and interchanged like a circus.

'Come on, you lot, gerroff,' said Eric. They needed no further invitation to get out of the vehicle.

'Come on, Amanda, take a look at these guys.'

'Hang on, Charlie,' she chirped. 'I need my Dad to get my chair.'

'Your chair?' said Charlie curiously.

'Aye,' she said. 'I canna walk,' she said, giggling, as Charlie turned a bright shade of red.

'I-I-I-I'm sorry, I didn't know,' said Charlie, feeling guilty.

'Och, Aye,' she giggled. 'Don't worry about it. I'll tell you all about it later,' she said calmly, smiling at him. Charlie composed himself a little.

'Papa,' she said.

'Aye, my little angel... I'll get it for you,' he said, instinctively knowing what she wanted.

Minutes later, they were nearly all off the bus coach.

Amanda's Wheelchair was outside, waiting for her with Charlie at its side.

Amanda's father came off with her in his arms and placed her in the Wheelchair. Charlie then pushed Amanda around, even though she could manoeuvre herself; he was trying to be a gentleman.

'Welcome to Sherwood Forest,' declared Robin Hood in his traditional attire. 'Who wants to join me as an outlaw?'

'Me!' all the children shouted.

'Great stuff!' he said. He reached into a large bag and handed out suitable Robin Hood outfits, which they put over their clothing.

The area was getting busy, with different coaches pulling up with other tourists and visitors.

The Stuarts and Campbells walked through another large wooden framed entrance.

On the opposite end, men and women were dressed in mediaeval outfits. The area was filled with various stalls and designated spaces where individuals engaged in different types of craftwork, such as creating pots and tools, cooking, and face painting. One man even forged swords, and another made bows and arrows.

The time went quickly. Charlie especially enjoyed sword-making with a man called Barnaby, whilst Amanda received a free bag of herbs from a kind old lady on the stall.

The evening was drawing to a close. After a meal, Randle invited them to the evening's festivities: a mediaeval pageant involving archery and jousting; it was a delight, to be sure.

In the end, Randle approached and spoke: 'Now, there is one more event set aside for future Dragonstoners,' he said.

Randle's tone arouses further excitement and expectation from everyone.

Charlie began to think. *What more surprises were there? Surely, it could not get any better than this. Why would the school do such a thing in the first place?*

'OK, five minutes, and we'll head into the forest.'

'The forest? Sounds spooky!' Emmanuel said.

The children exchanged glances of wonder and excitement while the adults, except Charlie's mother, eagerly anticipated what would happen.

'But it's getting quite dark now,' said Victoria.

'Perfect timing for the next activity,' said Randle.

The two families gathered their things and followed Randle into the darkness. It was eerily quiet.

The temperature was dropping, and there was a fresh smell in the air. As both families and Randle walked along, you could hear a procession of crickets and soil grinding beneath their feet.

At its lowest point, the sun shimmered a beautiful orange, and the moon was full and bright. As the sun set, some of the stars became more visible.

Lucy held tightly onto her mother's arm, afraid of the dark, whilst Olivia struggled to stay awake. Emmanuel and Charlie walked beside each other, but their destination remained unclear.

As he often did, Charlie's mind wandered again, thinking about the events before him. He longed for a time of castles, pageantry, swords, and armour.

A faint glow appeared in the distance after walking for what felt like an eternity. It was a small fire.

'OK; nearly there,' said Randle.

'What are we doing here?' said Mrs Campbell, somewhat nervous.

'Nothing to worry about,' said Randle. 'All will be revealed when we get there.'

Minutes later, they arrived.

Charlie noticed a stone circle beneath the fire, adorned with various symbols surrounding a larger one.

'Please—*tell* me what is happening!' demanded Victoria Stuart. 'This is all very peculiar.'

Randle courteously nodded and spoke, 'You are about to witness something marvellous, a rare event.'

'What?' Andrew demanded.

'It is an ancient rite, a druid ceremony performed for centuries. Don't be alarmed when you see them. They are peaceful people who work with and respect nature and humanity.' As soon as he spoke, people came from the woodland.

Their arrival was perfectly timed with the sunset.

Both families jumped when they first saw them. They were wearing long white robes with hoods covering their heads. They arrived wearing flower necklaces, removed them, and placed them in front of the families.

Still fearful, they joined together instinctively to form a protective barrier.

'Fear not,' said a voice. One person came forward and pulled the hood back. It was a beautiful lady with a smile that seemed to warm everyone around her. 'Blessed be, for it is an honour to receive such distinguished guests.'

'Blessed be,' said the rest of the group.

'*Why* have we been brought here? What *are* we doing here?' said Andrew, rising very tall. 'I never realised it was Halloween. Is this trick-or-treating or something?' he asked defensively.

'Hello, Andrew,' said a familiar voice. Another person came forward and pulled down his hood. It was Randle.

No one noticed him disappear, and they were shocked to see him dressed up.

'It isn't Halloween, and it certainly isn't trick-or-treating,' he laughed. 'It is as I said; you are here to witness a unique ceremony—that is all. I can assure you that not many people will see what you will see, and I can further assure you by mid-morning tomorrow, the whole thing will make much more sense. You have the option to receive a blessing from us. It's your free choice to stay or leave.'

'Let's stay, Mum!' pleaded Charlie. 'This looks very interesting,' he said, unperturbed by what was happening.

'Can we stay, Papa?' pleaded Amanda. 'I've seen documentaries on these kinds of things....'

'Please, Mum,' said Emmanuel.

'Well, I'm not too sure', said Victoria. 'After all, it is way past your bedtime.'

'Please, please,' they all begged together.

'What do you think, Andrew?' said Charlie's mum.

'Och aye, we'll stay if the children want to stay.'

'Mum, please!' begged Charlie.

'Oh, OK then. But I have to say, this is highly irregular.'

Randle gave them warm robes as it was getting cold. Charlie sat by Amanda's side.

'What do you think about this?' asked Charlie.

'This is cool. Something seems familiar about this,' said Amanda.

'I know what you mean,' he said.

A slow drumbeat filled the air, bringing a natural stillness to the gathering.

One of the druids entered the centre and sprinkled salt on the ground while muttering some strange words. Then, they walked around the circle three times clockwise. A second Druid appeared with a torch, muttered some words, and walked around three times with the torch ablaze. Then, a third came wafting a large incense stick, muttering words whilst walking like the others. A fourth person walked around, whispering many words while sprinkling water this time. Finally, another druid came into the circle's centre, lifted his hands high and said a few words.

The druids then retreated to the outskirts. The woman approached them with a large staff, spinning it around and pointing it towards the ground, filling the air with magick. As soon as she started, a chill permeated the area, and a tingling sensation went up through their spines; they shivered.

Both families seemed transfixed by the proceeding and were keen to see more.

The lady drew the staff around and appeared to make an invisible doorway in the air. One by one, they entered the circle.

Once they were in, the druids etched magical symbols at various circle points. Finally, two more people raised their arms and bowed whilst making further incantations.

Charlie looked up to find a shadowy figure sitting beyond the fire. The figure, smiling, winked at Charlie with one of its large, unfamiliar eyes before disappearing again.

'It was over there, again,' whispered Charlie to Amanda.

'There was what?' asked Amanda.

'That shadowy creature I told you about earlier. Did you see it?' Charlie quizzed, hoping she had.

'Sorry, Charlie, I didn't,' she whispered back regretfully.

'What is it?' he asked himself. He was now frustrated by his lack of knowledge.

Amanda's eyes jolted open, widening to the size of plates, and her mouth parted in shock. There was no denying that the sight before her was truly unbelievable.

'Look,' she pointed.

'Look at what?' asked Charlie.

Amanda was awed as she witnessed an ethereal golden figure illuminating the centre. The sight was so mesmerising that she couldn't take her eyes off it.

It came towards her, and then it disappeared again.

'See what?' asked Charlie.'

'I'd never seen anything like that before,' she said, explaining what she had seen to Charlie.

A deep sense of curiosity quickly replaced Charlie's surprise. He couldn't help but wonder why he only saw dark, shadowy things while she saw beautiful, glowing entities.

The drum stopped, grabbing Charlie and Amanda's attention.

One of the druids brought forward a large silver goblet. The goblet was held up, and magical-sounding words were spoken.

The beautiful woman who had spoken to them earlier and the other druids added various ingredients to the goblet before raising it high. The goblet was swirled around to mix the ingredients.

'So mote it be,' said the lead druid, followed by the rest.

'Come, my friends,' the lady spoke, 'drink with us this special night. It is our gift to you.'

'What is it?' demanded Andrew, sounding suspicious.

'It is a consecrated drink mixed with fine herbs and berries. It is an ancient formula passed down only by word of mouth.'

Charlie boldly stood up and strode purposefully towards the lady, unafraid and determined.

'It's an honour to meet you,' she said to Charlie.

'Thanks, you too,' Charlie nodded respectfully.

He took the goblet and sipped its contents. He rolled it around his mouth and then swallowed.

'Mmm,' he said. 'This is good. Come and have a sip of this,' he shouted.

Sure enough, they all went up to drink from the goblet.

'It is done. Blessed be, so mote it be.'

*

The day's events had exhausted them, so they appeared disinterested in the hotel.

Charlie and Emmanuel were sleeping peacefully in the partially moonlit room when, suddenly, something seemed to disturb Charlie's slumber.

Charlie panicked; his body stiffened, breathing quick and erratic, and his head turned from side to side until it became stiff. Charlie was blinded, wondering what madness possessed him in the darkness. He attempted to scream but was unable to. He tried to move again but couldn't. The only movement from him was a tear rolling down the left side of his cheek.

Charlie struggled to understand his situation. What was particularly unsettling for him was the feeling of powerlessness he was experiencing for the first time. Charlie had always been in control and confident, and this kind of anxiety was entirely new to him.

Charlie struggled to resist the madness, but it tightened its grip, and he began to sweat profusely.

He had all but given up. He couldn't even cry when, at last, he made a small whimper of a plea: 'Help!' Charlie croaked.

The shadowy figure flew into the room instantly and comforted him. It circled him so quickly that a cool breeze formed.

Oblivious to Charlie's plight, Emmanuel picked up on the coolness and wrapped himself further in his duvet.

Charlie momentarily forgot about his paralysis and wondered what he was seeing.

His rigidity subsided as the shadow's actions took effect; soon, he could move his fingers and toes, and within minutes, he was free.

'Thank you,' said Charlie gratefully as the shadow entity flew through the main door.

Charlie was exhausted after his experience. He feared returning to sleep, worried the paralysis might come back.

Four hours had passed, and Charlie was disturbed by something else. He tried to move his hands and arms, fearing that he might have become paralysed. Fortunately, Charlie could move them effortlessly, which immediately relieved him. It was then that he realised that the knock on the door was only his mother.

'Charlie, Emmanuel, it's time to get up!'

'OK, Mum,' said Emmanuel, surprising Charlie.

'Ooh, you scared me,' said Charlie nervously, 'I didn't realise you were awake.

'Yeah, I just woke up. I slept well, did you?'

'Er—yeah,' said Charlie, lying to his brother.

He knew he wouldn't believe him if he told him what had happened, so he didn't say anything.

After breakfast, the Stuarts and Campbells went outside to a fed-up-looking Eric, who was ready to take them to school.

CHAPTER EIGHT

DRAGONSTONE SCHOOL OF MAGICK

A small slit in the gate opened, and a pair of hazel eyes were looking through.

'Come on then! Open up!' said a frustrated Eric.

The guard's eyes narrowed as he sneered disapprovingly at Eric's tone.

The enormous wooden gate opened slowly, creaking as it divided down the middle. The surrounding wall was so massive that not even a fire engine's ladder could have reached the top.

Eric put the coach into gear and began entering the grounds. To the left, a large man occupied a small brick hut, sitting down and operating the gate controls.

The Stuarts and Campbells had their faces glued to the windows, trying to glimpse what had been a complete mystery until now. Their mouths went into a fly-catching position as they looked, astonished at what they saw.

'This is Dragonstone School, my dear friends,' said Randle. 'Marvellous, isn't she? Wait until you see the rest!'

The property's expansive grounds stretched out as far as the eye could see, with vast fields in every direction. Trees were neatly grouped, and deer roamed the lands. A massive building sat at the top of a long, gradual-sloping hill.

'Now, this magnificent structure was one of the first Renaissance buildings in England built in the early 1500s. It was completely out of context for the period, of course.'

'What do you mean?' asked Charlie.

'It means that in this country, we still had older mediaeval structures compared to Renaissance-inspired Europe, so this would have seemed very strange.'

'Oh, I think I know what you mean,' said Charlie.

'Interesting,' said Mrs Stuart. 'I like this more and more.'

'Aye,' said Mrs Campbell. 'I did have my doubts, but I think it will work out just fine,' she said, relieved.

The building was beautifully designed. In front of it, two enormous dragons were positioned in a protective stance. They looked menacing and magnificent simultaneously, and the children couldn't wait to examine them closer.

The school seemed deserted, as the term had yet to start. Charlie looked over to Amanda and noticed her staring into the distance.

'What's the matter?' asked Charlie.

'Oh, I could have sworn I saw a group of people over there. I think it must be my imagination,' said Amanda as Randle looked curiously at her.

A refreshing cool breeze welcomed them atop the hill, and Charlie breathed it in deeply, immediately relaxing. He stood outside the school building and listened intently for any signs of noise, but all was quiet.

There was peace in the area that immediately brought quietness and stillness; even the traffic couldn't be heard in the distance. It, coupled with the sun's warmth that gently caressed the skin, made for a perfect moment.

Charlie observed a serene landscape with birds fluttering from treetop to treetop and clusters of deer grazing in the freshly cut grass. The scene was remarkably evocative.

He turned around slowly, and the giant dragon that stood to the left of the main entrance greeted him. Although lifeless and made of stone, it startled Charlie and interrupted his moment of awe.

He steadied himself, examining the two dragons closely and then the school.

Charlie remembered Randle Fitwick telling him that the school was from the Renaissance. It certainly looked different from any other buildings that he'd previously observed.

Two massive towers joined the central part of the building. The adjoined building between the towers was filled with many classrooms. The central tower was taller than the side towers, approximately five times the width and beige. *Someone made this into a school*—wow, he thought.

Charlie then went over to join his family. They arranged a makeshift circle to discuss their thoughts about the school. They were all equally impressed and surprised. Emmanuel spoke.

'I can't wait to see inside. I wonder what the classrooms are like?'

Charlie looked to the other side, observing the Campbells discussing similar things, except Bruce, who had decided to climb the dragon.

'Hey...Bruce, get down!' shouted Andrew. 'Ya shoudn' be climbing up!'

Emmanuel laughed, Charlie grinned, and Lottie wished he'd fall off for his cruel teasing.

Randle said, 'Oh, I hope you like the school grounds. But before we continue, headmistress Hecate Winslow would like to see you all now.'

They enthusiastically followed Randle as he led them to meet the headmistress. Her unexpected letter piqued their curiosity, and they were eager to meet her in person.

Trusting Randle's guidance, they couldn't wait to see what the headmistress had in store.

All of them climbed up several steps except for Amanda, who her father pushed along the flattened pathway leading into the school. Shortly afterwards, they were all in a vast hall with two staircases leading upwards in two directions. Beneath the stairs were more doors leading to different areas of the school.

Some lift doors were also present. Dark wooden flooring, matching the colour of the doors, covered the vicinity. Surrounding the outer part of the wall were suits of armour from the Mediaeval period, all decorated with different colours and individual Coats of Arms.

Four broadswords were slotted in stands against the wall, but one was missing. It reminded Charlie of his attempt to make a sword in Sherwood Forest.

Unlit fire torches hung high on the thick stone walls, and there was no sign of modern lighting anywhere. Charlie was excited by the definite scent of an atmosphere from a bygone age.

'This pays tribute to the Keep that used to sit here,' said Randle.

'A bit like Nottingham Castle,' said Mrs Stuart. 'I mean, it was a castle before, but now it is a large mansion house.

'Yes,' replied Randle. However, it is good that the main castle gates and walls are still there. I hope they rebuild it one day!'

'This is a grand location for a school. Where are we going to live?' asked Andrew.

'All will be explained shortly,' he said reassuringly.

'This is impressive,' Emmanuel muttered. 'This makes Compton Comprehensive School look tiny.'

'Yeah, and just *look* at those shiny knight armour over there!' said Charlie.

'Ah,' said Randle. 'I'd noticed in the forest that you had a particular interest in swords. I bet fencing would suit you.'

'Fencing?' said Charlie, looking confused.

'Oh yes—of sorts—you'll see. The school offers quite a large range of facilities and activities for students to participate in,' said Randle, finally divulging some information about the school. 'Come on then, time is ticking; we mustn't keep the headmistress waiting,' said Randle, looking at his watch.

They all took the left-hand staircase to the top whilst Amanda got into the lift with her father. As they walked up, Charlie imagined himself sliding down the bannister, brandishing a sword.

Charlie noticed the area was quite dark despite the daylight coming in through the large window. It didn't bother him; it added to the school's ambience and mystery.

They all arrived at the top and went through a doorway. They walked through and found themselves in a narrow corridor that looked completely different from the main hall. It was brightly decorated with bright red carpet and subtle oil light fittings positioned every six feet. The corridor had golden striped wallpaper, a beautiful gold divider, and wooden panelling up to the floor. Four unique doors lined the hallway.

'Ah, here we are,' said Randle as Charlie noticed no name on the first door they came to. What made it stand out was the triangular wooden carving at the top of the doorframe. Randle knocked.

'Come in,' said the headmistress. Randle pushed the handleless door open, and they walked into a vast office with décor similar to the bus.

Hecate Winslow sat behind a semicircular desk with golden trimmings, similar to the wall divider in the main corridor. The top of the desk was deep red and highly polished. Victoria noticed the curved rings from the tree bark on it.

Charlie looked around and couldn't understand why no doors were leading in from outside the room as he saw in the corridor. *Undoubtedly, the doors would have overlapped into this room,* he thought.

'Welcome, welcome,' said the headmistress. 'Please come over here and be seated.'

They all approached a set of plush couches decorated with velvet cushions, each corner adorned with tassels.

'Make yourselves at home—after all, this will be your new home,' she said with some certainty. 'You must have so many questions regarding the school and why we do our business the way we do.'

Charlie looked at her, and you could see why she was a headmistress: She had an air of authority, and her voice was commanding but pleasant. She was elegantly dressed in a long dark green skirt and matching jacket, and an ornate brooch added to her regal appearance.

Victoria Stuart spoke.

'I must admit, it does seem rather extravagant just to come to a school interview.'

'My dear, you will find many extravagant *things* here at Dragonstone!' she swiftly responded. 'But first, a toast to your arrival, after which everything will be made clear.'

'Randle, would you mind?' said Hecate, signalling him to pour the drinks.

'Not at all,' said Randle pleasantly.

Charlie stiffened slightly after being reminded of the events that followed the drink in the forest.

Randle opened a cabinet and pulled out what looked like an old whisky decanter. He then took out the correct number of matching drinking glasses, placed them on a silver tray, poured the drinks, and carried them over.

'Don't worry, it's non-alcoholic,' Randle chuckled as Andrew looked disappointed.

'If there is anything with a bit more of a 'kick to it for the grown-ups, I wouldn't mind sampling a bit,' teased Andrew.

'Typical!' said Victoria Campbell.

'Oh, I'm sure you'll find this will have 'kick' enough,' Hecate reposted.

Randle handed the drinks out. They all had a sniff. Charlie swore the drink smell changed from liquorice to chocolate.

'Mm, this is nice; it smells nice too,' said Charlie. You could see that everyone else was enjoying it.

'A toast,' said Hecate, 'to our newest members of Dragonstone School of Magick and Jarv!'

'To whom?' Emmanuel queried.

'I'll explain later,' said Randle. 'Ah—this looks to be Percy's best batch yet,' he smiled.

An unexpected incident occurred when they emptied their glasses, leaving them all surprised.

'Ooh...I feel rather funny. What is this?' said Victoria.

'Me too...' said Victoria Campbell. 'What was that?' she said, staring at the desk.

'Oh, *not* again!' said Charlie as his ankles, wrists and heart all began to tighten up again, though there was an intense burning sensation before he dropped to the couch. Amanda passed out.

Those who remained standing began to sway. Andrew's vision blurred as everyone he saw started triplicating before he collapsed onto the couch. Emmanuel fell into an uncomfortable heap on the floor, and Bruce doubled over the couch's arm. Lucy, Olivia, Martha and Lottie were all fast asleep.

Charlie's rolling eyes were the last bodily movement that remained defiant. Before losing consciousness, Charlie heard Randle and Hecate whispering about him and a prophecy, before losing consciousness.

It had been thirty minutes, and the Stuarts and Campbells remained unconscious in the room. Randle and the headmistress were frantically running around, partly because of what had happened to their guests and partly because they were trying to put things in order.

'How long before they wake?' Randle asked.

'I'm not quite sure. Each case is quite different, though I'm sure they will be fine,' said Hecate.

'This has taken some time for the drink to have its effect,' he said nervously.

'It does seem unusually long,' said Hecate, agreeing.

'Yes, far too long,' said Randle. 'I hope that they are OK with this.'

'Ah, once they see our world, today will become but a memory,' said Hecate confidently.

'True,' said Randle. However, there was the unusual case of Mr Jones, who went slightly mad at what he'd seen. His mind couldn't accept this world. It's a good job that we had the memory blank potion here. Poor Eric had to drive to the South Coast to drop him off.'

'I remember him, poor fellow. I suppose he's happy now,' said Hecate reflectively.

'Are you sure the Astro-Mages are correct about this?'

'Oh yes,' she said confidently. 'Why someone would go to such lengths to invisibilize their charts is a complete mystery, not to mention quite worrying. What kind of person, or persons, would deny their family this rite is beyond me,' said Hecate. If it wasn't for Victoria's letter arriving at the school, thus breaking the dark charm, they could have been lost forever,' she concluded.

'More worrying is that there could be many more families or individuals in the same situation,' said Randle.

'Yes, yes,' said Hecate. 'I hear security has now been doubled at the Astro-Mages chambers, and Philbus is now in charge.'

'Philbus?' exclaimed an alarmed Randle.

'Yes, Philbus,' she repeated. 'Astrophos was furious that someone had managed to get into their space.'

'Well, I'll be surprised if they try this again with him in charge. God help them if he catches them. There hasn't been a need for an inquisitor for years. I suppose he'll be glad of the work.'

'I assure you, he's revelling in the role,' said Hecate.

'Once they discover how things work, should we tell them about the scrolls disappearing? Or should I say hidden?' asked Randle.

'Probably not a good idea; there are many factors that we do not understand ourselves, including why the dark charm broke. Cosmolos has a couple of theories that he's currently investigating. For now, let's see what happens. There could be other consequences resulting from this,' said Hecate sagely.

'How do you think they'd react to all this?' asked Randle.

'I have no idea. In most cases, it is generally well-received,' replied Hecate.

'Oh, yes, I have to say, we've influenced someone who will write about a great magickal adventure in approximately ten years. 'It will make our world more acceptable, but they will soon realise there is much more to understand about magick.'

'Yes,' said Hecate, 'there is so much for us to learn. The last of the greatest wizards died an age ago, taking the magick of the old with him. I would love so much to uncover more about the ancient mysteries.'

Fifty minutes had passed, and there was still no sign of consciousness.

Randle paced around the room anxiously while Hecate sat by her desk, tapping her fingers, and then drank cold water.

Suddenly, someone spoke.

'Och—my head,' said Andrew as if he'd woken up after a Friday night out with his friends.

Randle and Hecate breathed a sigh of relief and headed for the door. Moans and groans sounded from the rest, and gradually, everyone regained their faculties. Charlie was the last to wake up. He wasn't looking thrilled.

'What happened?' asked a startled Victoria Stuart.

'I have no idea,' said the other Victoria.

'This is getting beyond a joke,' said Andrew angrily. Too many strange things are happening here, and they still haven't told us anything! Have they?' bellowed Andrew. 'Let's go here, *drink this*, drink that,' he continued to rant. 'What have we got? A sore head and no explanation.'

'He's right,' said Mrs Stuart. 'Where have Randle and Hecate gotten to?'

'Aye,' said Mrs Campbell. 'They've done a runner.'

'This is like some sick practical joke. What a waste,' said Andrew, getting angrier at every breath.

'Look at the time,' said Emmanuel. 'We've been here over an hour.'

'AN HOUR!' fumed Andrew. 'Wait until I get my hands on them. I'll turn them both to haggis!'

'Is it me, or does everything seem brighter to you,' Victoria Stuart observed.

'Aye—you're right. Things do seem a little more vivid. Everything is sticking out a little more, and the colours are more beautiful,' she said, feeling less apprehensive.

'Drugs, I tell you. That's what they've given us. I bet they would have operated on us next,' said Andrew in a frenzy.

'No drugs, and they'll certainly be no operating either,' said a voice from the doorway.

'Who are you? Why have you done this to us?' shouted Andrew, curling up his fist and beginning to walk towards him. A man wearing dark blue robes with a prominent white beard stood at the door.

'Please forgive me for what you have experienced this past hour. This must be very confusing. My name is Cosmolos, and I'm an Astro-Mage.' Andrew stopped in his tracks as Cosmolos spoke. 'I am part of the group that decides who can come to the school,' he said before being interrupted.

'An Astro, what?' blurted Emmanuel.

'Astro-Mage,' Amanda said out of the blue. 'A Mage works with magick—my Grandma told me.'

'That is correct, young lady, perfect!'

'Magick? What utter tosh, rubbish, no such thing,' said Andrew, recapturing his aggressive tone.

Amongst the furore, Charlie suddenly realised he might get some explanation about his experiences.

'A trick, you think,' said Cosmolos. Cosmolos raised a shoulder-length staff he was holding. The top had a silver ring with a small silver ball at its centre that began to swirl around. A golden glow emanated from the sphere and grew slightly more substantial as he held it up.

'It's all a trick,' said Andrew, deciding to move forward to confront Cosmolos.

'Apanus,' said Cosmolos, pointing his staff at Andrew, and he began to rise.

'What the...' said Andrew, lessening his voice.

Everyone looked amazed at what was happening, and Cosmolos lowered him.

'Look, look,' shouted Lucy excitedly as some vines appeared on the border at the top of the room.

'Look over here,' shouted Martha, pointing at the flowers on the desk. Tiny white, pink and green spheres were circling the unusual-looking flowers. The spheres flew in and disappeared within the flowers. As the green globe left, a fantastic fragrance filled the room, bringing a sense of tranquillity.

'Er...aye...Er,' said Andrew, stuttering.

Both Victorias stood together, absorbing and enjoying the sweet aroma. However, Charlie was still a little apprehensive about the whole thing. Emmanuel was frozen to the spot, and Bruce sat down. His mouth was wide open, and he looked rather pale. Amanda and the other girls were excited as they moved around the room, chasing the phenomena and trying to examine them.

'Drugs, I tell you. We had these in the sixties,' said Andrew with a final bit of defiance.

'Drugs,' laughed Cosmolos. He swung the top of his body around with his staff and the other arm pointing at the door, which instantly flung open.

Miniature firedrakes flew and went immediately to the torches and fireplace. Once lit, the flames grew tall, and the heat became intense.

Andrew was about to open his mouth again when one of the firedrakes flew over and stung his bottom. Andrew began to run around the room with the firedrake in tow.

'Drugs, he says,' said Cosmolos chuckling.

'OK, OK,' shouted Andrew. *'Please* stop this...er... well, whatever they are.' Cosmolos closed his eyes and took a deep breath. Moments later, the firedrake flew off to meet its companions. The flames receded, and the room cooled down.

'Why? Why us?' asked Andrew.

'Why?' said Cosmolos, 'Because you all have magick,' he said.

CHAPTER NINE

A WORLD OF MAGICK

Silence pervaded the room. Cosmolos placed his staff back on the ground, and the metallic end slowly began to stop. Before it did, Cosmolos muttered something under his breath, and a pleasant cooling breeze entered the room.

'Air was always my favourite,' said Cosmolos. A *tut* of disapproval could be heard spitting from the fireplace. The air brought calmness, liberating the mind of any gloomy thoughts.

Both the Stuarts and Campbells stood united and speechless. The magick that unfolded around them brought a sense of fear and wonderment.

The atmosphere seemed tangible and bright. Furthermore, the vines on the ceiling pulsated to nourish the room. The glowing orbs encircling the blossoms shifted to new ones that suddenly emerged.

'This must be very confusing for you,' said Cosmolos. 'I then ask you to sit down, and I will try to explain it.'

Both families sat down, looking at Cosmolos to hear what he had to say. However, they were all a little preoccupied with the wonder that had suddenly entered their lives.

Before Cosmolos could say more, the main door to the room opened, and Randle and Hecate entered. Hecate was still wearing her dark green suit, but Randle had changed into his druid clothing.

'Feeling more comfortable?' said Cosmolos to Randle.

'Much. Though I do like a good suit,' he replied.

'Excuse me,' said Victoria, 'but can you *please* tell us what is happening? We've been waiting patiently, though now we deserve to know what this is all about.'

'I apologise for the distraction. I will begin immediately,' said Cosmolos. 'Thousands of years ago, quite a different world existed from the one you already know. Some have existed as mythology through legends such as King Arthur, Merlin, and Hercules. Back then, magick was real and practised daily by those who could. Powerful magicians such as Merlin, Gideon and a few others were important advisors to the kingdoms.'

'What happened?' asked Amanda.

'Well, those who had abilities were scoffed at by those who did not. A few centuries after Merlin, Lord Gideon Mortus became the most powerful wizard. He was wise and advised the ruling king of the time. However, an equally powerful wizard named Prince Zordemon, the son and heir to the king, had other ideas about what to do with the world's future. The story got confused over the years as to what happened. However, we know that Gideon made arrangements for those who had magick and those who did not live separately. Gideon didn't like the idea, as he knew that ordinary men lacked the insight to rule properly. Unlike Prince Zordemon, Gideon respected men's free choice and created an agreement, which I'll explain later. However, Gideon made sure that traces of magick in the Plainlands could be found.'

'What do you mean?' asked Victoria.

'Well, you can't obliterate magick; it is impossible. Magickal forces join together the whole world. However, Gideon ensured that those sensitive enough, visually or in a sensory way, could access these traces.'

'Like the cold, tingling sensations in the forest?' Victoria Campbell asked.

'Exactly,' said Randle. 'And more...'

Cosmolos continued. 'Enough magick existed to ensure that people retained some memory. Therefore, there has always been an interest in magick, and some can even practise it to an extent. Look at your world today. There is a surge of interest in the mystic arts. Even those who do not believe are always drawn to such things; this is the power of magick. Remember, magick can never be destroyed; it is always there. Ultimately, it is up to you to decide whether to use magick and, if you do, how to use it.'

'You mean for good or bad,' said Mrs Campbell.

'Yes,' replied Cosmolos. 'Sorry, as I was saying, shortly after a battle, Zordemon was defeated. A contract was signed, so magick became virtually redundant in the Plainlands. Hence, all kinds of witches, warlocks, wizards and magicians moved on.'

'So how does this place exist then?' asked Victoria Stuart.

'A good question! Gideon and his team of powerful wizards ensured that all those with magical abilities had a place to call their own—the Magicklands. These lands are a testament to their unwavering determination and commitment to provide a haven for all those who possess the power of magick. Thanks to their tireless efforts, the Magicklands is now a thriving community where magicians can flourish and live their lives to the fullest. Sadly, in the Plainlands, some Plainers sought to eradicate the very memory, and thousands of people were tortured and burned. Most of the literature was also destroyed. Many people killed were innocent, but some were real magick folk who chose to live in the Plainlands to keep an eye on what was happening.'

'I see!" said Victoria.

'Without their full powers, they were defenceless. History was rewritten. The old ways became stories, myths and legends instead of facts. Centuries of dumbing down have resulted in what you believe today to be real. Magick was seen as evil and something to be feared. Yes, there are dark aspects to it, as there are in all things, but there are beauty and intelligence that reaches far beyond the Plainlander way of thinking,' said Cosmolos.

'Fascinating!' said Victoria, focusing on every word.

'Plainers tend to associate magick with fear, which is completely wrong. In the modern era, the media and film-making have helped re-introduce the concept of magick, even though most of it is still, sadly, based on fear. People like to be on edge, excited by dark ways, distorting the true representation of what magick is about. It is quite devious, as it stops people from exploring their power and true potential; if you fear magick, why explore it?'

'Yes, I can see that!' Victoria said reflectively.

'Gideon knew that magick could not be eradicated, no matter how hard you try,' said Cosmolos. There is a prophecy, or should I say half of a prophecy, that has existed since those times. The story has become confusing over the years. Still, we know that Lord Gideon made arrangements, written in the agreement mentioned, for those who had magick and those who did not live separately. In addition, the prophecy states that balance will return to the world one day. Until this time, we have no idea how it will happen. Most folks have either given up or do not care. This realm has become a part of our lives that most magick folks do not care much about what happens to the Plainers; life here is very comfortable.'

'What do you mean a Half Prophecy?' queried Charlie.

'Well, for some reason, half of the prophecy disappeared off the face of the earth. What happened to it? Nobody knows. Over the centuries, a massive search has been under-way to recover the lost half of the prophecy as magick folk believe it will answer all their questions,' replied Cosmolos.

'Why us? What do we have to do with all this? How come we have magick? How do you know we have magick?' asked Andrew, now feeling calmer.

'Good questions; each person is born at a specific time. I assume you have all heard of astrology?'

'Yes,' they all acknowledged.

'Yeah, it's a load of old....' Andrew thought twice about saying what he was going to say. After all, he didn't fancy being suspended mid-air or attacked again.

'Ahem,' said Cosmolos, raising a brow as Andrew put on an innocent face. Cosmolos narrowed his eyes like the gate guard did to Eric.

'Well, the astrology that has become popular in the Plainlands only covers part of what occurs. Yes, there are predictive values, which, incidentally, most can be changed, but there are other deeper elements to their readings. Each person has a handcrafted chart or an Astro-Chart. Within these charts, there are signatures or traces of magickal potential. He explained that magick exists within families, and nearly all are born and live here.'

'What happened to us?' asked Victoria Campbell.

'Well, some families escaped us for some reason, but eventually, we caught up with them. That is why Randle and others you saw volunteer and become Trackers. I believe the name is self-explanatory.'

'So that's what happened to us then; we got found?' asked Emmanuel.

'Yes... eventually,' said Cosmolos.

'With magick not functioning as effectively in the Plainlands, it is difficult to keep account and track everyone. It is quite frustrating, to be honest. It is why we remain in contact with the Plainlands. Some here wish to cease all communications with the Plainlands and tell those with magickal abilities born there that it is tough luck. What they don't know won't hurt them, et cetera. Of course, this is nonsense as we all originated from the Plainlands. As you have recently found out, the school is a gateway to the magickal realms and was one of the first to be created. As you will undoubtedly find out, there are various ways to travel and communicate between communities, towns, cities, et cetera via magickal lines.'

'Fascinating,' said Victoria Stuart. 'You say we have magick. Does this mean we can do the things that you do?' Everyone seemed to listen more intensely.

"Yes, with some practice," said Cosmolos.

'How?' Emmanuel asked.

'Well, it is like anything; you must learn it,' said Cosmolos.

'That is why we're here, at the school, I mean,' said Charlie. 'But what about Mum and Mr and Mrs Campbell? Surely they don't come to school; they're too old.'

'Thanks a lot,' said his mother.

'Oh...er, sorry. I mean, grown-ups don't go to school like we do,' he said, recovering.

'You are absolutely correct,' said Hecate, joining in.

'Well, there is a special place for grown-ups called Dragonstone Grammar School of Magick, and for the very young ones, there is Dragonstone Tots. For those of Lucy's age, there is Dragonstone Juniors. Simple, but it works.'

'I see,' said Andrew. 'Do we go there full time?' he continued.

'Yes,' said Hecate. 'You have to, as you will be out of sync, magickally, with everyone else. You are never too old to learn.'

'Fantastic news!' Mrs Campbell beamed.

'So where are we going to live?' enquired Mrs Stuart.

'Those attending the school will live here. Our wonderful campus contains activities, societies, and ways to learn magick. It is quite similar to the universities in the Plainlands.'

'Great!' shouted Charlie as the rest cheered and looked equally excited.

'However, the rest of you will head to the Village of Wondle. Here, you will live with families with backgrounds similar to your own. Virtually all your neighbours are friendly and will help you settle in and adjust to your new life. Believe me when I say this world is very different from the one you are used to, and there are many things to learn,' said Hecate.

'What about Grandad?' Charlie asked.

'We are monitoring the situation,' said Randle. 'We have found, over the years, that the transition can be challenging for those who are too old, so we tend not to disturb them. Those poorly, like your grandfather, find that going through the transition could cause further health problems, as there are physiological and mental adjustments to our world. We'll have to see. It is not to say that all older people are discriminated against. Each case is treated individually. Of course, you are free to visit him anytime you like, as long as you don't miss any lessons. But a warning: discussing this world with your Plainland friends is forbidden.'

'When does term start?' asked Emmanuel.

'Oh, at the same time as the Plainlanders, or Plainers as they are also called, start their term. It makes it easier for families to visit friends over there. However, school residents will return to their families during the holidays—in this case, the lovely Village of Wondle.'

'Will Amanda and I be in the same class?' asked Charlie.

'Yes,' said Hecate. 'You are both different elements, but all classes are mixed now.'

'What do you mean by different elements?' asked Charlie.

'Each person born under a sign has a predominant element attached—Earth, Fire, Air and Water. Those born under these signs are assigned to an Elemental House. You all have a potential great ability to use this element, but one of the aims is to master all of them. Needless to say, there aren't many people who can. You can use your element for all things, including Dematerialisation Transport.'

'Demat what?' asked Charlie.

'You'll discover soon enough. You will learn that there are many forms of magick and their uses. This school also promotes the development of all creative endeavours like art and music, to name a few. There are also fitness activities to your liking. After all, magick exists in all things. What expands our minds and bodies expands our understanding of everything and enhances our magick. We are made up of many levels of being, and all of these parts must be satisfied somehow. As for myself, I have had many revelations and epiphanies whilst courting the canvases,' said Cosmolos.

'What do you mean by revelation and epiphany?' queried Amanda.

'It means that I've received and understood valuable insights or information about the different parts of magick whilst my mind was engaged in other activities. You will understand as time passes.'

'Now, before we go on, I must point out that you must decide whether to enter our world. You have received a taster of what could be, though you always have a free choice whether to enter the delights of our world or not. We will return you to your old homes if you choose not to, but the Magicklands will forever be open to you! We'll leave you a few moments with your families to discuss this and then obtain your final answer on our return,' said Cosmolos.

Seconds later, Hecate, Randle and Cosmolos turned around to leave the room. This time, the door opened automatically for them, and they left whilst both families returned to their family units to discuss what had happened.

It wasn't until they got back together that they realised the gravity of the situation. They all spent some time thinking, but the pull towards the magick world was too strong for them all.

Charlie took the longest to decide, worried about more paralysing experiences. However, what swayed him was that he could finally get some answers.

Cheers and celebrations could be heard from both families, and they huddled and shook each other's hands.

'Well, well, you all look happy,' said Hecate, who stood alongside Cosmolos and Randle. Do I take it that you've decided to join the magickal community?' she said cheerfully.

'Both the Stuarts and the Campbells will be delighted to enter this fascinating world,' said Mrs Stuart.

'Well then, let's not wait a moment longer,' said Cosmolos.

The energy of excitement was now bustling so powerfully that it was like magick.

Cosmolos raised his staff as he did before. Andrew gulped as he ended up in mid-air the last time he did that.

'Apocalypton!' said Cosmolos commandingly. Both families were looking excitedly at where Cosmolos was pointing.

Suddenly, the doors that Charlie observed that should have appeared in the first place appeared. 'Ah', said Charlie, now realising what had happened—*but surely these must lead to the main corridor*, he thought. Vines and leaves covered most of the walls and doors. Each door was decorated with a unique pattern.

'Charlie,' said Cosmolos. 'Choose a door!'

'Me? Why me?' he said, looking very surprised.

'Why not,' replied Randle.

'I suppose,' said Charlie.

He proceeded forward and examined the doors. Charlie walked past the first two doors, but nothing happened. He couldn't explain it, but he didn't seem bothered by them. Charlie then walked past the third and fourth doors, but nothing happened. Minutes later, he walked past them again, but there was nothing.

Then, Charlie saw the shadow entity, but its head poked out between the fourth and fifth doors. He walked towards where it was, and its head poked through the wall, looking at him.

'Look,' the mysterious being whispered. Charlie jumped slightly backwards as he was not expecting it to speak.

Charlie gazed hypnotically at the space where the creature was and then disappeared. He put his hand on the wall, and another door appeared.

All were shocked at what Charlie had just done, but Cosmolos stroked his beard.

'I choose this door,' said Charlie confidently. As soon as he spoke, the door responded.

'Welcome,' it said. 'Enter.'

Chapter Ten

THE ILLUSION LIFTED

The Stuarts and Campbells moved tentatively towards the door. Cosmolos, Hecate, and Randle followed behind. They found themselves back in the same narrow corridor as they passed through it.

'Oh,' said Charlie.

'What's the matter?' asked Emmanuel.

'After all that, I thought we'd enter some strange new land or something,' Charlie replied, disappointed.

'I see what you mean,' said Emmanuel.

The expressions of the rest of the family suggested that they were all thinking the same thing.

The corridor appeared quieter than Hecate's office, yet it felt more inviting and homely, like their first visit.

Randle led them back into the main entrance hallway. It was empty. Charlie was half expecting it to be bustling with people, but it was a ghost town.

As Charlie moved down the staircase, he looked round to see the knights' armour and swords. Like most of what they saw, the suits were brighter and more animated, and the swords shone vibrantly.

'Wow, look at that!' shouted Charlie. 'That's amazing!'

'That's nothing,' said Randle.

'Just wait until we get outside.'

Everyone's head lifted, and a gentle tingling sensation passed through them.

As they approached the door, there was a change in the atmosphere: a feeling of happiness and freedom. Hecate then walked to the front and stood at the door.

'Welcome, Headmistress. I hope you are having a great day. I see we have new guests in our world. It brings joy to my heart,' said the door in a helpful manner.

'Oh yes, Cyril...new guests indeed.'

'It is going to be a good year, I feel,' said Cyril, the door.

Both the Stuart's and the Campbell's mouths were wide open.

'The doors talk?' said a startled Mrs Stuart.

'Some... but there is more to them than what you think. You will learn more in your studies,' said Randle.

Expectations were building and building. Their experiences were a continual peak that never seemed to stop. Even Charlie's apprehensions eased as he was in awe of what he saw and heard. On reflection, he started feeling quite bad about how often he kicked the door at home. *I wonder if it was alive, and I never knew it.* He thought.

'It is like the whole place is alive—amazing!' said Amanda.

'I canna believe it,' said Andrew.

'Lovely, fabulous,' said Victoria.

'Look,' said Lottie, pointing at the pulsating vines, vibrating with energy.

'Why do these vines appear on the walls?' asked Emmanuel.

'They don't appear all the time, but come when they need to be here and help the school,' explained Randle.

'Uh?' said Emmanuel.

'You'll understand in time,' said Randle. 'By the way, you'll hear that phrase a lot! It wouldn't make sense if I tried to explain it to you all now.'

'Ah, OK...' said Emmanuel, looking confused.

'However, they are here to greet you and are happy to see you,' said Cosmolos.

'Oh,' said Charlie, not knowing how to respond. After all, they were just vines, or were they?

Still perplexed, he realised he knew little and decided to wait and see what else would happen.

'Don't try to figure it out,' said Cosmolos softly.

'Just enjoy it for now.'

'Hello, Cyril,' said Randle.

'Hello, Randle,' greeted Cyril. 'I will open up now.'

'Most kind of you,' said Randle.

'A pleasure,' said Cyril.

Charlie was now itching for the doors to open.

'Everyone here is very polite,' said Victoria.

'What a refreshing change,' she said approvingly.

'Aye indeed, everyone is so nice,' said the other Victoria.

Silence pervaded the hall. The door started to open, and both families moved slowly, nervous about what they would see.

Their movement was hesitant as they proceeded to walk outside, treading on the ground carefully as if it would not be there.

They walked down the many steps in front of the school, apart from Amanda, who went down the side pathway with her father.

'Well,' said Cosmolos. 'Aren't you going to turn around?' Both families' heads were fixed on the grass before them, frightened at what they were about to see.

Hearts were pounding, and breaths quickened.

Charlie felt his neck vein throbbing and panicked, thinking he might have another paralysing experience. When he realised this would not happen, he sighed in relief.

They turned around, their mouths dropping, frozen in awe. Bruce then tried to jump into his mother's arms but stopped because he was too big.

'Welcome to Dragonstone School of Magick!' said Hecate with genuine pride.

Well, this was the icing on the cake.

'I, I, I, don't understand...How...Er...What?' Mrs Stuart said, fumbling her words.

'This has got to be the most amazing thing I've ever seen,' said Charlie.

'I second that,' said Amanda.

'How could this happen?' said Emmanuel.

'I'm flabbergasted,' said Andrew.

'Well, let's show you around,' he said.

What they saw was very different from what they first saw when they arrived. The main building was enormous, and several buildings appeared. *How could something like this remain hidden from so many people?* Charlie thought. Even the landscape had changed, and the sky seemed more vivid.

Cosmolos walked to the front, raised his staff, and said, 'Venio taperatum megalus.' A large, rectangular object flew toward them from the other side of the main building, and they looked nervous as the thing came closer.

Moments later, the object landed within a few feet, and they all looked.

They still couldn't fully comprehend what was happening to them. It was pure shock on an unimaginable scale.

'Is that a...flying carpet?' asked a buzzing Charlie.

'Oh yes,' said Cosmolos happily. 'It is my personal favourite. There is plenty of room as we all have to get on.'

'We're gettin' on that? You mean we're gonna fly on that?' asked Andrew. 'Aren't we too heavy?' he said, sounding unconvinced.

'Yes, it is a flying carpet,' Cosmolos chuckled. 'The Arabians handcrafted it. Oh, this carpet can handle more than you think, so there's no need to panic.'

'Oh,' said Andrew, 'as long as you are sure.'

Andrew knew it was wise to say nothing else in front of Cosmolos.

'Well, come then, get on,' said Randle, sounding more like Eric than his usual calm self.

They walked tentatively onto the carpet, like when they took their first steps out of the school.

'What if we fall off?' asked Mrs Stuart.

'Don't worry, you won't; trust me,' he said softly, attempting to allay their fears.

'Why are we going on this?' said Amanda curiously.

'Well, can you think of a better way to see the school than to view it by air?' asked Randle.

'I see,' said Charlie. 'At least Eric isn't driving this carpet,' and they all laughed.

Without hesitation, they trod upon the glorious red carpet, its stunning golden patterns catching their eye. The crowning jewel of the rug was the magnificent golden dragon, meticulously crafted into the centre of a black square, commanding their attention and admiration.

Andrew was the last person to step onto the carpet. As he stepped on, the carpet took off. They all held onto each other for dear life as Hecate chuckled slightly.

'Don't worry!' Hecate said. 'Look!' Hecate was about to leave the carpet when Victoria Campbell shouted, 'Don't do it!' Andrew tried to grab Hecate as she leaned over the edge, but an invisible force pushed her back. 'See,' she said, 'it's perfectly safe.'

'Ah yes,' said Cosmolos fondly, 'the new shielding addition to this carpet, thanks to my old friend Astrophos. He's a great inventor and thinker, you know. Slightly erratic, but that makes him a genius and a good friend.'

Cosmolos stood commandingly at the front, steering by thought. The carpet flew up and up and over the building they first entered. Once past it, they looked around. It was a fantastic sight, to be sure: similarly, large buildings formed a gigantic circle. Cosmolos then guided the carpet to the centre of it.

'If you look towards the corners, you can see the Elemental Watchtowers. Each tower represents an element. I assume you can see which is which?'

'Ooh yes,' said Victoria, admiring the elemental display at the top.

'Allow me to give you a brief lesson,' said Hecate. 'The North Tower represents the Earth element!'

The pulsating vines covering the top of the tower, changing shape and moving, were visible. The vines knew they were there and waved them a big, leafy hello.

'South represents the Fire element!'

When she mentioned it, the flames roared to greet them and even changed colour, turning red, orange, yellow, green, blue, indigo, violet and purple. Andrew was relieved the fire didn't sting him on his bottom again.

'Wow!' all the children said.

'I've never seen fire do that before,' said Charlie. 'Impressive,' said Andrew.

Hecate continued. 'West represents the Water element!'

The water gently flowed over the top of the tower, resembling the patterns of mercury on a tabletop. It began to swirl around the centre, creating a whirlpool, and then it shot upward, forming a powerful jet. Then, it transformed once more, this time resembling a reverse whirlpool. As they flew past, it lightly sprinkled water on them. They felt the small platters of water droplets on their faces; it was refreshing, to be sure.

'And East is represented by Air!'

The East Tower had a visible covering of air. 'It appeared almost liquid, although it was clear enough not to be one.'

Like the other towers before them, the air started to perform its dance. It lifted upwards and spun around gently. Then, it got faster and faster until it formed a tornado, swirling menacingly. Two more miniature tornados emerged near the top of the primary tornado, looking like a pair of arms waving triumphantly.

'This is incredible,' said Mrs Campbell.

'Yes, the elements are powerful forces. They can be as gentle as a mother bathing her child or as violent as a storm on the sea. You will learn more about them when you start your classes,' said Cosmolos.

Cosmolos then reversed the carpet so they could see what was below. They saw a massive circular courtyard divided into four sections by a pathway.

On the outer edges of the yard, there were two study blocks on the left and two on the right. These blocks were situated inwards from the Watchtowers. The buildings were interconnected by corridors that linked the study blocks. Directly across from the main building was another large one, smaller than the main one.

'Lessons will be held in all these buildings. Each element block is dedicated to learning an element. The closest study block to the Elemental Tower belongs to that element. Now, we must move on,' said Hecate. But it will all make sense when the new term starts.'

'Agreed,' said Cosmolos. He turned the carpet around and headed down the field.

'To your right is where we hold our assemblies. We prefer them to be outdoors so students can breathe fresh air and remain alert. If it rains or snows, we have a magickal cover to protect us.'

Cosmolos guided the carpet to some buildings located at a distance, directly opposite the assembly area.

'These are the living quarters of our pupils. Magnificent, aren't they?' said Hecate, pointing to a series of small buildings that made up a miniature student village.

Cosmolos then flew up towards the centre of the vast field.

As you can see, the other buildings and marked areas of the fields are related to magickal and creative societies. There are too many to mention, though we want students to further their skill range and create new friendships. Some societies have changed, though you will get your complete listing when you start term,' said Hecate.

Cosmolos then flew further down the middle of the field until they approached a massive hole in the ground. There was no mistaking what it was: a vast underground arena.

'What is that for?' asked Charlie.

'Ah,' said Randle, 'this is what most students enjoy: it is the Arena of Orberon, often called The Orberon. Students can test their magickal abilities with various scenarios in a special space. It is fun and safe; it helps students revise and encourages them to learn new things. It is the most popular form of entertainment here at the school and, quite possibly, the most popular sport in the land. You can build alliances with anyone from your year. The rules will be explained later on. I'm sure your new friends will explain it all.'

'Sounds great! What are the school houses?' asked Charlie.

Hecate answered, 'There are four school houses, each representing one of the four elements. The House of Ghob represents the Earth element, the House of Gjin represents the Fire element, the House of Paralda represents the element of Air, and the House of Necska represents the element of Water. These are all ancient and well-respected Houses. The names come from the original founding Kings of the Elementals, dating back thousands of years.'

'Sounds fascinating! The schools where we come from all have houses, but nothing like this,' said Emmanuel.

'Yes, where do you think they got the idea for houses from?' Hecate said with a little chuckle.

'This all sounds very interesting. We have so much to learn by the sounds of things,' said Mrs Stuart.

'I wouldn't worry too much,' said Randle reassuringly. We find that most pick up the basics of magick pretty quickly. However, very few explore its potential. Don't panic. Take each stage as it comes and flow with it. The magick will guide you on your journey.

'Have you seen the time? We need to move on,' said Hecate.

'Yes, we must move on. There is more to the school premises, though you will discover more whilst here,' said Cosmolos.

'Where to?' said Mrs Stuart.

'The Village of Wondle!' said Hecate. 'You will now see your new and wonderful abode,' she said proudly.

Cosmolos immediately spun the carpet around and soared upwards. They felt the wind's forceful power as it hit their faces, and their hair flew back in response. It was a refreshing and invigorating experience, filling them with renewed energy.

The carpet paused and floated majestically in the air. Cosmolos raised his staff and spoke again. 'Portus megalus,' he said commandingly, and the air started to distort several feet before them.

A giant vortex appeared. As soon as it opened, rows of houses could be seen on either side of an open road. The image appeared grey and hazy but was still clear enough to discern their destination.

The carpet swooped towards the vortex, resembling a bird of prey.

'Amazing!' said Charlie.

The youngest girls screamed, and Emmanuel and Bruce cheerfully shouted as they did so. After a few seconds, they arrived in Wondle without any trouble. Cosmolos guided the carpet down the street.

A sense of eagerness filled them as they gazed upon the village they would soon call home.

Their eyes sparkled with anticipation as they envisioned a life in this quaint and charming community. Their hearts were filled with hope for a brighter future, and they knew that this village held the key to unlocking their dreams.

'I wonder which will be our house,' said Victoria Stuart.

'Aye, I wonder whether we will be neighbours,' asked the other Victoria.

'Yes, you are,' said Randle. 'We try our best to put families together that get on.

'It's such a beautiful village with gorgeous old-looking houses,' said Victoria Stuart in awe.

Chapter Eleven

A New Home

Cosmolos steered the carpet down the street as Randle began to explain.

'Tudor inspired,' he said. 'Oh yes, a wonderful place it is, so sophisticated and elegant. It is one of my favourite places, and I love to have a quiet drink in the *Old Witch Tavern*; it serves beer, ales and mead like no other.'

'Now you're talkin' my kinda language,' said Andrew.

'I didn't think druids did this sort of thing,' said Amanda.

'Oh yes,' Randle laughed. 'There is nothing wrong with enjoying some physical pleasures. As Cosmolos will tell you, it is all about keeping your life in "balance and proportion," Isn't that right, Cosmolos?'

'Indeed, this is true! Ah, here we are—your new home!'

Cosmolos and the families descended onto the back garden of the first house. Like everything else in this new world, it was vivid and beautiful, qualities not often seen in the Plainlands.

The air was fresh and clean. The flowers emitted a hypnotic scent, and the wind blew the long grass in the adjoining field at the back of the house. Beyond the grounds, there was a mixture of hills and woodland.

'Stuarts, you are in this house, and Campbells, you are next door,' said Randle.

Hecate had some errands to run in the village and thus departed.

Cosmolos dropped off the Stuarts and glided the magick carpet towards the Campbell's new home. Their houses weren't too far from each other, and they could happily chat away over the boundary fencing.

Their land was plentiful, and many flowers and trees existed, some known and others unknown.

'I've dreamt of a garden like this!' said Victoria, admiring the upward and downward flow of the water between two pond segments. At the top of the garden, a large tree stood firm. It had large overhanging branches that spread out as if to keep shelter.

'What tree is that?' asked Mrs Stuart.

'It's known as Crainus. It is a relative of the Willow, much older and wiser. It only exists in our world. Wide varieties of plants and wildlife exist here; each makes a valuable contribution to our learning, the environment, and ourselves. The school has a great mixture, and some are quite amusing.'

Amusing! How can plants be entertaining? Charlie thought.

'Lovely! I love a good garden. I'm not sure I could look after this myself, though.'

'Ah, my dear, one cannot be expected to look after this by yourself. There is help if you so require it,' said Randle.

'Help? From whom?' Victoria asked.

'The elementals,' replied Randle. 'What you saw at the school were the elements in their raw form. Each element has its kin and representation. They are experts of nature, which is the root of earth magick. There is more respect between our two kingdoms than there is with the Plainlands. Many stories have been written about Elementalkind, but you will learn the truth soon enough. Simply put, they can help or cause many grievances. Many younger pupils have not quite handled or summoned an elemental properly, and, in some cases, they've gotten their fingers burnt, literally! Fortunately, there are teachers on hand to help resolve any issues. However, many elementals assist us with day-to-day activities, one of which you have seen today.'

'That fire thingy,' said Emmanuel.

'Yes, that is correct. 'That fire thingy, as you call it, is a firedrake. They love smaller fires and love lighting and sitting within the flames. To them, it is the equivalent of sunbathing on a beach somewhere. OK, lessons later. You must be curious about your new lodgings, so let's go inside,' said Randle.

'The house is beautiful and so big,' said Victoria, with some delight.

Randle moved forward and whispered something to the door, which opened slightly.

'What did you say?' asked Charlie.

'Ah, it's a type of magickal password. You'll all have your personalised one when you start school. In the meantime, you will have to do with a key.'

At that moment, a set of golden keys gently oozed out from the front of the door, and a handle appeared.

'My password is now redundant,' said Randle. 'When you get your magickal password, you can enter as I have done.'

'When do we get that?' Victoria asked.

'When you go to your respective schools of magick,' Randle replied.

'Well, why wasn't a password needed at the school when we first came out?'

'Well, passwords will sometimes be used to access something personal or secure. It's efficient but complicated. There's no conning an access point that uses your password; the door will know whether you are lying. Cyril is aware of all the school members, so there is no need for the password in that instance,' said Randle.

'But what about the younger children? They don't have a magickal name yet,' said Victoria.

'It's no problem. The children will be with you most of the time so that they will enter with you, but they can have a magickally enchanted key to recognise all those in the family. Whilst you are on the grounds, the House Door and keeper will recognise you and allow everyone to move freely.'

'That's great!' said Charlie.

Victoria got the set of keys, and the family touched them to gain their magickal scent.

The house was impressive, large and spacious. It was Tudoresque, beautiful, and decorated with hand-crafted wooden furniture.

There were many rooms, including four living rooms, three dining rooms, and eight bedrooms, six of which had en-suite bathrooms and another main bathroom. There was a play area, an attic, and a drawing room full of old books.

'Are you sure that we are going to live here?' Victoria queried.'

Randle laughed. 'Of course! This house is tailor-made for you!'

'I see you have a TV here,' said Emmanuel.

'Is it the same as the TV we watch back, well, on the other side?'

'Just Wizard TV, I'm afraid. There is plenty to choose from. Trust me when I say you will be too busy to watch.'

'I'm thirsty,' said Charlie.

'I believe your food stores are well stocked. Let's head to the kitchen.'

They followed Randle into the kitchen, but before anyone could say anything, the fridge started to protrude further from the wall and opened. It was fully stocked with a range of drinks.

'There are a lot of drinks here. Where is the rest of the food kept?' asked Charlie.'

'In the cupboards, of course! However, things work differently here: you can access cold snacks like sandwiches from the fridge. The fridge is like a portal to various drinks and food items, provided the food is in the house. Upon arrival, we will stock your home with food and beverages for the week so you can settle into our world without worrying about grocery shopping. You have to cook hot food, as you do in the Plainlands. Any elementals you attract will gladly assist you with anything you need.

'Wow, that's different!' said Charlie.

'Amazing!' said Emmanuel.

'Might I suggest this drink if you are thirsty?' Randle leaned forward into the fridge and pulled out *Percy's Thirst Quencher for all Occasions—Magick Bean Root flavour.*

'Would you like a glass?' asked Randle.

'Ooh, yes, please,' said Charlie.

Everyone else was looking to see what other marvels would transpire. They weren't disappointed. A cupboard door swiftly opened at his request.

'I guess the glasses are in there, but I can't reach them,' said Charlie. Suddenly, part of the floor lifted him towards the cupboard. Everyone's mouths opened up like they did in Hecate's office.

'This is fantastic!' said Emmanuel, beaming.

Charlie picked up his glass, and the floor lowered again. He walked to the tabletop and started to pour the drink. It went from a bright red to a darker hue. Then, Charlie caught sight of the instructions on the bottle: "The darker the colour it turns, the thirstier you are; the more potent the thirst quencher becomes."

'Unbelievable!' said Charlie. 'We have nothing like this where we are from.'

'Oh, you must be thirsty,' said Randle. Charlie showed everyone what the bottle said.

Everyone else clambered towards the fridge to get a drink and see what colour their drinks would change into.

'Of course, there are drinks for all occasions, and they are all-natural ingredients, with a bit of added magick,' winked Randle. 'There are normal Percy drinks, however.'

'Is there any ice?' said Charlie.

'Ooh, over there in the bowl,' said Randle.

'The bowl?' said Charlie, looking somewhat confused. Charlie went over to the bowl and saw some blue, sweet wrappers.

'Aren't these sweets?' Charlie asked as he began to unwrap the blue wrapper. Then, low and behold, there was an ice cube inside.

'Now that's impressive!' said Victoria. 'Amazingly, the whole thing doesn't melt,' she continued.

'A true genius that Percy, he's thought of *everything*,' said Randle. 'Anyway, I must show you this,' he said, leading them to the drawing room. The bookcases were full of old-fashioned books. 'These books will help you understand the world of magick, though you must read these first. It covers some of the topics we've discussed and more. It is a kind of dummy guide to magick.'

'Thank you, Randle, though I have another question. I've noticed the word Magick is spelt with a K on the end of it and not a C as we normally see back in the Plainlands. Why is this?' asked Victoria.

'That's a good point,' said Randle approvingly. 'You see, we have spelt it with a K on the end because it defines real magick and sets us apart from other types. With the K, it gives the word more meaning, power and potency.'

'Intriguing!' said Victoria, speaking on behalf of everyone. 'I can quite honestly say that we are completely overwhelmed by this—incredible...amazing...speechless! Never in a million years would we have ever imagined a place like this to exist. Where we are from, places like these are pure fantasy! The more I think about it, the more I need to be pinched to ensure this is real,' she said excitedly.

'Mrs Stuart, you will find that all fantasy has its foundations. Well, some of what the Plainers call fantasy is reality!'

Charlie and the others listened and began thinking again about what was happening. Their circumstances were different and alien from what they had been used to. For instance, buildings with life in them, talking doors, magick carpets, and cupboards that seem to read your mind when you want something. *What else exists in this world? What other bizarre experiences exist here?* Victoria thought. The more she thought about it, the more confused she became.

The room went silent, and Victoria wondered whether she had done the right thing by exposing the family to this; it seemed to take her breath away.

Randle read the situation and spoke.

'I sense this might be a little overwhelming, and understandably so. It will take some time to get used to. I can assure you that you are in the best place where your potential can be fulfilled and your dreams are realised. There is a beauty here that cannot be found anywhere else; it is how things should be. Admittedly, not everything is perfect, but compared to the Plainlands, it is paradise. Much of the Plainlands is born out of fear, manipulation, and the absence of real colour and creativity. People are shaped and live by what others say they should be doing and live comparatively mundane lives. Many people exist without truly living up to their potential. It can lead to widespread depression because individuals may feel inadequate, unworthy and worthless, resulting in low self-esteem. Unfortunately, many people's unique talents and gifts are not recognised or developed, resulting in a great loss for humanity. Whilst not all actions and life choices are a complete waste of time, we could achieve so much more if we open our eyes to the possibilities! This is the magick of the Magicklands.' said Randle reflectively.

His passionate words made them reflect and calm them a little—everyone quietened.

Then, a knock at the door brought them out of their reflective thinking.

'Hey, how's it going?' said a familiar voice. It was Andrew.

'Hi Andrew,' said Victoria, pleased to hear his voice. 'Do come in.'

Charlie opened the door. The Campbells and Cosmolos were standing, waiting to go inside.

'Come in!' said Charlie.

He was pleased to see them, especially Amanda, whom he had warmed to.

They entered the house and looked excited.

'Amazing!' said Andrew. 'Absolutely amazing! I canna believe it! I reckon I will enjoy this place,' he said enthusiastically. 'Things seem so much more relaxed here, as well as cleaner. We had a look around the village, and it is immaculate. Back home, litter, dirt, and children are up to no good. This place is ideal for raising a family. I have to admit; this will take some getting used to.'

Victoria looked at Andrew. The roles had been reversed, as Andrew first showed the most concern.

Afterwards, they spent some time exploring the house and its ornate craftsmanship. The house was tall, had six floors, and had an oak staircase.

'I want the top room,' shouted Charlie as he ran towards the stairs. He suddenly stopped when he realised that Amanda could not get up. 'How is Ama...' Before he could finish, Randle pointed to another door that fit neatly under the first staircase. Charlie opened it, and much to his amazement, there was a lift.

'Hey Amanda, check *this* out,' he said excitedly.

'Yes,' she said, 'we have one the same at our house. This house seems identical to ours!'

'Marvellous! Did you check out the fridge,' he said whilst they entered the lift.

'Aye, it was great. Bruce was rather thirsty, and he opened the fridge. It looks like these Percy drinks are trendy here. I love the way they change colour.' Charlie pressed the button for the fourth floor whilst Amanda was talking to him.

'I had a *Percy Cola—Extra Fizzy*,' said Amanda. 'It was amazing, though bright blue did put me off, to begin with. Then, my brain fizzed with excitement once I drank it.' They both laughed, and the lift stopped. Charlie opened the door, and, remarkably, the elevator was not in the same place but down the corridor just outside a bedroom door.

'Wow!' said Charlie. 'It's like this house knows every-thing.' *How does it know everything?* He thought.

As Charlie approached the door, a handle appeared.

Charlie turned the handle, and the door opened.

'This is the best room I've ever seen,' said Charlie. It matched the rest of the house. Charlie began to explore. It had a king-size bed at the top of the room, a door leading to an en-suite bathroom, and an enormous walk-in wardrobe.

A giant TV screen was fixed to the wall at the bottom of the room. Charlie was amazed by the slim, sleek TVs in the Plainlands, which were a vast improvement from the bulky ones he was used to.

On one side was a large study desk, and on the other was a marble table. Although the table was made of marble, it blended well with the surroundings.

'I wonder what this is for?' queried Charlie.

'Not sure,' replied Amanda. 'I've got one the same in my room.'

Charlie looked puzzled but turned around and observed other parts of the room. There was a large window over-looking the back of the house. Small oil lamps, similar to those outside Hecate's office, dotted around the walls, and two unlit wall torch holders dotted around the room. *So, isn't it dangerous to have torches?* He thought.

'This bed is amazing,' said Charlie to Amanda. He took a run and jumped onto the bed before jumping around.

'It is huge and brilliant! Oh, this room is just for me, no more sharing.' I have to admit, I did have some fun with my Brother, so it wasn't all bad,' he said reflectively, thinking about the bunk bed he shared with Emmanuel.

'Just imagine having a bed that could fill a room,' he told Amanda. Suddenly, the bed started to creak, expanding its width and lengthways.

'Crikey me,' said Amanda as she quickly wheeled out of the way.

'What is happening?' Charlie bellowed as the bed continued growing.

Amanda wasn't waiting to see. She backed out of the room into the passageway and turned to face Charlie. The bed was about to hit the side furniture when Charlie shouted, 'Stop, please STOP!!' The bed stopped expanding. It had nearly covered the room, and the bedsheets had miraculously grown.

'Wow!' repeated Charlie, laughing and running around the bed. Amanda, Amanda,' he shouted excitedly, 'this is just blooming brilliant...I want to be here right now.' Charlie was brimming with excitement. He had forgotten all his anxieties and worries about the magical world at that moment.

'Charlie, Amanda,' shouted Victoria. 'We need to get going,' she continued.

'Going?' said Charlie. 'But we have just arrived,' he said to Amanda.

Victoria's mouth opened as she stood behind Amanda.

'Charlie Stuart. What have you done to this bed,' she said sternly.

'But...I...it...er...the bed, it just grew,' he said.

'What do you....' said Victoria.

'Ahem,' a voice came from behind her. It was Cosmolos. Moments later, there was a small audience in the hallway.

'I see you have discovered some of the wonders of the magick houses,' he said calmly. The rest stood stunned whilst Randle laughed.

'What happened?' asked Charlie.

'Well, you must have asked for it,' said Cosmolos.

'Ah, I did, but I was only joking about it to Amanda,' he said, looking puzzled.

'You undoubtedly have encountered the widely known adage: B*e careful what you wish for*,' said Cosmolos. 'This is never a truer statement in magickal law. However, this house is designed to cater to your needs and, most importantly, respond to your wishes. No harm can come to you in your house—I think it was having a little fun with you.'

'Cosmolos, why are we going now?' asked Charlie grumpily.

'Remember, this is just a visit, but don't worry, this world is your real home now, so there will be plenty of time to explore. For now, you must head back to the Plainlands to settle your affairs. Randle will explain what's to happen next.'

'Oh deary me,' said Victoria. 'I'd completely forgotten. It seems that we've been here some time!'

'And not a moment too soon,' said Hecate's familiar voice. 'Come along, please! I have some paperwork to do before the new term starts.'

Five minutes had passed, and they were all outside in the back garden and on the magick carpet.

Cosmolos raised his staff and said, 'Portus megalus.' A great vortex appeared, and back to the school they went!

CHAPTER TWELVE

FIRST DAY

The month had gone quickly, and the Stuarts spent some time concluding their business in the Plainlands with their family and friends.

Before they left, there was a big party at the house. Despite Lee's efforts to acquire some, Victoria was very vigilant and did well keeping the grown-up drinks away from the children. "Boys will be boys," she said, half-amused by their efforts. Ironically, she got a bit of a headache from drinking too much.

In the morning, she kept telling everyone to keep the noise down every moment. Emmanuel did his best to tease his mum by crashing cupboards, pots, doors and other items, much to her displeasure; he'd been hanging around Bruce too much.

The journey back to school took about an hour, and they were very apprehensive.

Randle, who seemed to pick up on these things, had said, "Although nervousness is understandable, plenty of help will be available. Reading your basic magic books will help.

Remember, keep calm; within a few weeks, you will be in the swing of things."

*

Eric honked the horn at the school entrance. The slit in the gate opened, and some steely eyes narrowed, looking at Eric, and Eric responded in kind.

There was a strong impression that the two didn't like each other, which amused Charlie.

The school gates opened, and the bus entered a bustling campus filled with children, families, and teachers.

The bus moved toward the school. 'Move out the blooming way, you imbeciles!' shouted Eric. Some children stuck their tongues out and gesticulated toward the driver to annoy him further.

Charlie and Emmanuel laughed hysterically. Even Randle seemed to have a smirk on his face.

The bus pulled into the parking area. Randle stood up to speak: 'OK, this is the plan—Charlie and Emmanuel will head to the main entrance, and you'll both be directed from there. The rest of you are coming with me to settle in at the Village of Wondle. You will be taken to your respective schools in two days to begin your magickal training. Oh, something else: only teachers and special guest visitors can use the Portus charm to leave and enter the school. It was recently added to the rules to prevent pupils from using it to play truant.'

'Where's Cosmolos?' asked Charlie curiously.

'He's in the Great City, where the Astro-Tower is. He shares it with Astrophos, who is helping him with a venture. I heard that he will be teaching some subjects at the school this year upon Hecate's invitation.

'I like him,' said Charlie. 'I have a few things I'd like to ask him, but hey, that's for another day.'

'A silly question, but what is the Great City?' asked Victoria.

'It is one of the magick world's finest achievements. There will be a visit there, and you will see first-hand,' said Randle. They all got excited.

'What about our school things?' Emmanuel asked.

'The school will provide you with everything you need,' said Randle. 'Sorry to hurry proceedings, but you must head to school for your induction. And don't worry; you are in competent hands.'

Charlie and the rest of his family spent a couple of minutes saying their goodbyes. Victoria was rather tearful, as she wouldn't see her sons until the holidays.

The act of severing the symbolic umbilical cord in Charlie created an unfamiliar feeling of insecurity. Life was no longer as simple as dealing with Vinnie in the playground, but he knew he would have to adapt.

A portal opened as Charlie and Emmanuel turned again to wave his mother and sisters off.

In a flash, they had vanished, and the brothers were on their own. Even Randle wasn't there to guide them. They felt alone, so they would have to fend for themselves.

Charlie moved closer to his brother for security and hurried past the dragons before standing next to the main entrance door.

Charlie placed the book he was reading, *Choosing Your Name* by Dr C Namewise, in his bag, and then a voice caught him unawares.

'Hello Charlie,' said Cyril, the door, 'how are you?'

'Oh, er, hello,' said Charlie, slightly uncomfortable in a conversation with a door. 'I'm fine, thank you—er, how are you?'

'Oh, all the better for the new term starting. I love talking to the teachers and pupils. I'm busy all the time, you know.'

How can he be busy? He's a door. Charlie thought.

'Well, it's good to see you again, and I hope you enjoy your year at school,' said Cyril.

'Thanks, Cyril, see you soon,' said Charlie.

Charlie couldn't figure it out but felt happy talking to the door.

'Charlie!' shouted a familiar voice.

Charlie turned around, and with her usual smiling face, Amanda was a few feet away from him. She was waving at him, and Bruce stood beside her, waving also.

'Hey guys, so glad to see you both,' said Charlie. 'When did you arrive?'

'Oh, ages ago. Eric dropped us off and said he would pick you guys up. It was a little boring standing here until everyone started arriving. Don't they look smart?' she said.

You could spot the first-years over the other children: they had no uniforms. The other children wore black trousers for the boys and black skirts for the girls. They all wore stunning blazers with bright white shirts and different coloured ties. Some wore capes with collars pointing upwards and had a metal chain connecting the two sides at the top. It reminded Charlie of a Count Dracula film he saw with his brother one late night.

'We do look a little out of place...' said Emmanuel. 'But I can't wait to get our uniforms. They do look rather good,' he beamed.

'First-years, this way,' announced an unfamiliar voice. There was a funny-looking man who was slightly stooped with a hunchback. 'My name is Goodwin Albright. I am the assistant to the Year Head. Follow me to the tailor's office so you can receive your uniforms,' he said in a dull announcer's voice.

They proceeded to one of the doors under the staircase. First, they went up, then down a similar-looking corridor.

Amanda pointed toward a ceiling decorated similarly to the Sistine Chapel in Rome.

A figure of the ancient god Poseidon held his fork of power, with all mythical sea-faring creatures swirling around him. It was as if Poseidon himself was observing the newcomers with curious interest. Afterwards, he dived into the sea, sprinkling a splash over everyone.

'WOW!' said Charlie. 'That was amazing,' he said, breathing in the sea air as all the first-years stood with mouths wide open.

'Come along now,' said Goodwin nasally.

They proceeded further along a corridor until they reached a door. The door opened automatically and greeted them as they went inside individually.

'Form a line, please,' Goodwin said in a dulcet tone.

A man came running out enthusiastically.

'Welcome, welcome, welcome, welcome! My name is Antonio Trapitoni from Trapitoni Tailors from the Greata City, the besta tailors in the land. Form a line and come standa on the marble stepa; say your star sign, and we'll take your measurements for your uniforms.'

Each pupil did as he said. As soon as he stood on the strange marble step, Charlie announced,' Aquarius!'

Then, the magickally enchanted tape measures whizzed around him, taking his measurements. One impatient tape measure even tapped Charlie on the arm as if to say, *Raise your arms. I need to measure your waist and chest.*

A stunned Charlie raised an eyebrow as well as his arms. The step glowed red when the tape measure finished, and he was ushered to a wardrobe. By some miracle, a perfectly formed uniform awaited him.

Steam escaped from the sides of the peculiar cupboard every time a garment was made. It resembled a well-organised production line, with a noise similar to a steam press.

After collecting their garments, they went to a changing area to wear their uniforms. Like most other children, Charlie had problems with his tie, but Antonio and some tiny helpers lent a hand. Whilst Antonio had no difficulties reaching, Antonio's dwarven helpers stood on boxes to help them. The dwarves said nothing and calmly went about their business.

They handed out cards that read and said aloud when he touched them, *'Antonio's Helpful Tips for Tying Ties and Looking Good.'* Charlie smiled and put one into his pocket to study later.

After a time, all the pupils were ready and looked immensely smart.

'Look at you,' said Amanda to Charlie, 'you look amazing!'

'Thanks! You're looking great, yourself,' he said, repaying the compliment.

'What house are you in?' asked Charlie.

'I'm in Necksa. It's a Water house. I'm a Pisces!'

'Oh, cool. I'm unsure what it all means, but it will make sense. I'm in Paralda,' said Charlie.

'Oh yes, Paraldians are Air signs,' said Amanda.

'Yes, I am an Aquarian, according to my astrology book,' said Charlie.

'OK, guys,' said Goodwin in a monotone voice. Let's go next door so you can get writing materials and equipment for your studies.'

They proceeded through an adjoining door in an orderly fashion and down an old, slightly crooked corridor. The firedrakes, which had fascinated Charlie so much, lit the torches as Goodwin led.

They entered a large, dark, circular room with no windows. The room was like a library with hundreds of bags labelled with glowing nametags in alphabetical order perched on shelves.

'Please go and get your bags. Those whose surnames begin with the letters A to M go from left to middle, and those who begin with N to Z go from right to middle. Don't all rush: we don't want any accidents or arguments.' Goodwin left the room, leaving the students to their own devices.

Charlie and Amanda separated, and Emmanuel ran up to meet Charlie. As Amanda wheeled herself over to her shelf, her wheel accidentally caught the foot of another young girl.

'OUCH,' shrieked the girl. 'Hey, watch it, wheelie,' Felicity said nastily.

'I'm really, really sorry,' Amanda said, apologising.

'You will be! Hey, girls, we got ourselves a crooky over here,' four more girls gathered around. 'I think she needs to be taught a lesson. Look at my *foot*. Well, at least mine can get better,' she said venomously.

Amanda was mortified and utterly dumbfounded by Felicity's reaction.

'Let's send her on a little journey,' she said with an evil grimace forming across her face.

Felicity grabbed Amanda's chair and, with the help of one of her other friends, Annabel, pushed it forward. The chair tipped over, knocking over three pupils as it crashed into the shelving. Amanda was thrown to the ground.

'Oi, you!' shouted Bruce.

'HEY,' shouted Charlie, whilst Emmanuel looked very angry. All three of them ran across the room. Bruce picked up his crying sister with Emmanuel whilst Charlie headed straight for Felicity, shouting, 'SHE'S MY FRIEND!'

Felicity went to kick him with her pointed shoes, but Charlie instinctively knew what was coming to him and blocked it with his leg. He then sent her flying with a forceful push of his hand from close range. Annabel tried to grab his hair. As her hand touched his head, he spun around, blocking her hand. Then, with an upward thrust and span around again, sweeping with his foot across her legs, taking them out, she crashed to the floor. The other two girls, Greta Gobbins and Phoebe Mulbright, were about to move to get him when Emmanuel and Bruce stepped in and grabbed them.

'I suggest you stop there if I were you.' The whole room looked on in horror; it went deadly silent. 'Anyone thinking about picking on Amanda or my other friends will get the same treatment. I hate bullies, and bullies hate me,' Charlie said, sounding very self-assured.

'Thanks, Charlie,' said Bruce. 'This is my Sister, and I suggest that if you don't want to feel my fist in your face, you better stay clear of her. DO YOU HEAR ME?' asked Bruce angrily.

'What's going on in there?' asked Goodwin.

'Nothing,' said Charlie quickly, knowing his actions were enough.

Felicity looked shocked and then gave a look that could destroy a building.

Her friends gathered around her in a final defiant show of force. They usually got their way, but they had met their match in Charlie.

'Are... are you OK?' asked Charlie softly.

Amanda wiped the final tears from her face and spoke, 'Just about,' she said. 'Thanks, Charlie. Where did you learn to fight like that?' Charlie began to explain to her all the training he had done since he was four. He then told her a similar story of Vinnie and little Tommy.

'That's amazing!' said Amanda.

'I tell you what: I'll teach you some basic defensive moves you can do with your hands. It's amazing what you can learn, no matter your disability. Bullies deserve only one thing,' he said, working himself up.

'Thanks,' said Amanda. 'I'll enjoy that,' she said, sounding more cheerful.

'Good moves, Brother,' said Emmanuel, approving.

'Thank you; I hate people like that,' said Charlie.

'I know what you mean,' said Emmanuel. 'Cowards, the lot of them... they always go for the easy targets. After that, I guess everyone will know who you are,' he laughed.

'OK, students; follow me. We need to go to the assembly area now as the headmistress, and some other teachers will now introduce themselves,' said Goodwin.

Everyone looked excited, and the atmosphere returned to normal. Still, Felicity and her gang huddled together, scowling, making provocative gestures, and whispering.

Charlie just ignored them, knowing better than to respond to petty gossiping.

They walked down a few corridors until they reached the outside. This time, they had a ground view of the school, which was awe-inspiring. It seemed so much bigger and more mysterious compared to the first time they'd seen it riding on the back of Cosmolos' carpet.

They then walked down some steps and entered the circular courtyard. It was amazing. There were statues, a fountain, and a range of flowers that weren't there before, along with all manner of creatures and light faeries.

'Ooh, look at these newbies,' said a voice.

Charlie, Amanda, Emmanuel and Bruce all looked around at each other. Charlie looked down at some flowers with sizeable yellow petal heads; they were talking.

'Flowers can talk?' said Bruce.

'Oooh, flowers can talk, nu, nu, nu,' said the first flower, Neil, cheekily.

'You're kidding me,' said Charlie, laughing.

'Don't laugh at me, you whippersnappers,' said the flower. 'Hey, Malcolm, wake up! Check these first-years out—it looks like they think they know it all,' he said.

The second flower opened its eyes and just looked. 'Achoo!' sneezed a flower at the end.

'What's the matter with him?' asked Amanda.

'Hay fever,' said another flower called Brian.

'Hay fever? But he's a flower,' said Charlie.

'I know, embarrassing isn't it,' said Brian.

'He's an embarrassment to the flowering world,' said Neil.

Charlie and his friends all laughed. However, Frank, the sneezy flower, didn't seem amused.

'Come along, everybody,' said Goodwin.

They looked around and realised that most had reached the outdoor assembly area, so they moved swiftly across. Panting, they eventually made it and sought to find their seats. Charlie looked up, and hundreds of pupils sat on chairs organised in a sloping arrangement, following the curvature of the hill.

'Hurry up and sit down,' said Goodwin. 'Your seats are just over here. Amanda, there is a gap there for you.'

'Thank you!' said Amanda.

'Emmanuel and Bruce, being in the year above, makes you second years. Your seats are in the next section up.'

'Good luck, guys...see you later,' said Emmanuel.

'You too, dear Brother, and you too, Bruce,' said Charlie.

'Be good,' said Amanda.

'Aren't I always?' said Bruce.

They all went to their respective seats and waited.

A lady approached the front stage area, and the chattering figures all went silent.

'Good morning to you all,' said Hecate, speaking through a magick microphone, but no speakers could be seen. 'I said good morning to all,' she repeated louder.

'Good morning, Headmistress Winslow,' they all replied.

'Better,' she said. 'I trust you all have had a great summer holiday and are eagerly awaiting the new term—first-years at Dragonstone—a very warm welcome to you all. I'm sure you will enjoy our school's delights, and I wish you all the best in your endeavours. Most of you are aware of the rich history of our outstanding school. However, there are some aspects of our magickal history that we do not understand. Enchantments remain in the older, mediaeval parts of the school and some from recent history. The function and purpose of most old spells remain a mystery, so we advise caution if you ever encounter them. One of these includes a peculiar door that has come to be known as The Door of Mystery. We advise staying completely away from this ancient enchantment, or you might disappear forever.'

Best avoid that then, thought Charlie.

'Any moment now, your Elemental Housemasters will be arriving. I can hear something now.'

They all looked up. In the distance, they could see something coming at them very quickly: a ball of flames scorching towards them at high speed. The first-years were screaming. The flames got closer and closer, reaching the stage where Hecate was and rising ferociously into the air. The ball of fire landed next to her, transforming into an Egyptian man wearing ancient clothing, much to the shock of the new students.

Several small Fire elementals hurtled towards the pupils, who ducked out of the way. The elementals danced in the air and then disappeared.

'Let me introduce you to Artuk Ra, the Fire housemaster.' Immediately afterwards, the earth appeared to distort and reshape as something else came hurtling towards them. As it approached, the ground shook violently, shaking everyone in sight. Standing before them was a stern-looking Native American Indian.

'May I introduce you to White Eagle, Elemental Master of the Earth House! He will join us as the new housemaster, replacing Dr Hume, who is looking after his newborn child. Can everyone please give White Eagle a warm Dragonstone welcome!' The students roared like dragons and then clapped.

Something else came swooping down from the sky and landed on White Eagle's arm.

'WOW, that's why they call him White Eagle,' said a voice amongst general mutterings. 'Yeah, they're really rare,' said another child. Perched on White Eagle's arm *was* a white eagle. The bird was scarce in the Magicklands and extinct in the Plainlands. 'It's beautiful,' said Amanda. The eagle bowed its head and then flew off.

Now, all the students from all the years were sitting on the edge of their seats, waiting to see who was coming next.

The sky began darkening, and a large grey cloud approached in the swirling wind. Torrential rain began to fall, followed by sparks of lightning and thunderclaps.

'That's new,' said one of the third years.

This time, two people appeared. A man dressed in ancient Greek clothing and someone else familiar to Charlie was Cosmolos.

'May I introduce the returning Elemental Housemaster of Water, Archimedes! Also, our new Air Elemental Housemaster, Cosmolos, the great mage and astrologer, has kindly taken on the role this year. Cosmolos has generously allowed older students studying advanced astrology to look through the famous astroscope as part of their studies of astronomical phenomena. It will be a wonderful addition to your magickal training and learning. Thank you, Cosmolos,' said Hecate. Cosmolos bowed his head in response. Charlie smiled.

'Now, a real treat for you... For those undertaking your knight training, we have a special addition to our team.'

Charlie's eyes widened, and he went all tingly. Did he hear correctly, or were his ears deceiving him? *Did she say knight training?* He now understood what Randle meant when discussing the fencing-type activity at the beginning of the year.

'And our special guest is...Sedrick the Viking, also known as Sedrick the Brave and Sedrick the Strong!' The students gasped in awe.

'Wow, great, brilliant!' said the students, amongst other appreciative gestures.

'He's my favourite by far. How enormous is he?!'

'He's huge! I've only seen him in posters,' said another child. 'I've got the latest one with me.'

'And here he is, making a special appearance... Sedrick the Viking!' The pupils were looking left and right. There was a bang, and a massive blanket of smoke appeared; even teachers waved their arms, trying to clear the misty air.

The smoke slowly dissipated, and the pupils sat on the edge of their seats.

Standing there, mighty and strong, was Sedrick. He easily towered over the other teachers, and he looked to be over seven feet tall. He seemed as broad as he was tall, wearing chain mail that covered his thick muscular frame; Charlie just about fell off the edge of his seat.

'I bid ye welcome warriors of the future. By Odin, the mighty Thor and the lovely Goddess Elin, I will make you the best of the best,' roared the Viking's voice. 'Let us see who can make the magickal class of knight. I am looking for one amongst you all to receive a special prize. But that is a long way off,' he said, scanning the audience with his piercing blue eyes.

'Well, I'm glad he got your attention,' said Hecate, who approached the front of the stage. She stood next to Sedrick and was like a dwarf by comparison. However, she appeared unfazed by his enormous size.

'I am sure that you are all looking forward to your new term at school, and it is great to see more magickal families joining us from the Plainlands. I am certain you will all do your utmost to help them settle in; we don't receive Plainland families daily. I trust you will all go and settle into your accommodation, that is, bar the first-years, as you are now eligible to decide your magickal names. Please follow our Head of Estates, Winston Denton, to the main building. He will take you to the magickal booths to give you your name. I hope you have had time to think of something appropriate. If someone else has your name, the booth will tell you. Once you have your name, you may proceed to your campus accommodation. I'm sure you will find it to your satisfaction.'

Charlie remembered reading about the magickal names in his book: it allows access to the dormitories, other personal information, and secured items. The book also said that with the name comes the real power that will help enhance your magick. It was a perfect system as the name was magickally enchanted to be inaudible to everyone other than the user. He thought of a name before attending the school, and, as it happened, he got one quite quickly.

Winston led them back the way they came, heading towards the talking flowers.

'Is it me, or have the flowers moved?' said Charlie.

'Is it me, du du du, mi mi mi,' teased the first flower they'd encountered.

'Oh, yes, they like the sun,' said Winston, 'just like me,' he said, in his calm, Jamaican swagger.

'You mean, they move around?' asked Charlie.

'Oh yes,' said another voice coming into the fray. 'They are a rare species commonly known as un-potted plants. They move according to where the sun is,' said the gardener.

'Good morning, Reginald. How are we today?' asked Winston.

'Absolutely marvellous! It has been a wonderful summer. I had a little problem with the trickster trees hiding my tools, though I got them back eventually—China, of all places. Oh! More first-years, I see. Hello, I am Reginald Bloom, the gardener,' he said in a very well-spoken voice.

'Hello,' said Charlie and Amanda, as well as some of the other pupils.

'Anyway, I must be orf... see you at the meeting, Winston.'

'Always rushing around, Reginald; you should take it easy,' said Winston.

'Easier said than done, anyway, pip, pip,' said Reginald as he moved quickly down the courtyard and into the grounds.

The pupils headed towards the school to see what was in store.

Chapter Thirteen

A Magickal Name

Charlie, Emmanuel, Amanda and Bruce walked towards the rear entrance of the school's main building, discussing the marvels they had seen.

Charlie was impressed by how the elemental housemasters could transform from their respective elements and back into human form.

He loved Sedrick the Viking and was in awe of him. Furthermore, Charlie couldn't believe he was learning to use swords and become a knight with Sedrick as his teacher, but he was excited to start.

Emmanuel, Bruce and Amanda were equally impressed, though the white eagle fascinated Amanda. The talking and walking plants were something else. No one believed they could do so!

Charlie gazed at his emblem and noticed his house's badge. The emblem showcased the ancient unicorn Pegasus, a lightning bolt, and other magical details. The badge was in a slim yellow circle, forming the emblem's outer edge. The house motto, Cogitatio est Magicus, meaning *thought is magick*, was inscribed on the outer ring of the badge. Charlie was about to open his bag when Winston spoke.

'OK, first-years. You need to follow me and stay close to each other. We are heading down to the depths of the school through the Earth corridors.'

Winston wore a loose, round-neck purple tunic, white long-sleeve undergarment, and a short, black hat. The garment was held together with a twisted gold and white cord tied around the waist. He wore a purple cape hanging off the shoulder and flowing to the ground.

Winston confidently withdrew a wand that resembled a twisted breadstick. The middle of the wand featured a single, bright, silver, thin strip with something painted on it that curled around the middle. A red jewel was firmly embedded at the bottom, with various engravings etched towards the bottom edge. As he lifted it, you could not miss the sight of a noticeable yellow gemstone protruding from the top of the wood.

'Fotios sapheara,' said Winston, and several balls of light emerged from the wand.

They flew down the corridor, hovering at appropriate distances, lighting up the darkest areas of this strange, spine-chilling tunnel leading into the earth.

The walls were slimy and unnerving, composed of mud, rock, and vines. The earthy odour in the atmosphere seemed very dense but not oppressive.

As they went further into the tunnel, the only sound was the patter of footsteps, and the daylight faded away.

Charlie asked, 'Where are they taking us?' as he pushed Amanda's chair.

'I have no idea. This is a bit scary, don't you think?' replied Amanda.

'It sure is, Amanda. I don't remember these corridors being mentioned in the magickal name-thingy book we got.'

The scared first-year students continued their journey until they reached a levelled area.

They approached an archway with a curved stone top and entered a large, unusual room. The students entered slowly but surely.

'Telios,' said Winston loudly, making some students jump.

The spheres of lights came back to him speedily and re-entered the wand.

Momentarily, the room darkened, followed by screams from some pupils.

Seconds later, a red light filled the room, only illuminating the lower half.

'What is this place?' Charlie asked Winston.

'This is where you "give" your magickal name,' replied Winston.

'But why do we have to come to this creepy place?'

As soon as he spoke, a gust of wind moaned through the area, causing everyone to freeze in place.

'Ah, this is one of the oldest parts of the school. No one knows how long it has been here. Magickal names have always spoken to earth kind. They take your name to where it needs to go and embed it in the magickal energies. It is a kind of grounding, a confirmation of your power. There are places like this at many points of the school and the Magicklands. Your parents will visit a similar place, Charlie,' said Winston.

Charlie stood back, surprised that he knew his name and family.

'He's from the Plainlands,' uttered one child.

The thing Charlie was trying to avoid was out: he was not born here in the magick realms.

Felicity smiled devilishly and looked like she was scheming something, but Charlie didn't see.

'So what?' said Winston, uncharacteristically.'

'Now everybody, go and find a booth. Don't be frightened; approach it with the highest respect, then listen.'

They scattered down the maze of corridors, trying to find a booth, and all entered the strange enclosures individually.

Charlie entered his.

The natural-looking cubicles began to close, creating a type of chrysalis effect.

'Speak your name,' whispered the booth, and Charlie uttered it.

'Accepted,' said the booth. 'Speak of this to no one... until it is time. Close your eyes and trust,' whispered the voice.

As he closed his eyes nervously, something touched his throat very quickly. Charlie opened his eyes immediately and felt like he had a frog in his throat.

'No person will hear your name. The words can be spoken casually, but no one will hear it when it counts.'

'Thank you,' said Charlie. The booth unravelled itself, and Charlie left.

Minutes later, it was all done. Everyone had given their name and could now go about their business.

Until it is time? What does it mean? Charlie thought to himself.

Winston lit the way again, and they quickly departed.

'Thank goodness for that. That was too creepy. How weird! How strange!' said Emmanuel. Everyone agreed.

'Where do we go now?' said Bruce, who was still regaining some composure.

'Now everybody, to your residence, follow me please,' said Winston.

'Great!' said Charlie. 'I'm bursting to see where we are going to live. If it is anything like the new house, it will be great,' he enthused.

After passing the un-potted Plants, which had moved to bask beneath the sun's rays, they proceeded to the halls of residence beyond the courtyard.

Charlie and his gang took a left turn down a pathway and passed through a large arched gateway, leading them into a miniature city of student accommodation.

The buildings on both sides of the path were designed similarly to the main school building.

The structure was ten stories tall, each room with a protruding balcony.

'This is incredible,' said Charlie.

'Aye.' said Amanda. 'And just think, no parents telling us what to do,' she smiled.

'But...but... I don't know how to cook,' said Charlie, slightly panicked by this.

'Well, I think it is the same as our kitchens in Wondle, but we will have to see,' said Amanda.

'Good point!' he said, feeling more cheerful. 'Do you know what? I think this is going to be really good. I wish my old friends could see this place,' he said reflectively.

'I know what you mean. I miss some of my friends, too,' said Amanda.

'Hey Charlie,' shouted a voice across the way. Charlie looked around and saw his brother waving at him from a balcony at the top of one of the buildings. Charlie waved back.

Next to Emmanuel was Bruce, who sat on a reclined chair with his feet up. He said hello by holding up a Percy drink with a straw sticking out from the top.

'Watch this!' exclaimed Bruce. He held the drink down, and a straw grew upwards to greet his mouth.

Bruce made a cheeky wink to imply, "This is the life," and then started sipping the drink.

'I wonder what flavour drink that is or what it means? It's turned black!" said Charlie, raising an eyebrow.

'I've no idea, but the colour suits him,' said Amanda as they laughed.

The main path was surrounded by a grass field that flowed in and around the dormitories and beyond.

Various trees were dotted around the garden, and neatly placed pots and hanging baskets held beautiful flowers tended by light faeries.

One of the faeries waited for a bee to leave before disappearing within the flower. They illuminated the area, creating a serene atmosphere.

The air was fresh, and the soft wind carried a sweet scent.

Winston walked with a floating scroll that flashed up, which students were going where each time they reached a building.

The process took a while, though Charlie was just a few blocks from his brother.

Winston read the following names, 'Thomas Feldrew, Amanda Campbell, Nicholas Rhoads, David Moarns, Steven Coldwell, Samantha Rome, Imogen Braithwaite, Charlie Stuart, Raphael Guessepi, Timothy Morden, Helen J.V. Kennedy, Parveena Badhan, Elaina Marcounis, Michael Shaw, Melay Cheung, Pierre Alfonso, Heinz Mogol, Freya Antony and, Melissa Jones.'

'It's about time,' said Charlie. 'I can't wait to see my room. I hope it is as good as my room in my new house,' he said eagerly.

'Me too; I hope the bed stretches out like in your room,' laughed Amanda.

'Now I've read your names; the door will recognise you as you enter and leave. However, you must use your magick name to enter your bedrooms. Full instructions on how to use your room are in your rooms. Enjoy!' he said as he walked down to the next block with the rest of the children.

Charlie and his group walked into the building, and moments later, they were all standing in the hall. It was like the main entrance hall of the school, with dark wood on the floor and walls, but the rooms were square. The ceiling had a circular mediaeval chandelier, though its flames were extinguished. Charlie was fascinated.

'Greetings, house,' boomed a voice.

All the children jumped at the sound of his deep voice.

'I am Sebastian, Guardian and Keeper of the House.'

'Hello, Sebastian,' said the children congregating around the door.

'If you require an early wake-up call, please let me know the night before,' said the faceless door. At 9 pm, the door will automatically lock, so if you are late, you will have to use your magickal name to get in.'

'Thanks,' said Charlie. At that moment, something else caught Charlie's attention.

'Er... Sebastian—what is this?'

'Charlie Stuart, welcome. Of course, you have taken the wondrous journey from the Plainlands. The item you speak of is a scroll porter: you send messages with it.'

'Oh!' said Charlie.

'Here, Charlie,' said another pupil. 'I've got to send this to Mum. She worries a lot, so I promised to send her this.'

The child took the rolled-up parchment to the machine, placed it vertically and said, 'Incedo, Mum.' The scroll dematerialised into light blue sparks with specks of orange and then vanished.

The boy brushed his brown hair and proceeded to wait.

'Fantastic!' said Charlie, but before he could say anything else, something else materialised into one of the pigeonholes on the wall behind the machine.

The name Thomas Feldrew appeared on the parchment that had arrived.

Thomas went over to the pigeonhole and said his magickal name.

The scroll flew out at him and landed in his hand. As it did so, a green seal with a golden crested crown vanished, and the scroll unravelled itself, keeping firm as it did so.

The following words appeared:

Hello, my little darling. I am glad you have arrived safely. I can't believe you have your magickal name—you're all grown up now, sweetums. May your magick flourish.
Go get 'em, Tiger! ;o)
Love, Mum and your family

A pair of magick lips flew out, kissing him on the cheek and leaving a red mark on his freckles.

'I wish she wouldn't keep sending those; it's embarrassing!' said Thomas, wiping the red lipstick off.

Everyone laughed and playfully teased him, and Thomas went a brighter shade of red.

'That is just brilliant,' said Amanda.

'So you are both from the Plainlands,' said Thomas enthusiastically. 'Oh, sorry, my name is Thomas; my friends call me Tom. Tom shook hands with both Charlie and Amanda.

'Hi Thomas, er, I mean Tom. My name is Charlie, and this is my friend Amanda. Yes, we are both from the Plainlands,' said Charlie proudly.

'Great!' Tom enthused. 'I've never been, so you'll have to tell me about it.'

'Yeah, sure,' said Charlie, feeling more at ease now he had befriended his first Magickland friend.

The other children seemed interested in them, so Charlie and Amanda shook hands with everyone.

'Do you know lots of magick?' asked Amanda.

'Just a bit: everyone's magick begins to work once you have your name, you see. Mum made me remember the

sending spell and expects a letter daily—she drives me up
the wall! I see you're with the Air House,' he said to Charlie.
'And you, Amanda, are in the Water House,' he said, observing their badges. I'm in Earth House. I hear it's harder
to travel than by Air; you're lucky.

'Er, OK,' said Charlie, unsure how to respond.

'Ah, sorry, Charlie, you probably have no idea what I am
talking about. Well, I'll tell you as much as I know as we go
along,' said Tom helpfully.

'Thanks,' said Charlie. 'We would appreciate it.'

'I don't know about you, but I'm dying to see my room,'
said Tom.

'What room are you in?' asked Charlie.

'I have no idea. Let's check the board,' replied Tom.

Everyone hurried over to the main notice board to check
their room numbers.

'Brilliant, Charlie, you're on the top floor next to me,'
enthused Tom.'

'So who am I sharing with?' inquired Charlie.

'Sharing?' Er, no one shares; we have a room all to ourselves. Great, isn't it!'

'You're *kidding*!' replied a stunned Charlie.

'Gosh, you certainly have a lot to learn about the Magicklands. The board says you are in 10a, and I'm in 10b. This
building will be our house for the next few years, apart from
the holidays. You know all about that, I assume?'

'Yes, Tom, Cosmolos told us all about it when we first
came,' said Charlie.

'You've met Cosmolos?' said Tom curiously.

'Yeah, we took a ride on his carpet when we had a tour of
the school,' said Charlie.

'Wow! You never! You *lucky* thing! I've always wanted to go on one.'

'Oh right!' said Charlie, sounding confused. 'I thought that everyone would have had a go on one?'

'They're quite expensive to buy. Normally, all the top households have one—well, all the decent ones.'

'What do you know of Cosmolos?' Charlie asked.

'He's a mage, the next stage above a magician and below a wizard in terms of magical power. There haven't been many true wizards for centuries, though mages are mighty. He's a brilliant astrologer, and he looks after everyone's chart. Some say he knows everything about everyone. He works with Astrophos, another great mage.'

'Ah yes, he is the guy who invents things,' said Charlie. 'That's right. He's brilliant!'

Charlie, Tom and Amanda proceeded through double doors leading to other rooms. The first door led to a communal room where everyone could socialise.

There were lovely sofas like the ones on the bus and in Hecate's office. Pictures and posters of different magickal folk left by the previous occupants were on the walls. One was of Sedrick, a magickal knight, holding up a trophy that read, "3 x Winner of the Orberon."

A TV hung above the massive fireplace in the sitting area, and there was a large kitchen. On one of the tables, there were some board games. As Charlie glanced, he saw a game called Wizopoly.

'Hey, Charlie, look at this!' shouted Amanda. Charlie was so preoccupied he failed to notice that Amanda had wandered off.

'Over here,' she said excitedly. Charlie and Tom walked over to Amanda.

'See... what do think to this?' she said. 'WOW! Er, what is this room?' asked Charlie. 'It's called the Room of Reflection,' replied Tom.

'A what?' asked Charlie and Amanda.

'Come in and see. The stained glass windows change colour according to what you need or think of at the time and help you solve problems. It is very clever. I'm not too sure how it works. ' Tom said to Charlie, 'think of something you would like an answer to.'

Immediately, Charlie thought about the shadowy thing and his hotel experience. The light in the room turned green, violet, and then purple. Charlie's mind went unusually still, and then he opened his eyes.

'Good, isn't it? Whatever you were thinking seemed quite important. I know purple means important magick stuff. Sit long enough, and you should receive a solution to a problem you are looking for. That's if you can figure out what it is trying to tell you.'

'I like this room,' said Charlie.

'Me too! I might pop down here in a wee bit to see what it can do,' said Amanda.

'What room are you in?' asked Charlie.'

'I'm in 9a, just below you, Charlie,' she chirped. The view from our rooms must be great, so I'm glad I'm not stuck on the ground floor.'

'Come on, let's go and see our rooms,' said Charlie as all three proceeded toward the lift.

On their way, they noticed a drawing room similar to, though much larger than, the one in his new Magicklands home. It had a regal feel, and there were enough tables for everyone.

The books seemed old; you could smell their age. They somehow made you feel quite important.

'I like this space,' said Charlie. 'We've got one at the house,' he said.

'Yeah, me too; there are many books here, and even more in the main school library. I saw it in the summer when I came with Mum and Dad,' said Tom.

They spent a few more minutes looking around. Charlie was impressed with the executive toys that moved by themselves. There was also an orrery hovering in one corner.

A few more minutes passed, and they walked into the lift.

'Floor nine and floor ten, please,' said Tom.

Amanda got off first, and then Charlie and Tom got off their floor.

'I'm bursting for the toilet,' said Tom. 'See you in a bit.'

Tom ran towards his room, clutching himself in desperation. He said his name and ran in before the door was fully opened.

Charlie walked speedily to his bedroom, said his name, and entered. He suddenly realised that he finally had his own space. He had never slept alone, let alone had an entire room to do as he pleased.

'This isn't going to be as bad as I thought,' he told himself again.

As Charlie entered the room, he was greeted by the things he had brought from his old house, and he examined them.

He took out his favourite sports poster and stuck it to the wall. He felt comforted that he had something to remember the old world by.

Charlie couldn't be bothered to unpack the rest of his things, so he ran and jumped onto his double bed. 'Grow,' he said to himself. Nothing happened. 'Rubbish!' he shouted out. The expanding bed was a luxury he'd have to wait for in his new house in Wondle.

As Charlie lay there, he heard a whooshing sound followed by a thud. He turned to his left and saw a scroll porter with a pigeonhole. Inside the pigeonhole, there was a scroll.

Charlie catapulted out of bed, remembering how Tom retrieved his scroll. He said his magickal name, and it flew towards him. Surrounding the middle was the same seal. It said *Magick Mail Postal Service*, and then the seal vanished.

Hello son, Mummy here! Charlie's eyes widened, and he felt excited to hear from his mum so soon. *Randle showed me how to use this thing, and I must say, it is somewhat more impressive and quicker than the postal service back home.*

Anyway, all is well here, and I now have my magickal name. It took me four attempts to get it to accept it, and poor Mr Campbell was at it for nearly an hour for his.

We're settling in OK, and if I were you, have a read of 'Invoking Family Helpers'. Mini the Brownie is adorable and a great help. You best read about them before you go around invoking them.

Randle is helping us out quite a bit, which is excellent; otherwise, it would have taken us ages to get everything sorted. We're heading to the local pub for something to eat. Andrew insisted, as he wanted to try the local magickal ales.

Anyway, best of luck to you, sweetheart. Your sisters say hi, and I've also sent a letter to your brother.

Write soon—lots of love, Mum.

Charlie saw some parchment paper left on the side with instructions on how to use them by Reginald Gimbus, Head of Postal Service for Plainlanders.

Charlie was about to use his first spell in the magick world and was excited by the prospect.

But what if this doesn't work? He thought. He started to panic. *What if my magick is rubbish and I look stupid in class?!* he pondered.

Charlie picked up some spare letter parchment and said, 'Speak.' The paper gave a slight vibration.

'Hi, Mum!' Said Charlie as the words began to appear on the paper. Charlie went all goose-pimply as he did so. *Everything is going better than expected, and I've met a new friend, Tom; he's been very helpful.*

I live on the top floor, room 10a, next to Tom, and Amanda's room is just below mine.

The bed doesn't expand like at home, though I am sure there are plenty of exciting things to discover.

I'll write to you soon. Love Charlie. Xxxx

Charlie double-checked his instructions and declared, 'Finished!' He rolled up the scroll and placed it vertically in the scroll porter.

Charlie felt slightly nervous as he was about to utter his first incantation. Still, he took a deep breath and shouted confidently, 'Incedo, Mum!' Instantly, the scroll vanished before his eyes.

Charlie felt proud that he had successfully used magick.

'It works!' he shouted. Even after all that he had seen, he was still somewhat sceptical. But when using magick, he confirmed that he had officially arrived in the magick world.

Buoyed by his experience, Charlie sent messages to his brother, Amanda, and Tom. It was the most fantastic thing he had done, and he wanted to learn more about magick.

Emmanuel had written to him saying he should examine the shower, so Charlie ran into the large and cosy bathroom.

An unusual-looking shower cubical dominated the right-hand corner of the room. Another set of instructions was posted on the cubical. 'Marvellous,' Charlie said to himself as he read.

Charlie's eyes lit up, but before he could finish, there was a knock at the door.

'What are you up to, Charlie?' shouted Tom.

'Come in,' said Charlie.

The door opened, and Tom entered.

'Does this shower do all this?' asked Charlie.

'Yeah, though some are better than others. We are lucky to get these deluxe models,' said Tom.

'I've never seen anything like it,' enthused Charlie.

'Blimey, I guess you have nothing like this in the Plainlands?' said Tom.

'Not quite,' said Charlie. 'I understand why you call it the Plainlands.'

'Anyway, are you heading down to the common room? Amanda has already gone down as she's hungry,' said Tom.

'I'm starving, too,' Charlie said as his stomach started to rumble.

They left the room and headed toward the communal area.

'Hey Tom, hey Charlie,' said Amanda, waving and shouting simultaneously.

Tom and Charlie walked over to her table, where she was reading Dr GT Spellbinder's magick book,' *Beginners Guide to Spells and Incantations.*'

'I sent my first scroll,' said Charlie, all excited.

'Aye, me too,' said Amanda. 'I had this feeling that it wouldn't work, but... but it did. Incredible!' she said, beaming.

'Just look at the timetable: We've got *Introduction to Meditation, Basic Spells and Incantations, Magical Tools, and The History and Magickal Practices of Magick.*'

'Where did you get the timetable from?' asked Charlie. 'They're in the school bags,' said Amanda. I guess you haven't looked yet?' she chuckled.

'Crikey, I forgot all about it. I'll check it later on.'

Charlie headed to the fridge and thought of a bacon sandwich. He opened it, and it was there. *Fantastic*, he thought, 'but it's cold!' he said aloud. He immediately saw a sign: "Hot food can only be obtained in the main canteen." He gave a small sigh and went to sit down to eat his food.

The Re-Fillable Cups impressed Charlie the most. They *allo*wed you to choose from just about any drink except a Percy alcoholic one.

He then picked up the cup and said, 'Tea, white and no sugar.' Sure enough, the tea filled up from the bottom upwards, creating the perfect cup.

Something then caught Charlie's attention: a child vanished from sight.

'Tom! Where has that girl gone?' he said, panicking. 'They're playing Wizopoly.'

'Wiz what?'

' Wizopoly. It's a game. You go around buying famous magickal places with fake money. But sometimes you have to go and barter for a property,' he said casually.

'Oooh, that sounds similar to a game in the Plainlands. Why do people keep disappearing?' asked Charlie.

'Well, how else are people going to have their turn,' said Tom, looking as confused as Charlie.

'What do you mean?' asked Charlie.

'When it is your go, you go into the game. It is great; even sitting in the dungeon can be fun.'

'Incredible! So, let me get this right. The game, somehow, shrinks you, and you end up in it.'

'Yes,' said Tom. 'This looks like the latest version: the buildings are brilliantly enchanted. They look just like the real thing, as do the people.'

Charlie and Amanda looked at each other, impressed, and quietly ate their food.

The rest of the afternoon and evening went quickly.

In their spare time, they explored the campus. However, there was little to do, as the Orberon and societies were closed until the weekend.

Afterwards, they spent some time in each other's rooms, each reflecting the characteristics of its tenants.

Nightfall came, and they were all exhausted.

Charlie had asked Sebastian if he could wake them up early, to which he courteously agreed.

Having felt the weight of the day, they all went to their respective rooms and collapsed in their beds. The first day was over; the lessons were about to begin.

CHAPTER FOURTEEN

HISTORY OF LEGENDS

The night was tranquil. Charlie deliberately opened his window and took a deep breath, savouring the pure, refreshing air that carried the scent of freshly cut grass and autumn blooms. The stars in the sky shone brilliantly. Charlie was too exhausted to appreciate their magnificence and eventually dozed off, snoring audibly throughout the night. Time moved slowly, but it couldn't hold back the dawn of a new day.

As the day broke, Charlie was abruptly awoken by the curtains in his room that flung open and the sun's rays blinding him. Suddenly, an ancient-sounding horn blared, startling him.

'AHH!' Charlie screamed as he leapt out of bed, assuming a martial arts stance. After a few deep breaths, he calmed down.

'Crikey,' he shouted. 'That was the wake-up call? I need to have words with Sebastian,' he said, sighing and laughing before taking more steady breaths.

Despite the early shock, Charlie acknowledged that the wake-up call had done its job and proceeded to the bathroom.

Charlie suddenly remembered his brother's note about exploring the shower. He removed his Dragonstone pyjamas and placed them on the rail. Then, he walked into the odd-looking shower cubical and closed the door.

'Shower,' he said aloud, following the instructions.

Water came rushing out from all directions, moving, circling, caressing, tickling; it had a life of its own. A jet came from above, stimulating his head, and he grabbed some Leprechaun Soap and then some Leprechaun Shampoo.

It was a fantastic experience compared to his old shower, which was like a hosepipe in a sewer.

'Slightly warmer,' he said, and the shower responded to his command. 'Much better,' he said.

Charlie then prepared himself. 'POWER SHOWER!' he shouted, wondering what marvel would happen next.

The water now gushed in from all directions, cleaning and refreshing him; it suspended him two inches off the ground before gradually lowering him.

'Stop,' repeated Charlie, and the shower responded. 'WOW, that was amazing!' he yelled to himself.

'Oh yes, dry,' he said, issuing his final instruction. In came a warm yet powerful airflow.

Seconds later, he was dry and heard a scroll arrive.

Charlie quickly put on his Dragonstone robe and headed into the room to read Tom's scroll.

Hey Charlie, I'm heading down for breakfast soon. Are you coming?

Charlie quickly responded.

Ten minutes later, Charlie had put on his uniform, though he still hadn't worked out how to tie his tie properly. He wished he had one of the dwarves with him to help.

Breakfast consisted of cereal called Gobby Brisks, which didn't sound too appealing to Charlie or Amanda but tasted good! By the end, they all decided to head to the main canteen the next day to treat themselves to a full English breakfast of egg, bacon, tomatoes, beans, toast, and a nice cup of tea.

Time was ticking, and they knew they had to head to class. They collected their things, put their bags on their backs, and left.

Hundreds of students were rushing around, checking their timetables, some fumbling as they looked.

'I wonder why we are doing meditation?' asked Tom.

'Aye,' said Amanda. 'At least it is not a too strenuous start to the day,' she smiled.

'Sounds good to me, too,' Charlie said. 'My old kickboxing teacher said that some martial artists use meditation to help them focus better. It makes sense, I suppose,' said Charlie, replying to Tom's query.

'How long have you done that for?' Tom asked.

'Oh, since I was four,' said Charlie confidently. 'My dad took my Brother and me before they separated,' he said. 'I enjoyed kickboxing, so I hope they do it here. I've not practised for days,' concluded Charlie.

'You seem pretty good from what I've seen,' said Amanda, referring to the Felicity incident.

'Ha-ha, thanks. I got into a fight at the end of term at my old school with a bully called Vinnie and his stupid thicko gang. I told Amanda about it yesterday.'

'What happened?' asked Tom.

'Well, they avoided me until the end of the term,' said Charlie.

'Brilliant. You must have scared them.' said Tom.

'I hope so,' said Charlie, smiling.

Moments later, they arrived at the top of the sloping hill, heading towards the rear side of the main building.

'What class are we in?' asked Charlie.

'Er, let me have a look,' replied Amanda.

She pulled out her timetable, which was printed on parchment paper. The front listed all the lessons for the day, and the back displayed a school map. There was an animated compass that would ensure you never get lost. Additionally, student notifications would appear. It was a fantastic piece of magical invention.

The day's first lesson was meditation with a kind old teacher, Mage Siddhartha, Master of Meditation, Visualisation and Second Sight. The mage taught them the importance of meditation and visualisation.

The two were different, but meditation was a way of relaxing so you could visualise or image accurately. He explained that 'to image' was an advanced form of visualisation as you use all your senses: smell, taste, touch, and sight. Furthermore, he explained that it was necessary, as it is one of the keys to performing all levels of magick. It helped to increase the power and efficiency of the spell or enchantment. With the meditation, he said, "Stillness, quietness, reflection, observation, focus, clarity, answers, sharpness, bliss, knowing, enlightenment; these are just some of the many benefits. In time, I hope you see and feel the benefits of doing such a practice," and they would understand this in time.

Mage Siddhartha materialised several items on the students' desks. Seconds later, the objects levitated, rotating very slowly. When the items vanished, they had to write down what they remembered about them; the more thorough the detail, the better.

Afterwards, he took them through an exercise to meditate and focus on their breathing so everything else was blanked out. It was called 'Meditating on the Breath'.

Mage Siddhartha then told them to write down what they remembered about the objects in the first task. Much to their surprise, they remembered considerably more detail about each object.

Of course, many struggled to keep their focus, and many snored. However, he wisely told them not to force the exercise, allowing distracting thoughts to pass through, not to fight them, and above all, to *relax*.

After their first session, Charlie, Amanda, and Tom grabbed a quick bite, but they had to rush off as they ran late.

'You're going to be late, you're going to be late,' teased the un-potted Plants.

To Amanda's surprise, Amanda got out her timetable, which said, *'This way,'* in a quirky voice.

They moved to the Earth element block as quickly as possible, where the rest of the class and another teacher waited.

'Sorry we're late, sir,' said Charlie. 'We were eating, and we forgot the time,' he said, embarrassed.

'It's not a problem; don't panic. However, as you missed the introductions, I am Astrophos, Mage of Magick, Scrolls and Technology.

'Oh, you're the guy who designs all the cool things,' exclaimed Tom.

'In a manner of speaking, yes,' said Astrophos. 'Curious!' he said, looking at Amanda. 'Amanda, could you please see me after class?' he said, rubbing his beard, inspired by an idea.

'Er, me? Well—OK, sir,' she said, sounding uncomfortable.

'Good, we must get on now,' said Astrophos. This is great!' said Tom.

'Let's make haste. This way, much to do,' said Astrophos.

'Sir, where are we going?' asked Timothy Morden.

'Into the Great Wood, of course...exciting place, you know,' said Astrophos.

'Why?' asked Timothy.

'You'll see,' said Astrophos, leading the way at some pace.

They walked beyond the assembly area, across a field, and into the woods.

Various trees, some unique, had amazing exotic flowers that delivered breathtaking fragrances.

The sky was cloudless, the air still. The sun warmed during the beautiful Indian summer that graced them.

'What are those... and those--and those?' Charlie asked eagerly, pointing at strange creatures that darted in and out of the area.

'They are Elementals of the Woodlands,' said Tom. 'They help to take care of the forest.'

Amanda got very excited and shouted, 'Look over there, is that a gnome?' she asked eagerly.

'It certainly is,' said Astrophos. 'It is a tree gnome which lives inside the holes at the top. They're friendlier to humans than most elementals. They are exceptionally curious and like to see what's what, especially when new visitors arrive.'

'Look, he's waving,' said Amanda as she waved back to the gnome smoking a pipe, which emitted yellow smoke.'

'SIDNEY!' shouted another voice.

'What is it, Matilda, my sweet?'

'Don't you, Matilda-sweet, me! Where on *earth* have you been?! With Rumbus again, drinking no doubt!' she said whilst she clouted her husband with a rolling pin, knocking the pipe out of his mouth.

The students laughed as they continued further along a pathway.

'Now, students, please do not tread or venture onto here.' Astrophos was pointing to an area with withered and scary-looking trees. They were surrounded by grass that initially seemed inconspicuous.

'This is Carnivorous Grass,' said Astrophos. 'Some old Warlock put a curse here. It's a long story,' he said, shaking his head.

As the students carefully walked past, it was evident that fear had taken hold of them.

After a few minutes of walking, they ventured into a densely wooded area and eventually arrived at a less compact region.

In the middle of this space stood a magnificent tree unlike any other. Its branches appeared to be made up of different trees, creating a miniature woodland in itself—a beautiful yet confusing display.

'This is the Lord of Trees, The Eternal Tree. It was the first tree that shaped the woodland and forest beyond. The tree is unique as it can give you any wood from any tree—it's one of its kind. It must be approached with the highest respect.'

'This is amazing,' said Charlie, as some wood elves entered and left the Eternal Tree.

'Why are we here, sir?' asked Steven Coldwell.

'A good question... You are probably wondering what this has to do with Magickal Tools, yes?'

'Yes, sir,' some replied, whilst others nodded.

Astrophos raised his staff and spoke.

'What is this?' asked Astrophos.

'A staff, sir,' said Tom.

'Precisely. What else can you tell me about it?' asked Astrophos.

'Er, it's used in magick,' said Parveena.

'Yes. What else?'

'It is made of wood,' replied Charlie.

'Where do you get wood from?' asked Astrophos.

'Trees!' said Heinz.

'Yes, so we need to get our wood from that tree, sir,' enquired Charlie.

'Very good,' said Astrophos.

At that point, the students appeared nervous. Their nerves were intensified when a scurrying wind whistled hauntingly through the branches.

'Please approach the tree one by one and do it respect-fully and cautiously. The wood elves are very protective of the tree. Once there, you must say your magickal name, and the tree will provide you with the branches you require to create your staff and wand.'

Charlie remembered reading that some elementals can change form and appear in any size they choose. They seemed pretty small at this time, with a faint glow around them.

'There is one more critical instruction: you must ask the tree if taking the wood from it is OK. If it agrees, it will release it to you.'

More elementals appeared, watching, observing, and producing strange sounds.

Some magickal creatures looked strange, and some looked frightening; you could sense the pupils' nervous-ness.

Suddenly, a three-eyed elemental transformed into a rainbow of light and vanished as it accelerated towards the sky.

'Show respect, and there will be no problems.' Astrophos reminded them to bow and thank them, regaining their attention.

One by one, they took tentative steps toward the tree. All you could hear was the soil crunching beneath them.

When it was his turn, Charlie suddenly saw the myste-rious shadow creature appear unexpectedly. 'Here we go again,' Charlie said to himself. He approached the tree courteously and said his magickal name. The shadowy crea-ture went into the tree. As it did so, the tree opened up, and Charlie walked inside. The tree closed.

'Charlie! Where has he gone, sir?' shouted Amanda.

'Sir, what's happening?' said a panicked Tom. 'What's happened to Charlie?'

Felicity smirked as if to say good riddance whilst David looked panic-stricken. Astrophos just watched and said, 'Wait... all is well.' The tree opened, and Charlie walked out with his branches.

'Are you all right?' asked a worried Amanda.

'Well, that was strange,' he said, looking like he'd been dragged through a hedge. Well, it wasn't far from the truth!

Astrophos took Charlie to one side and asked him what had happened.

'Well, I walked towards the tree and somehow got pulled inside.'

'And?' said Astrophos sharply.

'Well, I did as you said, sir,' said Charlie, sounding like he had done something wrong.

'Did anything else happen?' queried Astrophos enthusiastically whilst smiling.

'One of the elves, a gnome, and some other elemental creatures came forward and gave me these.'

'Fascinating!' said Astrophos.

'The next thing I knew, I was heading out.'

Astrophos followed in the footsteps of the wise Cosmolos, who rubbed his beard in deep contemplation.

'You've been given a piece of ancient bark from the Arterious tree, scarce and ancient; a great privilege, indeed.'

After a short walk, they returned to the school and headed toward the workshops. The walk wasn't without gossip about the woodland incident. Astrophos distracted the pupils by pointing out the various plumages around the school grounds.

The students went to a workshop to mould their staffs and wands from the newly acquired branches.

Astrophos mentioned to the class the importance of creating their magickal weapons by putting their 'mind, heart, and soul' into them. 'It is this that gives them special magical energy and power,' he said.

The machines clunked away to help smooth and shape the wood. Some dwarves assisted in operating the machinery, and hand tools were used to add some personal touches.

Astrophos mentioned they could add to their designs as they acquired more knowledge about magical workings and symbols, but they were complete now. He instructed them to take their wands and staff back to their rooms and activate the magick using unique power words within each Elemental Quarter.

Charlie's Arterious wand was deep red with black tones. The wand had ruby tips embedded securely at both ends of the wood. The ruby at the top of the wand was pointed like a pyramid, allowing it to focus and direct the spell's energy.

Charlie engraved the symbol of Air, a triangle pointing up with a horizontal line connecting the upper part.

Charlie informed his friends about what happened in the woods. Astrophos cancelled his meeting with Amanda because he had an essential appointment in the Great City.

The next lesson was basic spells and incantations with Guildus Grey. After making their way to the classroom, they waited outside.

'Come in,' said a voice sharply. The door swung open, and they entered.

'Sit down,' said the teacher abruptly.

'I am Guildus Grey: Mage of Spell Casting and Incantations. You must listen carefully to your instructions, and I expect you all to do well, but only some will make the grade. Astrophos has informed me you are all in the process of crafting your magickal tools. You will learn you won't need a staff or a wand to perform magick. In time, you might choose not to use these tools at all, but they are handy. Pay attention, and stop chattering at the back while I'm talking! I hope you will learn more about manners in your etiquette class,' he said to Felicity.

She had been discussing joining the cheerleading squad. Although Charlie, Amanda, and Tom found it amusing, she wasn't happy with Guildus for showing her up.

'Open your Spellbook to the first chapter, *Sending and Calling Objects*, known as the lazy spell. These are the most basic of what we call Non-Personal or Level One Spells, but we'll go into that at some other time,' he said mechanically.

Guildus stood at the top of the class, and his clothes matched his name: grey. He didn't wear robes like all the other teachers but wore an old-fashioned suit with a thick grey cape and a strange-looking hat resembling a beret. He would have looked like an obscure artist if he'd worn brighter clothes.

'Now, let's start with the less dangerous activity of the two spells we are learning today: calling an object to you. The spell you will use to summon objects is written on the paper. Make your intentions clear, speak loudly, and the object should come to you.'

'Where are the objects, sir?' queried Charlie.

Guildus ignored him, but then a group of items appeared at distant locations within the classroom.

'Here are the objects, Stuart,' he said rudely. 'The spell used is derived from the Latin meaning to come. Everyone looked at the word "Venio", which they all started muttering.

'In addition, it is essential to use the techniques you learned with Master Siddhartha— sight or visualisation, sense, smell, etcetera!' said Guildus.

'Sir,' Charlie interrupted. 'Why must we use visualisations with our spells and incantations?'

'That's a good question, Stuart. Using words and images focuses energy and generates power for the task.'

'OK, sir, I understand,' he said, following his instructions: Charlie was to summon a ruler, Amanda a small cushion, and Tom an eraser.

'Now take a deep breath; see the object; say the incantation with some meaning, and summon,' said Guildus.

'Venio ruler,' said Charlie. Nothing happened. 'VEnio ruler,' the ruler twitched forward.

'Come on,' said Guildus, 'give it a bit more oompf!'

'VenIo ruler', he said purposely. The ruler hovered and stuttered in the air before crashing down on the desk in front of him.

'FANTASTIC!' screamed Charlie.

Amanda managed the same as Charlie; Tom's object made a 'loop the loop' as it came over. David Moarns summoned a piece of chalk. It flew three feet, landed on the floor, and then moved slowly over to him. The class watched as the chalk drew a line, etching its way. Guildus shook his head with trepidation.

'I think it will be easier for you to go and pick it up. On the other hand, maybe I should make a cup of tea.' the teacher said sarcastically. 'Well, at least yours is moving, unlike *some* people.'

Felicity was screaming, but her small ball was defiant not to make the journey.

'Probably scared to go near her,' laughed Charlie.

She wasn't the only one. Raphael Guseppi and Timothy Morden's objects were levitating and swirling, and Steven Coldwell's was 'ping-ponging' its way across.

'May the gods help us,' said Guildus. 'I see plenty of practice is required. Dare I take us on to the next activity? Oh well, better get this one over and done with.'

Guildus raised his ornately crafted staff made from Silver Birch and made the objects that hadn't entirely made their way land on their desks.

'Now, I might be tempted to put protection or deflection spell up for this one. We are now going to send the objects back from whence they came. First, see it in your mind's eye. To complete the process, you need to use the word "Reverto" as an incantation to send the object. Derived from the Latin revertor, meaning 'to go back', this refers to returning an object to its origin. You can reflect someone else's spell on them in this advanced form. It is useful, especially if someone is casting a curse at you. Alternatively, you can use *reverto scorpus*, as it adds precision. Scorpus is also derived from the Latin *scopus*, meaning target. It helps to take deep breaths. Just close your eyes. See the place you want to send it to, then say the short incantation. One, two, three, go!'

Disaster! All the objects flew at speed in all kinds of directions. They hit each other, slammed into the walls, or passed out of the windows. They would have hit Guildus if it weren't for the teacher's mastery in stopping the objects.

'Shambles, shambles, where did they get you a lot from?' he said, thinking aloud. 'Dear, oh, dear... try again calling it to you and then sending it,' he said to the students' surprise. 'You're going to need the practice.'

Charlie couldn't quite figure out Guildus Grey. One moment, he seemed pretty insulting, while the next, he appeared to encourage them. Suffice it to say he was right; more practice was required.

The session finished with some progress, but everyone seemed worn out by the experience.

After a short break and drinking some *Percy Pick-Up Juice*, they went to their final session, The History and Magickal Practices of Magick. Amanda got out her timetable to see where the last lesson of the day would be.

'Oh, we're in the Earth elemental block, fantastic!' said Amanda.

'I wonder what it's going to be like in there,' said Tom.

'Do you know who is taking us for that lesson?' asked Charlie.

'You should get out your timetables, you know...er, let me look. It is Mage Brimstone-Greenback. Oh, hang on, it's changing. It's Guildus Grey,' said Amanda.

'Oh no, not that miserable git,' said Tom.

'It says he is just covering the lesson as the main teacher is poorly.'

'Good, as long as we don't have him every lesson. I think he'd do my head in,' said Tom.

'I quite like him,' said Charlie, surprising his friends.

Though Charlie's thoughts were elsewhere, Tom moaned about Guildus as they proceeded to class.

Upon arrival, there was a group of students waiting to head inside.

'State your name,' the door said sharply, making some students jump. Each student gave their name, but for some reason, the building didn't like some of the students.

You can easily understand why it was called the Earth Block. It was a combination of the school's main entrance and the Earth corridors, where they gave their magickal names.

Vines and root-like objects moved and wiggled around, and small and unusual insects went about their business; everything seemed to pulsate. It was also dark, so each student moved tentatively through the strange corridor.

As they walked, a strange creature appeared before them. It was a mud sprite. The beast stopped and gazed at the students with peculiar, wide eyes. It scratched its crooked nose, which stuck out magnificently from its massive head, accompanied by a bulging forehead. Then it gestured towards them by lifting its short arms, which only had three fingers. The elemental didn't say anything but waved for them to follow.

They walked along the corridor, avoiding the cold, damp walls. Charlie gazed upward, convinced he saw statuesque faces on the muddy ceiling.

After walking past three rooms, they arrived at a fourth. The door opened, and they entered. To their surprise, the classroom looked ordinary: plain wooden tables and chairs.

There were no windows, but old-fashioned gas lighting nicely lit the room.

'Sit down, please,' Guildus said unenthusiastically. 'For anyone who bothered to look at their timetable parchments, Mage Brimstone-Greenback has been feeling unwell after his holiday. The Headmistress has asked me to cover this lesson. As I was informed at the last minute, I have no lesson plan. Is there anything that you would like to discuss or learn about?'

Charlie flung his arm up quickly, much to the surprise of his classmates.

'Ah, Stuart, one of the students lost in the Plainlands, what a shame. I'd imagine you wouldn't have any idea about magickal history. Remember, I haven't got all day to explain everything,' he said sarcastically. Charlie ignored his taunt.

'Sir, could you please tell me more about the Half Prophecy and the times of Lord Mortus and Prince Zordemon.'

'Well, well, Stuart, there is hope for you yet. Does anyone object to this?' No objections came from the rest of his classmates.

'Very well,' said Guildus. He walked over to the main bookstand and rubbed his hands along the spines of the books, looking for the correct one. Guildus muttered something under his breath, and a book popped out.

'Ah, here we are,' he said, pulling the book off the shelf.

He took it to the front of the class and put it on the desk. He looked at the index, touched the page number, opened the book to the correct page and said, 'Projectum.'

To the class's amazement, an immersive 3D projection of the prophecy appeared. Impressively, the image floated around the room, hovering over the desks for the students to see. Then, like a ghost through a wall, it moved through the students to the next student to peruse.

After the students had examined the scroll, the projection moved to the front of the class, where it remained. Charlie was the last to investigate it.

'I see,' said Charlie.

The scroll was not an ordinary piece of parchment. It was a full manuscript with two sides that joined when rolled together. Wooden handles were attached to each side to open and close the scroll. The Half Prophecy stood out with a neatly torn edge and a faint glow, indicating its eagerness to reunite with its sister half.

'There are questions about the Half Prophecy because there is such a precise cut along the middle. Some say the Half Prophecy was deliberately separated, and the other half hidden elsewhere. However, do you see the fold that comes out? Some say the prophecy isn't split, and the fold seals the scroll. Of course, the text indicates otherwise.'

'What does the text say?' asked Charlie.

'The prophecy is also an agreement created by Lord Mortus to say that Plainlands and magick would be separated, thus respecting the free choice of men. However, Lord Mortus, like Merlin before him, possessed the gift of foresight and prophecy. He claimed that the Plainlanders would struggle alone and that their world would descend into chaos. The Prophecy suggests that a "man born of dragon" will help bridge the gap between the Plainlanders and the magick world. The scroll says this man could intervene if the Plainlanders could not rule sufficiently without magick. There are several problems with this, one of which is how a man can be born of a dragon. A second problem is how, on earth, one man can change an entire world established in its ways. It is impossible. The second part of the prophecy suggests revealing more about this person.'

'Oh,' said Charlie, fascinated by the story.

'People have searched high and low for this object, and no one has ever found it. There is much speculation about what the other half of the prophecy contains. Because it is enchanted, some say it will bring unique powers back to the world; as for what forces, if any, nobody knows. One thing's for sure: the Plainlanders could never rule properly. They have fought many wars through ignorance and fear and disrespected the planet greatly. Nothing has happened to say this will change. No one cares anymore; only obsessives about finding the Half Prophecy. Our worlds live side-by-side, and the Plainlanders cannot affect our society. Yet another reason why magick folk do not care what happens to Plainlanders.'

The class listened intently, and you could tell by Guildus' voice that he was interested in that period of history.

'What about Prince Zordemon?' Charlie asked.

'Well, as you can imagine, Prince Zordemon, heir to the throne, wasn't particularly happy with Lord Gideon's plans, as they would mean he'd miss out on ruling the kingdom. King Harold agreed it had to be, as it respected the free choice of men. Also, humanity had something to learn from their decision.'

The lights began to dim as Guildus continued to speak.

'It was said that Zordemon was furious and set to disrupt proceedings. Stories claim that he was brilliant and kind. However, if you ever decided to challenge him, you would need the gods' mercy to protect you. You see, Zordemon was renowned for his knowledge and use of the deadliest form of dark magick known as Blackfire. Not much is known, but it was one of the foulest and most devious ways of magick ever. The scripts exist today and were embalmed with some evil protective magick that prevents them from being destroyed. They are kept secret and guarded by the best magickal knights. Oh, Prince Zordemon has been deleted from the Plainer history books.'

'Sounds scary, sir,' said David.

'Oh yes, very,' said Guildus. David froze to the spot as some of the first years caught their breath at Guildus' tone of voice.

'What happened to them all?' asked Helen.'

'Well, maybe this could explain it.'

Guildus summoned a book with magick, which flew from the shelf into his hand. Guildus pulled out a thin red wand, showing the marks of the original tree carvings. It had a dark blue crystal sticking out of the end of it. He pointed at the book, which immediately flicked to the correct page and said, 'Projectum megalus!' The room transformed itself into a re-creation of the times of Zordemon. Simultaneously, the students seemed to glide into the background.

'Wow, this is fantastic,' said Helen excitedly.

The scene starts with Zordemon killing his father. He stands over him with a cold, chilling smile that oozes naturally from his perfectly formed mouth. His followers, known as Dark Keepers because they are renowned for their knowledge of dark magick, join him. The most expert of these is known as the Lordos, comprised of men and women of prominence and nobility.

The forces of the Prince and Gideon Mortus engaged in grand-scale fighting. Blade and spell spewed blood and guts, making some children's stomachs churn.

Thank goodness Mum doesn't see this! Charlie thought they had never heard of eighteen rating certificates. Guildus continued.

'In the end, reports by the last known powerful wizard, Ferdore, stated that there was an explosion so powerful that everyone was obliterated within the area.'

Charlie imagined a magickal nuclear explosion. The final scene showed the prophecy/agreement signed by Ferdore and the newly appointed King William I, known in the Plainland's history books, after killing King Harold on the battlefield.' As soon as the enchantment finished, the class returned to normal.

'You'd be interested to know that half of the original prophecy will be displayed in the Great City Museum later this year.

'Really, I'd like to see that!' said Charlie.

'It is more of a historical artefact now, but it's still a big attraction to the public. It moves from city to city; it never has a home. The Great City Museum has petitioned for years that the scroll should remain with them,' said Guildus.

'Right, this is the end of your lesson and school day. You may leave, and please don't be late for your next spell session with me,' he said as if it was inevitable.

Chapter Fifteen
KNIGHT FEVER

Wednesday seemed to have come around quickly. Charlie, Tom, and Amanda had spent time practising spells, using adapted and charged staffs and wands. They were almost level pegging in ability, but Charlie, who had a promising start, seemed to struggle. However, they ended up being playfully competitive.

On Tuesday, they had taken lessons in etiquette about the benefits of being civil to each other. Importantly, they learned that no matter what you gave out, magickal or otherwise, good and bad, it would return at some point.

Ancient languages were interesting as they discussed how writing had power. The final lesson fascinated them as they learned about their star signs and the skills and natural abilities that came to them.

The first lesson was with Cosmolos, the new Housemaster of the Air House of Paralda. Before learning about the qualities of the Air element, the Kings and Lords of the Watch Towers. were discussed.

Charlie was an Aquarian. He loved that Aquarians were renowned for being forward thinkers with the potential to be creative genii. However, his sign indicated that Aquarians could have their heads in dreamland most of the time, which he could understand. Charlie did not understand what gregarious or humanitarian meant, which typified his sign. However, he made a point of reading up on their meaning at some future date.

Cosmolos strongly encouraged them to seek a society that would help them develop their talents differently, as "it opens up the creative centres and unlocks part of our magick."

There were a few arguments about using the Wizopoly board in the halls of residence, as Giuseppe, David, Helen and Melay were hogging it. Despite the occasional moans and groans, Charlie had skillfully devised a rotation system to use the board. Besides, neither he nor Amanda had been shrunk and put in a game before, so they wanted to try it as soon as possible. Coincidently, the timing couldn't have been much more perfect, as it was Charlie, Tom and Amanda's turn to play on Wednesday evening between 7 and 8 pm.

Knight training, also known as KT, was to be the most popular subject of the day. The night before, you could hear students pretending to be knights. Amanda, however, didn't see the point and decided to attend an alternative lesson.

'Where are you heading for healing arts, Amanda?' asked Charlie.

'Oh, it's in the main study block and then over into the woods. Where do you go for KT?' asked Amanda curiously.

'Yeah, we've got to head right down, past the arena, over the bridge and beyond the trees. There is a special place arena for it.'

'Fabulous!' said Amanda.

Charlie instantly thought back to Sherwood Forest, where he had helped make a sword, and wished he had lived there during mediaeval times. Well, he was finally going to get his wish.

'Oh, Astrophos said he wanted to see me after class. I have no idea why, though I hope I am not in trouble,' she said, slightly concerned. 'Maybe they think I am not good enough or something.'

'I'm sure you will be fine,' said Tom reassuringly. 'I hope you are right,' said Amanda.

It was Amanda's first time separating from her new friends, but she didn't seem to mind.

'Well, good luck, and if you break a leg, maybe I can fix you up,' she laughed.

'Thanks, Amanda, though I'll do my best to avoid that,' he said, laughing back.

'OK, I'll catch you in a bit,' said Charlie.

'Yeah, good luck, Amanda,' said Tom.

'Thanks,' said Amanda, looking through her bag. 'Oh no,' she said. 'I've forgotten my book on chakras... I'll quickly head back to get it. You guys go, and I'll see you both for lunch.'

'OK, I'm looking forward to having fish and chips,' said Charlie.

Charlie and Tom went through the archway and headed towards the training area. Amanda wheeled herself back, humming cheerfully in the warm breeze.

However, something was about to happen that would change her day.

'Oi Wheelie, by yourself, are you?' said a familiar, unkind voice.

Amanda's heart seemed to stop, and she turned around, hoping Charlie would be there.

'Why are you doing this to me?' asked Amanda calmly. 'If it was for running over your foot, I did apologise. It was an accident,' she said, defending herself.

Neither Felicity nor Annabel replied. No matter what Amanda said, it wasn't going to change anything.

Felicity fixed her steely blue eyes on Amanda, giving her a cold, evil stare before delivering a pronounced slap to the top of her head.

'Ow! Leave me alone,' begged Amanda.

When Annabel swung at Amanda, Amanda lifted her hand to defend herself, something Charlie had taught her.

'How dare you raise your hand to me, you freak!' said Annabel cruelly.

Felicity and Annabel were just about to attack Amanda when Felicity suddenly screamed. Annabel stopped, and Amanda turned her head to see what was happening.

Another girl stood behind her, hands on hips. She was slender and pretty, with light olive skin and long, dark brown hair. 'If you want to fight someone, try me instead,' the girl said confidently.

'Who are you?' demanded Annabel, as Felicity still held her head from the slap she received.

'Her friend,' the girl quickly responded.

Amanda recognised the girl from class and the student accommodation, although she always kept to herself. At this point, Amanda was just grateful for her help.

'Now, what are you going to do about it,' the girl reiterated. They were outnumbered; Felicity's other friends arrived as backup.

'Felicity said nastily, 'Five against you and wheels.'

'I'm surprised you can count that high,' said Amanda's saviour sarcastically.

'Now you're going to see what we are going to do,' said Felicity, sounding victorious.

'What, you and those pathetic no-brain thicko friends of yours?' the girl said, winding them up further.

'We'll see who's the thicko in the end,' Felicity retorted.

There was a momentary standoff, watching who would make the first move. As predicted, Felicity put one foot forward.

'Oi,' shouted a voice. Everyone looked round to see where the sound was coming from.

'Up 'ere,' shouted the voice. 'Starting on my little sister again, eh?' said Bruce, with Emmanuel beside him. 'Touch her, and you'll eat your lunch through a Percy straw. I suggest you move away quickly, or I'll be down before you can say Cosmolos,' said Bruce. 'I've never hit a girl, but....' He just stopped the conversation there.

Felicity was furious, but there was nothing she could do. She backed away, defeated, and her friends followed. Minutes later, they disappeared into the main grounds, and Bruce and Emmanuel made their way down.

'Thanks for sticking up for my sister,' said Bruce.

'No problem,' said the girl.

'Yes, thank you so much. She seems to have a grudge against me,' Amanda said.

'Yeah, I saw what happened on the first day. I was going to jump in then, but you were in good company,' said the girl.

'What's your name?' asked Emmanuel.

'Imogen. Imogen Braithwaite. And your name?'

'I'm Amanda, as you know, well, Amanda Campbell. My brother Bruce and Bruce's friend, Emmanuel Stuart, is Charlie's brother.'

'Nice to meet you all,' Imogen said, feeling more relaxed.

'Where is Charlie?' queried Emmanuel.

'Oh, he and Tom have gone for KT. It's the first year's turn, first thing Wednesday. I'm not interested as I'm looking at doing the healing arts,' said Amanda.

'Well, I was heading to KT, though I'm going to the next healing arts class afterwards,' said Imogen. 'I enjoy all the fighting stuff. Growing up with a knight dad and two brothers rubs off on you. I tell you what, I might as well come with you to healing arts now and then head to the next knight's session,' said Imogen.

'Well then,' said Amanda, 'next week, all four of us will head to knight training, though I'll probably watch. Then we can head to the healing arts session afterwards. You never know; Charlie and Tom might be interested.'

'That sounds like a plan,' said Imogen. 'Crikey, look at the time; we're late, so let's go.'

Amanda and Imogen split off to head to class, whilst Bruce and Emmanuel enjoyed their free period, not doing much.

*

Tom, Charlie and dozens of other students were waiting in a specialised area designated for training. The area looked mediaeval, with solid wood huts and buildings. There were also stables and a workshop where swords and armour were made.

'Hello there, again,' said a voice.

'It's you from the forest, the blacksmith,' said Charlie.

'Yes, well remembered,' said the smithy. 'I don't believe I introduced myself. I am Sir Barnaby, Chief Blacksmith, Swordsmith and Magickal Knight of the Realm. Nowadays, I prefer to focus my skills on fashioning the best blades and armour I can. I prefer working here to the Great City; the open air and fields inspire forging new blades.'

'Fascinating!' said Charlie.

The students spent a few minutes getting changed into their sports gear. They were all wearing shorts with matching house T-shirts or sporting vests.

'RIGHT, YOU BUNCH OF DUNG WORMS! Let us see what you have got.'

All the students came out of the changing area to see Sedrick.

Sedrick, with his enormous frame, came into the training area. None of the students cared about how he spoke to them; most were in awe of him. After all, he was a hero in the Magicklands.

'Oh, he's ginormous!' said Michael Thorpe.

'He certainly is!' said Felicity Rhoads.

'I am told that Dragonstone produces some of the finest warriors! I'm here at the request of my friend, Sir Barnaby. After all, he does produce the best armour and weaponry you will ever see. You will be learning some of the greatest training methods developed over centuries. My knight associates will also visit to show you tricks of the trade. The aim is to keep you fit, focus the mind, learn great skills, and, above all, find the ones who have the potential to make the magickal knight grade. I'll stick you in the dungeons if you mess around or misbehave! Do I make myself clear!?'

'Yes, sir!'

'I can't hear YOU!'

'YES, SIR!' shouted all in unison.

'As the Greeks say, "In a healthy mind lives a healthy body." Right, follow me; we need to warm up your muscles,' said Sedrick.

Sedrick led them around an obstacle course, and the group struggled to keep up with him. Huffing and puffing, they followed Sedrick, whose blond hair flowed behind him, and his beard swayed from side to side in front of him.

After a few minutes, everyone was out of breath except for Charlie, who was used to physical exercise through kickboxing. Some grasped their hips, some doubled over, and others complained about getting a stitch.

'By Odin, I've never seen such a sight. By the end of the year, you'll be able to run to the Great City and back.'

They then spent a few moments stretching, and Charlie was impressed by his flexibility of Sedrick as he was so big.

'Now, go and get your weapons. We will start with the swords.' Barnaby came out pushing a large trolley full of wooden swords.

'Wood?' said David, looking confused.'

'So, you want to wave metal on the first day, eh? I'm afraid you can't wield steel until you become competent with wood. No, no, definitely not. I want no deaths or limb-lopping on the first day, thank you.'

The students picked up some wooden swords and started swinging them around.

'Ouch!' shouted Chris, as his friend Oliver accidentally hit him on the leg.

'Sorry, mate,' said Oliver, chortling.

'And you wanted real blades?' said Sedrick, laughing away with his deep voice. However, he did make his point.

'Now give yourselves plenty of space, though make sure you can see me.'

Sedrick demonstrated a series of lunging, striking, and defensive manoeuvres, which they all copied. Well, they tried.

'You, keep that arm high,' he shouted to one pupil.

'You! What on earth was that? You couldn't squash an ant with that hit,' he said to another.

'No, no, no, no, no,' Sedrick sighed again.

They spent half an hour practising, moving, swishing, and slashing.

Apart from Charlie, they were all getting tired.

'Goodness me, you're fit,' said Tom.

'Ah, this is nothing. You should see what we do in our kickboxing class. I have to admit, I haven't done any training for a couple of weeks, though trying to learn about the Magicklands has been exercise enough,' said Charlie.

'Now, I would like a volunteer to come and spar with me,' said Sedrick.

'Don't we need armour or something, sir?' said Felicity Rhoads.

'Don't worry, I'll not be hacking off your head with an axe or putting you on the end of my two spears,' he laughed. 'No armour yet; it will help keep you on your toes and sharpen your senses. Now, who wants a go?' No one responded.

'You go, Charlie,' whispered Tom.

'Me? Look at him—he's huge,' giggled Charlie.

'Ah, I see I have found one,' said Sedrick, looking straight at Charlie. 'Well, you seemed to find something amusing; maybe you were laughing at me!' said Sedrick to a stunned Charlie.

Charlie gulped and realised that everyone was deadly silent from fear.

He looked at his sword and then at a grinning Sedrick.

Sedrick lunged with his sword. Charlie turned to the side to avoid being hit. Sedrick raised his brow.

Despite all his training, Charlie was still petrified and unsure of what to do.

He lifted his sword to strike, but Sedrick casually deflected his hit. Sedrick moved forward, clipping Charlie's leg, but instead of falling over, Charlie cartwheeled to the side.

Sedrick maintained his grin and composure as Charlie spun around with his sword to hit Sedrick.

'Trying to be clever?' said Sedrick as he lunged forward simultaneously with Charlie, clipping him on the arm.

'Come on, Charlie!' cheered some of the crowd, finding their voice. 'Charlie! Charlie!'

Sedrick lunged forward, though Charlie, gaining some confidence, used a roundhouse manoeuvre, forcefully kicking Sedrick's sword to the side.

The children gasped, seeing the movement as contempt, but Sedrick said approvingly, 'Good. I see we have a warrior among us.'

Seconds later, Sedrick lunged, twisted, and spun at Charlie. He magnificently manoeuvred his sword whilst Charlie attempted to keep up. In a flash, Charlie was on the floor with Sedrick's wooden blade pointed at his chest, his sword lying four feet away.

'You move like a warrior, but you have no skill with a blade. We will change this. Well done!' said Sedrick. The cheering stopped.

The rest of the class practised, and you could hear many screams as wood and flesh collided.

'You did really well, Charlie,' said Tom. 'I think you took him by surprise with your spin kick. You could tell by his face.'

'I was nervous,' said Charlie.

'Well, you never showed it,' said Tom.

'Right!' shouted Sedrick. 'Your first lesson is over... now for your cool-down.' Sedrick took them through several stretches before they went to the showers.

Gossip spread throughout the first years about how well Charlie had done against Sedrick, even though they knew there would only be one winner.

'Nice one, Charlie,' said David Moarns, who had bruises on his right arm and legs.

'Hi Charlie,' waved a smiling Felicity Rhoads. *Well, she's nothing like the other Felicity,* Charlie thought to himself as he waved back at her.

Most of the students congratulated Charlie, who made him feel more welcome and settled at the School; Charlie loved this session and couldn't wait to return.

'What time is it?' asked Tom.

'Oh, crikey, we're running late. We need to meet up with Amanda. She's probably all alone,' said Charlie.

They hurriedly gathered their things and headed towards the canteen quickly.

There was some commotion in the cafeteria as some children gathered around Amanda.

'Hey Amanda,' shouted Charlie.

'Hey Charlie, Tom, look at this!' said Amanda.

'What's happened to your...?' asked Charlie.

'Eh?' said Tom.

'Astrophos,' said Amanda, beaming.

'Well, that makes sense,' said Charlie.

'Good, isn't it?' winked Amanda.

'How long did it take him to do it?' Charlie asked.

'Not long at all,' said Amanda. 'He was amazing!'

Astrophos magickally altered Amanda's chair. Crystals were embedded in the sides, a controller with buttons was attached, and her house emblem was imprinted on the seat.

'It is brilliant,' she said. 'I can get around so much easier. It even has some special features I'll show you later,' she said. 'Oh, by the way, this is Imogen Braithwaite, a new friend,' said Amanda proudly.

'Fantastic! Hi Imogen,' said Charlie. 'I've seen you in the halls of residence.'

'Hello, Imogen. I'm pleased to meet you,' said Tom. 'Fire House, I see.' He observed the red emblem on her blazer.

'Oh, yes; a Leo,' said Imogen playfully, boasting.

After shaking each other's hands, Amanda tells Charlie and Tom about her encounter with Felicity Phelps and how Imogen, her brother, and Emmanuel rescue her.

Charlie felt mortified but relieved by the presence of people willing to help.

This conversation prompted Charlie to check Emamnuel's progress and whether he enjoyed Sedrick's training.

Tom then told Amanda and Imogen about what had happened during the lesson. Amanda was pleased, and Imogen was impressed that he'd lasted the lengthy duelling Sedrick. She explained that her father was a knight who regularly saw Sedrick in the Great City. They were friends.

Eating dinner seemed like a joyous occasion, as the menu included roast chicken, Yorkshire puddings, mixed vegetables, and *Lord Quimbus's Finest Roast Potatoes* covered in delicious gravy.

First-year students could be heard muttering as they talked about Charlie's encounter with Sedrick, but Charlie ignored the fuss.

Charlie looked at Amanda and Imogen, who were laughing and talking. He was pleased that Amanda had found a good friend, and he wanted them to do girl things together.

With the afternoon upon them, Amanda pulled out her timetable to see what wonders lay ahead.

The class schedule disappeared, replaced by a map and different societies, so they decided to see what was available.

CHAPTER SIXTEEN

THE DOOR OF MYSTERY

After receiving carefully crafted insults from the un-potted plants, they walked to the rear of the school, where hundreds of tents and marquees were magickally erected.

Some students and teachers beckoned them to join their society. They displayed magickal signs, floating heads that spoke, illuminated signs, and unique fireworks.

Every tent had something that symbolised its society, and some stalls looked just like the society they represented. The Painting Society's tent was a massive easel with a giant brush stuck in the ground and the society banner flying above it.

Charlie, Amanda, Tom, and Imogen had never seen such an impressive sight before and were thrilled to be there.

Amanda now had the freedom of her magickally enchanted crystal-powered wheelchair. It had various settings, including walking, running, and spinning quickly to change direction.

'WOW!' said Tom. 'Look over there, what society is that?! Let's go and look,' he continued excitedly. He had observed three people around various canvases, drawing pictures without the aid of brushes.'

'How are they doing that?' asked Charlie.

'They're psychic artists: they use the power of their minds to create the pictures,' said Tom. 'I've heard of them but not seen any before.'

'Look,' said Amanda, 'they have their eyes closed. That's even more amazing. ' She said this as they approached.

'They're not just closed,' said Imogen, 'they're blind.'

'BLIND!' shouted Charlie, stopping the artists and everyone else in their tracks.

'Sshhhh,' everyone else said.

The lady artist turned around, and her face looked like it had just been burned. She smiled and turned to the canvas, and a picture was developing.

"What?" exclaimed Charlie. "How...? Why...? It is impossible!"

'What is it?' said Imogen.

'It is my old house in the Plainlands.' Charlie froze on the spot, and a shiver went down his spine.

'You're kidding,' said Tom.

'I'm not,' said Charlie, sounding more disconcerted.

'There is more,' said Amanda. 'I've looked on the societies listing, and there is no mention of them.'

'Really...so what are they? Eh—where have they gone?' Tom asked.

They all looked at where the artists were, and they'd all disappeared.

'*Really* strange,' said Charlie.

It was an 'add on to the list of strange experiences' that baffled even his Magickland friends.

Imogen brought everyone back to earth, diverting their attention to the many societies before them.

Sure enough, they mingled with the crowd and the maze of tents. They included the Magick Book Society, Spell Casting Society, Witches for Women, and Magician Society for Boys. Also, there was the Wizopoly Society, Etiquette Society, Jousting Society, Archery Society, and Martial Art Society, which interested Charlie. There was a Poser Society, Painting Society, Singing Society, I Am the Best Society, Language Society and many more. You could set up your own, provided you had ten aspiring members.

It took some time to walk around the tents, and the societies were more than just organisations to join; they were desirable places to learn. Making learning fun was part of the school's policy.

The teachers strongly encouraged these activities to 'maximise learning and creative potential. By doing so, "you open yourself up to greater magick and greater creativity", 'Whatever that meant,' said Charlie, who couldn't quite understand the statement.

Charlie was excited about the prospect of joining a society. There were some tough choices, but he and Tom chose to join the extra knight training and martial arts, including kickboxing, MMA, and spellcasting.

Charlie remembered what Cosmolos had said about trying something different, so he thought rowing seemed interesting. Tom thought about joining the Woodland Society. Amanda and Imogen also decided to try martial arts and spellcasting and join the healing arts and Magick Book Club.

The Orberon was slightly different, as nearly everyone entered a magickal team to gain extra credit. Charlie wanted to learn a little more about the mysterious Orberon. Coincidentally, there would be a demonstration to launch the annual tournament.

Having popped their names down, they looked around the society buildings beyond the trees to the far right of the Orberon. All events started the following week.

After a few hours on tour, they returned to the canteen for a snack.

The temperature dropped suddenly, and there was a smell of rain in the air. When a familiar apparition appeared before him, Charlie suddenly looked up: it was the shadowy entity.

Charlie paused and took a deep breath, observing what was happening. He understood that it was there to help him whenever this entity appeared.

'You OK?' Amanda asked Charlie.

'It's back. The entity that has been following me and helping me.'

'Really?' said a surprised Amanda.

'Eh?' said Tom, whilst Imogen just looked confused.

'I'll explain later,' he said, '...this way!' He began to run.

'What are we doing? Where are we going?' demanded Imogen.

'No time to explain,' said Amanda.

They quickly followed the entity that only Charlie could see.

The ghostly figure glided along, always maintaining a reasonable distance between them.

They crossed the courtyard, brushing past Reginald Bloom.

'Slow down, do you hear? And don't you dare tread on those poppylop flowers?' said a furious Reginald.

Having completely ignored him, they ran out of the courtyard and past the earth tunnel, the elemental Fire tower, and a pathway leading to some small woodland area.

'Where are we going?' demanded Imogen.

With the entity on his mind, Charlie ignored her.

The soil and twigs crunched beneath them, and they eventually approached some mediaeval stone walls and trees.

Whilst racing and weaving in between his friends, Charlie suddenly slowed down and came to a stop. His friends followed suit. The thick woodland and tall stone walls surrounding them prevented any view of the school, and the dark sky added to the creepy atmosphere. The surroundings resembled a graveyard without any gravestones.

Charlie and his friends made their way through some overgrown bushes.

'What is this place?' asked Amanda.

'I have no idea,' said Charlie.

'Are you going to tell us what this is all about?' asked Imogen impatiently.

'I will,' said Charlie. 'Later, I promise,' he reassured them.

'Of course! Don't you remember what Hecate said on the visit?' asked Tom. 'The school is built upon an old fortress that used to be here. It must be part of it.'

'Yes, Randle, the tracker said that the main entrance to the school was part of the old castle,' said Charlie.

Approximately fifty yards in front of them was a perfectly preserved door, with a couple of stone obelisks two feet in front of the doorframe. A dusty, cobbled pathway leading up to the door and an intersecting path formed a cross-shape. Some bushes and grass blended with the open landscape in each quarter section.

'Ah, I think I know what this is,' said Imogen.

'What is it?' asked Tom enthusiastically.

'Hecate said in the assembly that there are old enchanted places that we should avoid at all costs. This must be The Door of Mystery. My Dad says that people have disappeared in there,' said Imogen.

'Really?' said Amanda.

'I think we should do what Hecate says,' she continued.

'So why isn't it guarded or boarded up?' asked Tom.

'I have no idea,' replied Imogen. 'Maybe they are too afraid to go near it to bother.'

'Charlie, what are you doing?' asked Amanda as Charlie approached the doorway.

'Stay away,' said Tom, sounding very concerned.

'You're crazy,' said Imogen.

Charlie ignored them and proceeded towards the door.

With the dull, grey gravel crunching beneath him, he stepped over the threshold at the path's intersection.

Everyone stood still, and an eerie wind swept through, sending shivers down their spines.

Unexpectedly, the door clicked, and ground and an accompanying scream ensued. Imogen and Tom grasped Amanda, sitting in the chair before them.

Charlie reached for the iron door handle with a shaking hand.

The door opened automatically, revealing many rooms and images that spun and contorted so quickly that they made Charlie feel nauseous.

He felt the door pulling him in without hesitation and immediately took action. He firmly grasped the right obelisk to resist the force, but the room was relentless in its pull, growing stronger with each passing moment. He refused to give in and held his ground, determined not to be overcome by the powerful energy.

'Help! I'm being pulled in!' screeched Charlie.

'Charlie needs help!' said Amanda, so they quickly moved forward to prevent Charlie from being sucked into oblivion.

'Leave it to me,' said Amanda, as if having thought of some cunning plan. She sped ahead, veering off the main pathway and onto the old garden that was level with the ground.

With body mid-air, clinging on for his life, Charlie turned his head round, and with eyes squinting, he looked.

'What...? How...? Why...? Is it?' he said, but he quickly turned back as he was getting an aggressive headache.

'Hang on, Charlie!' screamed Amanda. 'When I come around, grab the back of the chair, and I will pull you away.'

'You're crazy,' said Tom.

Charlie tried to have one more look, but Amanda arrived. The images from the room were moving so quickly and violently that he felt like he was going to be sick.

Amanda slowed before the entrance and said, 'Grab the back of the chair as I pass. Do it quickly, or we will both get dragged in.' Charlie nodded in acknowledgement, finding it difficult to talk.

'NOW!' shouted Amanda.

With a struggle, Amanda was behind him, and Charlie reached out and grabbed her chair. Amanda instantly selected the highest setting and pulled off.

Still, the ordeal wasn't over: Amanda's chair got caught in the door's pull, and it started to draw her in. Tom and Imogen ran forward to help.

'Wait there!' yelled Amanda.

Amanda reached underneath the arm, and there was a crystal that would only be used in emergencies. She quickly twisted it. A bright red light circled the tyres and the chair, boosting them forward and pushing them away from the gravity of the door, which was trying to pull them in like a black hole sucking in a planet.

As they pulled away, the door slammed shut, and it went deathly quiet until Charlie emptied the contents of his stomach.

'Are you OK?' asked Amanda worriedly.

'Just about,' said Charlie, wiping the remaining sick off his face.

'I thought you were a goner there,' said Tom.

'Me too,' said Charlie.

'Next time, listen,' said Imogen angrily but concernedly.

As Charlie composed himself, he felt annoyed at what had happened.

He felt betrayed and gullible that he should trust in something he knew nothing about and that no one else could see. Was it some joke or his imagination?

Then he remembered what he saw, which settled him.

'Thank you,' said Charlie to Amanda.

'That's OK, we're even,' she started giggling.

'Are you going to tell us what it is all about?' said Imogen, sounding very fed up.

'Let's head back; I think I need to freshen up,' he said.

'So what did you see?' asked Tom.

'I'll explain that later,' Charlie said, feeling perkier.

Charlie took a long shower in his room and changed into his usual jeans and T-shirt.

More thoughts accumulated in his head. Should he tell them what he saw or thought he had seen through the door? He knew he'd have to explain about the entity because he promised to do so. It didn't matter as he knew Magickland people would accept this phenomenon more than plainlanders.

*

Charlie spent a few moments replying to a message sent by his mum. He also sent one to Emmanuel, thanking him for looking out for Amanda and saying they should meet soon to catch up.

Charlie wore his new white trainers and met Amanda, Tom, and Imogen. He then discussed the entity's story and actions to help and guide him.

'Well, it didn't seem particularly helpful an hour ago. You could have gotten yourself killed!' said Tom.

'I agree with Tom, apart from...er...there is something else that I haven't told you all,' said Charlie.

'What's that?' asked Amanda.

'I think the entity was trying to show me something,' said Charlie.

'What?' asked Imogen, trying to hurry proceedings.

'Well, you might think I'm crazy,' said Charlie. 'It doesn't make any sense.'

'What doesn't make sense?' asked Tom.

'Spill the beans,' said Amanda.

'Should I get some dinner first?' said Imogen sarcastically.

Charlie took a deep breath and... 'Hey guys...,' said a voice.

'Not now, David,' they all said together.

David knew he'd interrupted something and promptly moved on.

'Where were we?' said Imogen.

'I saw the Half Prophecy,' said Charlie.

'What?' said Tom. 'How? It's under lock and key.'

'Do you think the room is some kind of strange TV that shows you things?' asked Amanda.

'How could it?' said Imogen. 'It was trying to suck Charlie in.'

'True. OK, maybe some teleportation device,' said Amanda.

'Maybe it is,' said Tom, 'that would make sense.'

'You don't understand,' said Charlie. 'Understand what?' asked Imogen.

'I saw the Half Prophecy,' he said again.

'We know,' said Amanda, looking confused.

'The OTHER half,' said Charlie. 'I'm sure of it!'

Stunned silence hit them, and they just looked at him.

'Are you sure?' asked Amanda.

'That's impossible!' said Tom. 'The other half is of legend. People have searched for centuries and haven't found it. Are you sure?' he said sceptically.

'The room was spinning quickly. Maybe it was a trick of the mind; after all, Guildus only showed us this the other day,' said Imogen.

'I had thought of that,' said Charlie, 'but don't you think it would be a great place to hide it? 'After all, it is one of the oldest parts of the school, and who would be crazy enough to go in there to find it?' Charlie posed some excellent questions.

'Are you one hundred per cent sure?!' said Amanda.

'Pretty sure,' said Charlie. 'But yes, as you said, it was moving rather quickly, and my eyes were half-closed as it made me feel sick, but I'm sure I saw it!'

'OK!' said Tom. 'We need to do some research!'

'I agree,' said Imogen. 'We need to find out when it was built.'

'Hang on. Say everything checked out; what do we do then? Do we tell the teachers?' Tom asked.

'Much more to the point, how in the Magicklands do we get it out?' said Imogen. 'It would be the greatest find in history. I say, tell no one.'

'I agree,' said Charlie.

'I think we should check the drawing room and the main library as there is bound to be something there.' said Imogen.

Plans were in motion, and they were all getting very excited.

Helen walked over to them, carrying an object in her hand: the Wizopoly board game.

'Thanks, Helen,' said Charlie.

'No problem,' said Helen, walking back to her friends.

'Fantastic!' said Charlie.

'I've been looking forward to this; after all, enchantments don't work in the Plainlands,' said Amanda.' This is going to be interesting.'

'Sounds quite dull living without magick. Very plain,' said Tom.

'Yes, it does, though it isn't all boring,' he said.

'What do we do?' asked Amanda.

'Well, here are your wallets,' said Tom.

'They're tiny,' said Charlie.

'Not in there, they aren't,' replied Tom quickly.

'But how do we get into the game?' asked Charlie.

'Well, when it's your turn, you roll dice to get your number to move around the board. When you have that, you say enter, and you will end up in the game.'

'I get it,' said Charlie and Amanda.

'Let's play!' said Tom excitedly.

Sure enough, they played for two hours. When they entered the game, Charlie and Amanda were fascinated. Everything seemed natural, and they loved the Magickland money.

Amanda liked the miniature horses and carts they could sit in as they moved to each area. However, from an average human's perspective, they were like solid metal pieces on a plain board.

The game's enjoyment had made Charlie, Amanda, Tom, and Imogen forget about the Half Prophecy until they all returned to their rooms. It would play on their minds well into the night.

Chapter Seventeen

THE ORBERON

Over the next few days, they brought exciting new lectures, including Signs and Sigils 777, Nordic runes, more spell practice, and Magickal Powders: A Beginning and an Introduction to Spells for Specific Things (ISST).

Charlie knew little about spellwork and the Magicklands in general. What comforted him was the thought that his Magickland-born friends also had a lot to learn.

The ISST session explained that magick has different levels. The first was learning the beginners' summoning and sending spells. However, the next level was more complicated. It requires additional study, whereby magick could be used for personal life projects that couldn't be summoned like a book off a shelf.

Witch and Sorceress, Hegarty Blood, was a lovely old Hedge Witch and an expert in forming complicated spells. She was a stereotypical witch dressed all in black and with a pointed hat. She lived by the seaside in a cave, making spells, potions, and lotions for health.

As Charlie soon discovered, Hedge Witches prefer to work alone. Like some teachers this year, she was new to the school but never stayed on campus beyond the school day, as she liked to return to her cave.

The teacher started what was to be a long speech and lecture about her brand of magick. She explained to the class, "To achieve success in life, like a good job, relationship, or even becoming a first-class witch or Mage, you must know what you want. Dedicate your time towards your goal, and seek help when you become stuck. Don't hesitate to ask for help when you need it. It's perfectly okay to seek assistance, so don't try to handle everything alone. Remember, seeking help can often lead to better and faster results."

She added, "You can summon anything and everything! It depends on your faith in the magick that works in the unseen realms, your focus, and the amount of attention and dedication you put into your work. She warned that you get what you wish for, so be careful what you order."

She highlighted that second-level magick is not only about bringing what you desire or need. It adds energy and vitality where you want it. You can help others, nature, and the world. A simple act of kindness can bring untold fortune, so it isn't always necessary to formulate complicated spells.

Finally, you use magick only for good. "Never use it to bewitch others or against their will. Remember, what you give out will return threefold. It applies not only to magick but to thought and deed, too, especially when your intent is powerful," she said.

The group was confused by what she said, though she reassured them they would understand in time—a statement often used to encourage them not to give up, as magick can be overwhelming.

The class started. The pupils were given a Moonometer, each placed in their school bags before collecting. It was like a watch but had a more prominent face, with the moon imprinted and surrounded by various astrological symbols.

Charlie looked at Hegarty and put his hand up.

'Yes—young man and you are?' For the first time, he'd met someone who didn't know who he was.

'Charlie Stuart, Madam,' he said.

'How can I help you?' she said, smiling at him.

'What does a Moonometer do?' asked Charlie.

'It tells you the moon's phase, position, and planetary influences,' she responded swiftly.

'Why is the moon important to magick?' asked Charlie.

'That's a good question. The planet and the universe flow in cycles, just like the seasons. The moon has a massive influence on the planet, including controlling tides and emotions. Did you know most crimes are committed during the full moon?'

'Really?' said Amanda.

'And your name, young lady?' asked Hegarty.

'Amanda Campbell,' she replied.

'Hello Amanda, and yes, it is true. The moon's influences are much more extensive than you think,' the teacher said. 'Like the changing seasons, the moon has its cycle. The moon goes from nothingness into fullness and from fullness into nothingness. Let me explain. When the moon is heading into fullness, it is called the Waxing Phase of the moon, and when it reduces to its smallest element, it is called the Waning Phase. If you want to bring things into your life, like a new job, money, relationship, or gift, the best time to work on this is on the waxing moon. The energy works to pull and bring things into your life. If your spell requires power, it is the best time to do it on the full moon. If you wish to eliminate or remove non-useful things in your life, such as a bad habit, it is advisable to work during the waning phase when the moon's power helps to shift things out of your life. However, it's important to remember that you should never banish people from your life, as the energy you release will eventually return to you and possibly remove someone you need. If someone is annoying you, then there are more intelligent ways of handling them; see me first,' she said. 'Lastly, the best advice I can give you is to work from your heart and not out of hate. It achieves the best results long term and increases your power threshold.'

The class session continued, and the students asked about what she said.

She emphasised the importance of planting the seeds of magickal knowledge, no matter how complex or difficult it may seem. It will challenge their minds and spirits, but eventually, they will understand it.

Hegarty finished the session by asking them to think of an enchantment they would like to work on. Charlie wanted to discover who the shadowy entity was, so he spent some time with Hegarty, formulating a simple, revealing spell for this purpose.

Much to the class's relief, the next session wasn't as mind-boggling as the last: it was magickal powders.

Professor Lambert Snuffle, the teacher, was from the Magickal Powder Institute. He was large and looked like a typical mad scientist, with crazy, big hair and a white lab coat.

The lesson was fun as they could create powders that could do almost anything, from vanishing people to providing quick getaways such as teleportation. It could make you faster and your opposition slower; it is a fantastic level-one magickal aid.

The possibilities were endless. It involves combining herbs, woods, metals, and crystals, to name a few.

Professor Snuffle was an eccentric, passionate, and a very loud speaker. You could never fall asleep in his class. He discussed the history of magickal powders and demonstrated some of them.

The first powder he took moved him from one part of the class to another at high speed. The lesson's finale involved him walking on the ceiling and down the walls. The students were excited, and mischief was on everyone's minds.

Unfortunately, using magick and magickal powders to escape the school grounds was impossible, and the students groaned and moaned.

The first thing Professor Snuffle had them do was attempt to create a defensive shield powder. This powder protects the magician or objects for a few minutes against all kinds of magick and weapons. 'Great in emergencies,' said the Professor.

They began working in the laboratory, surrounded by test tubes, liquids, and ingredients.

The session was divided into two parts. First, the components were placed together and then ground into a powder resembling black sand. Although the students tried their best, the outcome of their experiment would be revealed only the following week.

*

The students found great joy in studying freely in various societies.

Charlie decided to teach Tom some kickboxing moves and was pleasantly surprised to see that Tom was picking up the basics quickly. However, Charlie had years of experience and was already ahead of the others.

Sensei Lee, the head of the martial arts club, was impressed by Charlie's skills and considered pairing him with some older students.

Charlie was new to spellcasting, though he was determined to learn. Tom, Amanda, and Imogen joined this session and worked hard to send and call objects.

The practice session went pretty well, but Charlie still struggled with aiming his spells accurately and often hit unintended targets, which frustrated him. Moreover, it annoyed the others, particularly David Moarns, who seemed to bear the brunt of the stray spells.

Tom had problems calling objects to himself, which either moved far too slowly or so quickly that he hit himself with the small ball he was using.

The girls seemed to do far better, though there was a lot of work for everybody to do.

'Relax, Charlie,' said Imogen, 'you're concentrating too hard, so it won't work,' she told him.

Afterwards, Charlie loved knight practice, learning a few defensive and offensive moves from one of the older pupils, Robert Ambrose.

It was the perfect build-up for the next big event: the launch of the Orberon over the weekend.

Because they were so busy, the one thing they didn't do was research the Half Prophecy further, and it was beginning to play on Charlie's mind.

*

It was almost seven on a Saturday evening, and time flew by. Charlie, Amanda, Tom, and Imogen waited in the canteen, drinking hot chocolate from the refillable cups.

'So what happens at the Orberon?' Charlie asked Tom.

'Well, I can't believe you have not heard of the Orberon; it is the coolest thing ever. I think you need to see it to believe it,' said Tom.

'I agree,' said Imogen. 'My Dad is superb at it. I hear that Sedrick will also be part of the launch.'

'Really!' said Tom excitedly. 'I've only seen him on TV. Well, I've never actually been to an Orberon before.'

'Really, wow! My Dad used to take me all of the time. He is part of the Black Dragon League of Knights,' said Imogen.

'That's incredible!' said Tom.

Charlie and Amanda exchanged a perplexed look, wondering what their friends were discussing.

*

The temperature dropped slightly outside as the sun lowered in the distance.

Charlie put on his Dragonstone leather jacket and zipped it up, tucking his scarf into his coat and putting on his matching gloves and hat. Amanda, Tom, and Imogen also proudly wore their house clothes.

They exited the building and joined the stream of students walking towards the arena.

The area was clear, except for large flags representing the school, The Orberon, and The Great City, and one flag representing all the elements and magick that blew imperiously in the air.

As they walked down the field, you could see students heading down passageways to the arena.

'The parchment says we need to go to the west entrance to get our seat,' said Amanda, so they did as she spoke.

They headed down until they reached the entrance to the inner part of the arena. Charlie had never seen it before and certainly wouldn't be disappointed.

They arrived at the lowest level, the same level as the participants, and Amanda had a special place that offered a fantastic view.

Charlie's mouth dropped, and he couldn't believe the vastness of the gigantic stadium.

'This is amazing!' he said, excited like he had just entered the magick world for the first time.

'It certainly is. I can't believe a thing this size is underground,' said Amanda.

The stadium filled up slowly, and various entrances on different levels made it easier for students, teachers and visitors to find seats.

The lights were bright as the sun finally set.

Mumbles and mutterings were rife, all filled with excitement and expectancy.

'What time does it start?' asked Charlie.

'Oh, about 8.15 pm,' said Tom.

The lights dimmed slightly, and a familiar figure entered the scene: Sedrick, wearing unfamiliar, neat, fashionable clothing. His hair was washed and tied back, and his beard was trimmed.

'Ladies and gentlemen, students and teachers, I, Sedrick, three-time winner of the Orberon with the Black Dragon League, say in traditional magickal voice, Hail and Welcome,' he said, speaking through some magickally adjusted microphone.

'HAIL AND WELCOME,' shouted the crowd.

'We have a treat for you tonight. The best duellers, jousters and fighters of magick are coming together to entertain you.'

'Fantastic!' said Charlie, as did some other children.

As the event progressed in the stadium, the lights began to dim. The once bright and vibrant atmosphere was replaced by a deep red and blue hue filling the stadium.

People in the audience struggled to see as the lights continued to dim even further until they eventually went dark.

The sudden darkness surprised everyone, causing a hush over the crowd. Then, just as suddenly, the lights came back on. The sudden brightness caused everyone to either squint or shut their eyes entirely as they adjusted to the sudden change in lighting. When the lights dimmed, a jousting partition mysteriously appeared.

The knights stormed in on horseback from the four entrances of the arena's lowest part.

The knights went straight into the action: The knight with red markings galloped towards his opponent in blue markings. They struck each other on the chest and knocked backwards with every hit, and the crowd bellowed as they did so.

'Get him!' the Fire house cheered for the knight in red, the colour of their house.

'Put his fire out,' teased the Water house, supporting their man in blue.

The knights turned to make another run, and the horses galloped as fast as their legs could carry them. Smash! The red knight blocked the blue knight's lance, knocking him off his horse. The whole stadium erupted with another roar.

'One to zero to the reds,' shouted Sedrick as it flashed on the mainboard.

'We've got this in the Plainlands,' shouted Charlie over the crowd's noise.

'Just watch this,' shouted Tom.

The blue knight quickly got up, minus his horse, which had run back down the entrance.

The red knight bore onto his opponent when he remarkably jumped over the thrusting lance of the oncoming red rider like a high jumper would over the high bar.

He pulled his sword mid-flow, landed on his feet, and struck the red knight from his steed.

'One all,' said Sedrick. 'Who is going to be the mightiest today?' he bellowed.

'WOW! How did he do that?' asked Charlie.

'That's a Magickal Knight,' said Tom.

Then something surprised Charlie: The red knight took out his sword and shot a large magickal red pulse straight towards the blue knight, who raised his shield and blocked it.

The man in blue reciprocated, this time sending a spread of blue pulses, just like an old Gatling gun. However, his opponent blocked some with his shield and deflected the rest with the sword.

Suddenly, the knight in red sneakily put something into his armour, and, at great speed, he zoomed towards the blue knight, knocking him to the ground. The crowd erupted once more.

'Two one to the reds,' said Sedrick.

'Roast him!' shouted the Fire House, so he obliged.

'That's curious,' said Imogen, whispering something to Amanda.

The red knight swung his sword up and around. His sword glowed red and caught fire, and its flame was directed towards his opponent on the ground. Within seconds, he was in flames; the crowd gasped.

The warrior on the ground grasped his sword and pointed it upwards, magickally dragging himself backwards.

'So you have this on the Plainlands?' asked Tom.

'Er, not quite like this,' said Charlie, laughing. 'This is so much better,' he said, grinning like a Cheshire cat.

Imogen was cheering away, and Amanda, entirely baffled by the whole experience, still managed to scream very loudly at various points.

The knight quickly picked himself up. Then, there followed a series of close combat manoeuvres. Large swords rushed, clashing and sparking different energy colours.

It was breathtaking while simultaneously producing a magick involving attack and defence, trying to defeat each other.

Everyone sat on the edge of their seats, observing the combat spectacle.

The knight with blue markings suddenly caught his adversary in a magickal net. The knight clenched his fist, and his rival in blue made a flinging gesture, sending the red knight crashing to the ground.

'Two all! The one who strikes the next point wins the match.'

Combat resumed. Bludgeoning maces were swinging, striking each other's shields and armour. Each knight shot multiple red energy blasts the size of a mace head towards each other with equal skill.

Swords clanged and clashed, with magickal and metallic sparks flying everywhere. Some even hit the side of the arena, making the children very apprehensive.

Then suddenly, the Fire house knight produced a cunning move: whilst avoiding the blows from the blue knight, he twisted on the spot, took out a dagger, and, like a wand, pointed at his lance on the floor behind his challenger.

The lance came hurtling towards the man in blue. He was unaware of the lance spinning towards him like a helicopter blade. Within seconds, the lance knocked the blue knight off his feet and onto his back.

'Three two to the reds; he's the winner!!'

Roars from the crowd came as Sedrick made his announcement.

Charlie glanced around and noticed that Water house appeared to be somewhat disappointed. The Fire house held up signs saying, "You're Fired," "Fire Rules," "Your water has evaporated," and "Let off some steam," to name a few. The only remaining blue sign was from one of the older children saying, "You need cooling off."

The blue knight looked dejected, though he got up, bowed to his opponent, bowed to Sedrick and then bowed to the crowd.

Everyone applauded, including Charlie, who had never seen such a thing.

It wasn't over. Sedrick spoke again, 'Now for the task! Release the Lionoth.'

A peculiar-looking creature appeared from nowhere. As the name implied, it looked like a lion, though it was at least ten times the size of a typical lion.

Its claws began to protrude outwards as it sat on its hind legs. The more they extended, the more evident it was that these were not just ordinary claws. They resembled sizable needle-like spikes that measured around three feet in length. Then, armour-like structures started materialising along its body, transforming its tail into a spiked club.

'That's an apparition enchantment,' said Tom.

'You're kidding,' said Charlie.

'But it looks so real,' said Amanda.

'The killing of beasts for recreational purposes was outlawed two centuries ago for being barbaric and against the natural laws. They can only be killed if your life is in danger or if they're a danger to anyone else. My Dad told me,' said Imogen.

'That's brilliant,' said Amanda.

'Yeah, the enchantment is genuine, and the more advanced you become, the more dangerous the charms. They can do serious damage, though, but as far as I know, no one has ever died before,' said Tom.

'Well, that's good to hear,' laughed Charlie.

Two other knights joined the fray.

The first knight had yellow markings indicating that he was an Air sign, and the second knight displayed green markings indicating an Earth sign. All four knights were on their horses, circling the beast in the middle of the arena.

Sensing imminent danger, the beast let out a mighty roar and started pacing around, causing the children to panic and scream in fear.

Its claws remained remarkably straight, and then Charlie noticed that some mercury-type substance started oozing.

'What's that?' said Charlie.

'Not sure,' replied Tom.

'Ooh, poison is now coming out of the Lionoth's claws; the knights better watch out,' said Sedrick.

Without warning, the beast lunged towards the blue knight, who, by the skin of his teeth, moved quickly out of the way, and the red and yellow knights thrust their lances into the beast from behind, having no effect. The Lionoth swished his tail, knocking the yellow knight's lance onto the ground.

'Come on, Air!' shouted Charlie.

The Lionoth swung round, and its javelin-like claws slashed into the armour of the red knight.

'What? That is magickal armour,' exclaimed Tom. 'I thought it was supposed to be impervious to everything.'

'Not everything,' said Imogen, frowning again.

'Ooh, the beast's poison can get through the armour,' said Sedrick softly. The red knight fled quickly, and the other knights kept their distance.

The red knight unsheathed his sword, which erupted in flames. The blue knight dodged the fiery blast while the beast was struck in the face.

The Lionoth raged as it stood on its legs and lunged toward the red knight. Thankfully, The yellow knight, being of Air, sent a strong wind, pushing the knight out of the way, and the Lionoth skidded on the surface, missing him.

The blue knight yielded his mace this time, swinging it around furiously. The head was frosted with a significant spike sticking out of the top. He threw it at the creature, and the yellow knight accelerated the rate at which the mace flew, using a miniature hurricane as a propulsion mechanism. It stuck in the beast's forehead.

The wounded creature became angrier and started chasing everyone wildly, and the knights went in different directions to confuse it. It focused on the green knight, and the others regrouped around.

Unexpectedly, another person entered the arena, holding a spear in each hand.

'It's Sedrick,' shouted a student. 'WOW.'

Charlie was now on the edge of his seat, as was most of the arena.

He came in with each spear above each shoulder. He was going to perform a double spear throw. 'Articus,' said Sedrick as he released the spears and the heads frosted over as he threw them. They moved with such force that the spears penetrated the natural body armour of the Lionoth and into its heart.

The beast whimpered its final breath, and the magickal apparition enchantment vanished.

Cheers erupted from the audience as Sedrick raised his arms in triumph, yowling as the Lionoth had previously. It turned out that the Lionoth's weakness was ice and steel to penetrate its armour.

'That was scary,' said Charlie.

'Sedrick's the best,' shouted David, who sat two rows above them.

The red knight turned and approached where Charlie and his gang were sitting. He stopped in front of them and took his helmet off.

Charlie, Amanda, and Tom were shocked and unsure what to say. Imogen looked at the knight and said, 'Hello, Dad.'

'Hello Imogen, didn't quite get the beastie this time, eh?! I must brush up on my ice; what, what,' he said chirpily.

'Yes, Father,' said Imogen, looking somewhat embarrassed. 'Don't forget to send your mother a message. She's sent you three scrolls already this week,' he said.

He wore his helmet and trotted off to meet Sedrick and the other knights.

'Your father is the red knight,' said Tom in disbelief.

'Yeah,' she said. 'I wasn't sure, to begin with, though when he summoned the lance that knocked over the blue knight, I knew it was him,' she said coolly.

'How cool! Of course, he's Sir Michael Braithwaite. Brilliant!' said Tom. 'Just flippin' brilliant!'

Imogen became embarrassed as some other students started chatting and pointing at her.

'Thank you for coming,' said Sedrick, wearing his full Viking gear.

'The Orberon is officially open at Dragonstone School of Magick, and you can put your teams together. Get plenty of practice in now.'

'Give us more,' shouted the students. 'More... more... more... more... more...'

Sedrick was unmoved, and the event finished shortly afterwards.

After returning to their accommodation, Imogen and her companions gathered in her room, where they found three scrolls waiting for her, just as her father had mentioned. A fourth scroll then appeared unexpectedly.

'I guess I better reply,' she said.

'Yeah, you don't want to worry her,' said Amanda.

They discussed the Orberon and considered forming a team. Since they all belonged to different elemental houses, this was perfect for them, even though they couldn't participate fully until the second year.

Charlie and Amanda wanted clarification on the Orberon, so Imogen spoke.

'Well, it works like this. Each team that enters has four members, and they compete against another team. Typically, one member does the duelling, though everyone can duel. Some teams change and rotate, so each member has a go each week.'

'I see!' said Charlie.

'Each scoring hit earns a point during the game when the knight hits the ground. Three hits to the ground, and the opponent is out, with points awarded to the other team. At the end, there is a 'Task' to complete, like the knights having to slay the Lionoth. It typically involves all team members coming together to help. In the league, a panel scores points in other areas, such as effort, cooperation, courage, and ingenuity—there are more.

'I see!' said Amanda.

'Oh, the first team to complete the task fastest gets a ten-point bonus; it is awarded at the end of the week. The Orberon tests your skill and the ability to work as a team. It is terrific because it keeps you on your toes and makes you work for your team and house. It also makes you spend a lot of time studying magick. In many ways, it is like the societies: it helps make learning fun,' Imogen continued.

'Well, how does it work for your house?' asked Charlie.

'Each team member's score goes to your Elemental House Score. The house with the most points wins. So, in the end, you have a team and house score,' said Imogen. The knight with the most individual points becomes Knight of the Year. Also, there is a duel-off between the top knights to become the ultimate champion,' said Imogen.

'So why don't you group everyone from one house?' asked Amanda.

'Well, they say it is vital to work with other houses to achieve things. Still, it is also important to see the value of all the elements working, as they are all needed,' said Imogen. 'Of course, we can all use all the elements ourselves, though the element we are born with is our strongest. Some great magicians and wizards learn to use all elements equally, though this takes years of practice and learning,' she said, concluding.

'I think I get it,' said Charlie. 'I can't wait to start!' he said with a sparkle in his eye.

CHAPTER EIGHTEEN

THE GREAT CITY

The first-year students were excited about their trip to the Great City, and Charlie was so eager that he asked Sebastian, the door, to wake him up on time. The trip had been rescheduled a few times for various reasons, such as damage to the river flume. Additionally, Eric had an accident caused by mysterious crocodiles entering the flume vortex.

It had been a few weeks since Charlie sent his mother a letter, and he was pleased to receive a response. He was relieved his friends couldn't see the giant pair of enchanted red lips that flew out, giving him a whopping great kiss on his forehead.

Charlie appeared to be having difficulty using magick to move objects and was falling behind the rest of the group. However, Astrophos reassured them that learning new spells can be frustrating, especially when "one finds it challenging to grasp them." It was important to remember that everyone learns at their own pace, and with time and practice, students could master the spells just like anyone else, even Charlie.

Guildus Grey seemed to be getting quite aggravated with some of the class. Conversely, Siddhartha got more patient as the weeks trundled on.

On October 31st, people celebrate Halloween, which originated in the ancient Celtic festival of Samhain. This festival was considered a Greater Sabbat. Western witches and other practitioners from different magickal practices enjoyed celebrating it. It differed from the one he'd learned in the Plainlands, though he couldn't wait to join in. Still, he'd have to wait another week.

Researching the Half Prophecy became a chore. Still, one crucial fact they discovered was that the oldest parts of the school existed when the prophecy was written so that it could have been hidden on the school grounds.

The more he thought about it, the more he was convinced that he had seen it. It remained a fundamental problem, but what could they do about it? How could they access the room without being sucked into oblivion? They researched as much as possible but couldn't find a piece of magickal text that mentioned that type of magick, but they weren't giving up.

Another annoying question Charlie asked was, *Why me?* After all, he was just some lost child from the Plainlands. Why did the shadowy thing take him there? Also, why wasn't the second-level spell that he created to confirm who the creature was working? *Maybe I was terrible at levels one and two magick,* he thought.

Most importantly, what would it mean if he did retrieve it? He'd wanted to ask Cosmolos, though something told him not to, just in case he thought he was crazy; his friends all agreed with his decision.

What concerned him most was that he might get told off for going somewhere he shouldn't have gone. The last thing he wanted was to get detention or be banished back to the Plainlands.

Charlie realised he knew nothing of the Great City or why it was so great. He was so busy that he never bothered to ask. His mother had told him, "You've got to see it to believe it."

In general, his lessons were fascinating. Charlie and his friends had been through all the elemental blocks for their lessons, and they were all incredible. Each block was constructed with precise representations of the elementals.

From now on, students were encouraged to refer to their respective houses with their proper names. Charlie belonged to Paralda, so he was a Paraldian. Amanda belonged to Necksa; hence, she was a Necksonian. Similarly, Tom belonged to Ghob, so he was a Ghobdinian, while Imogen belonged to Djin, making her a Djinzarian.

The Necksa Building looked like an aquarium with glass walls surrounding it. The walls held water with sea creatures; sometimes, you could see water elementals swimming around. You could also spot water faeries skilled in healing magick and caring for aquatic plants. Tom was amazed to see them travel on dragonflies from one place to another.

Amanda managed to see a water nymph. Water nymphs like to be alone and live near natural water sources. They are believed to have the power to aid in healing and prophecy.

There were so many creatures and elementals to learn about; it was fascinating, and the block was perfect for learning all about them. There were rooms dedicated to the seas, oceans, rivers, lakes, ponds, and streams. The least favourites were water bogs and swamps as they were very smelly. The ice and snow rooms weren't popular, though snowballing was fun. The seas were the most popular because you could wear the Dragonstone swimming outfits for class. Charlie thought the fourth floor was brilliant, as you had to row your boat to the classrooms.

Archimedes' office was located at the bottom of the first floor. It was easily recognisable as a waterfall covered the door leading into his office.

The Paralda building was just as fascinating. As soon as you walked in, you were greeted with a gentle, refreshing breeze that helped you relax. The main corridor was long, and the walls were made of old rock. The rocks' edges were covered in layers of mist, creating clear, pure air you could see moving.

The room's ceiling was designed to resemble a clear blue sky, with soft white clouds moving gently along, resembling cotton wool. The block was surreal, with some classrooms without floors and desks hovering mid-air. Although the students were nervous about entering this room, they felt relieved that no one would fall through this enchanted sky.

Certain classes made you feel drifty, sleepy, or very relaxed, whilst other rooms weren't as pleasant as the winds became more violent and stormy. Amongst all this, birds and other Air elementals were flying through. The ones that caught their eye were the sylphs and zephyrs that made regular appearances.

The sylphs looked like beautiful ladies inside bubble-shaped structures and were friendly and cheerful as long as no one provoked them. But if they got angry, they would go crazy like a storm. On the other hand, zephyrs were male creatures who controlled the winds and flew gracefully in the air with sylphs. They could be playful and fun, but if you got them mad, they could change their appearance and look scary with frowns instead of their handsome appearance, just like the female sylphs.

It was Charlie's domain, as he was an Air sign. He also looked forward to lessons with Cosmolos, a powerful mage. Charlie tried to visit the building as often as possible in his spare time, as he found it inspiring. After all, inspiration was one of the primary strengths of the Air element.

The last of the elemental buildings was the Djin Building. As Cosmolos told Charlie whilst on the magick carpet, it was named after King Djin, the King of Fire and its elementals. For centuries, King Djin had been demonised by some as fire had always been seen as the domain of hell. Of course, fire can burn and get out of control, but the other elementals can get out of control, too. Without fire, things wouldn't grow, motivation wouldn't happen, and neither would a warm heart exist. "A duality", as Cosmolos explained, "is the nature of the elementals, just like people."

All students knew about the firedrakes, as they could regularly be seen lighting and relaxing in the flames, which was their favourite pastime. Like all other elemental environments, fire has faeries, like firedrakes. They love to be near flames and bask and dance in them. Unlike firedrakes, they are hard to spot due to their pale orange hair, pasty skin, and bright eyes. They stand a few inches tall. They have various magickal uses, particularly in level two magic and some in level one magic, including wish fulfilment, divination, and shape-shifting.

Cosmolos kept repeating that elementals are independent entities that can be summoned but not controlled. You can request their help, and they will either accept or deny your request depending on the worthiness of the task. However, they are known to change their minds. Finally, Cosmolos said that elementals could not be deceived; "Try so at your peril." However, the more devious elementals can be banished.

Of course, Fire was Imogen's sign, just like her father at the Orberon. All the signs seemed important, but it was apparent that they were more complicated than they thought.

*

The internal post announced that all students would receive a new addition to their uniforms: fresh wizard robes for ritual celebrations and magickal work, such as spell-casting. The students loved the idea of dressing up in magicians' robes.

In the weeks that passed, Felicity Phelps and her crew failed at having a go at Amanda. Her adapted wheelchair made it easier for her to get away from them. She enjoyed circling them, running over their toes, and feeling no guilt.

Charlie thought he had seen everything about the magickal world, but a late October morning proved him wrong.

Charlie, Amanda, Tom, and Imogen waited for the flume rail at the main canteen. They were heading towards the Great City, and Tom explained that the rail was like the London Underground but on water.

Charlie was finishing the bacon on his plate when he dipped his egg yolk into his mouth. He loved eggs and bacon, which reminded him of being at home with his mother. Then he spoke.

'Where do we leave from?'

'Oh, the flume rail port is right at the bottom of the school near the river,' said Tom.

Amanda pulled out her timetable, and a map appeared showing the way.

'Look, it's right down here,' said Amanda. 'How come I'd never seen this before?'

'Well, Dad said the flume network had broken down. Crocodiles weren't the only things found there. Someone had mysteriously placed water trolls and gremlins to disrupt the tube. No one knows why. It took ages to clear them out, and that's why it has taken us so long to get to the Great City,' said Imogen.

Twenty minutes later, the four of them left the canteen.

'Oooooh, you're going to the Great City; do you think you're great then?' said Neil, the insulting Un-Potted plant, opening his mouth wide with his fingers and sticking his tongue out. They realised not to engage with him, so they continued walking on the freshly gravelled path.

'Fancy a lift?' asked Amanda.

As she spoke, two boards emerged from the sides of the wheelchair, which had a footstand at the rear.

'Brilliant,' said Charlie, 'let's go!' he said enthusiastically.

'It certainly beats walking,' said Tom, laughing.

Charlie hopped on the back, Imogen to the left, and Tom sat on the right. They descended towards the flume rail, honking an old-fashioned horn so students could get out of the way.

The air was crisper than it had been recently, so Charlie's gang wore winter overcoats, hats, scarves and gloves.

It was autumn, and the summer flowers had almost wholly disappeared. A few evergreens and everoranges remained unchanged year-round, while other plants would bud in autumn and winter.

As they descended the hill, they laughed and fell off occasionally as they went over the lumps and bumps in the earth.

They passed the Orberon, the knight's training area and society buildings, and eventually, they could hear running water.

'Over there,' said Charlie, seeing the port platform. They stood there waiting for the flume's arrival; he couldn't wait to see it.

After standing in the cold wind, the platform filled with first-years. Without warning, a crack in the air appeared, and a flume arrived out of nowhere.

It was a long train consisting of several carriages, each designed like the Dragonstone bus coaches, with a round-bellied red body. Inside, it was different, with many more seats but no luxury perks like a minibar.

The door opened, and a voice sounded as a man exited.

'Hello, Charlie,' said Randle.

'Hey Randle, great to see you,' replied Charlie.

'Hello, Amanda, lovely to see you too,' said Randle.

'Hello, Randle,' smiled Amanda. 'Are you taking us to the Great City?' she said.

'Yes, there is no one better to show you around,' he announced proudly. It's just a shame the pathway was clogged with many things. Water trolls are so stubborn and dangerous if you don't watch them. I have to admit this is the first time someone has done this. By the gods, I have no idea why,' he said, sounding very annoyed.

Randle began introducing himself to the other students when another voice sounded.

'Bloomin' hurry up,' said Eric.

'Oh no, not Eric?' said Charlie and Amanda, laughing together.

'I'm afraid so,' said Randle, smiling.

'Who's Eric?' Tom asked.

'He was the driver who brought us here. He's quite miserable, though quite funny,' said Charlie.

'You'll see,' said Amanda.

Randle finished what he was saying, and they all got on.

'About bloomin' time,' whinged Eric. 'If they move any quicker, they will stop', he continued. 'Right, I'm only going to say this once,' announced Eric over the tannoy, 'No litter, no fighting or no stupid anything. I'll chuck you out mid-journey, or worse, leave you stranded in the Plainlands. I can do that, you know.'

The doors closed, and the school pupils waited in anticipation.

The flume pulled off slowly, picking up speed as it approached the tunnel. There was a slight lift of the flume and a crackle in the air, and it entered a watery vortex, racing as it travelled.

'We'll be arriving in one hour,' said Randle.

'That's too long with this lot,' muttered Eric.

The journey seemed shorter than an hour, though they had already checked their bags and money.

Charlie's mum sent him money through the post, and he was pleased to see that he had the equivalent of one hundred pounds or what is known in the magick world as a grundle. A grundle comprised one hundred groans, and one groan comprised one hundred onks, similar to pence.

'Brilliant, you've got a grundle,' said Tom. 'I've got ninety groans,' he chirped. What have you guys got?' he asked Amanda and Imogen.

'Eighty groans,' said Amanda. '

Two grundles', said Imogen

'Wow! Two grundles! Drinks on you, Imogen,' said Charlie playfully.

The journey was mostly uneventful, but it seemed to pass quickly.

'Well, we'll be arriving any second now, and there might be some turbulence,' said Eric, smiling. 'Three, two, one....' There was a rumble, a sharp shake and a crack—the flume had arrived at the Warlock's Portside Station. Some students had fallen off their seats, and some looked rather green.

'That miserable git,' said Helen. 'Look at him laughing,' she said, glaring at Eric.

From outside the flume, all you could see were windows cluttered with young faces scrambling to see outside. They were in the equivalent of a bus and rail station with flumes of all colours and sizes from everywhere. The students quickly left after the water rail dockworkers secured the transport.

They saw many boats and ships in the port. Then they heard a loud noise, and the water engine disappeared. Most students wrinkled their noses at the pungent odour of fish and were eager to move on.

'This way,' said Randle.

Moving through a wide alley, they arrived at the main street called Percival Way.

'Hurry now; we have much to do,' said Randle.

Quickly, the children hurried along and approached a gate in the city wall.

'Ah Randle, old chap, great to see you,' said the gateman.

Charlie met a guard who wore an old-fashioned uniform similar to the one the Queen's guards wore at the palace he had seen on television. The guard held a large pole with a spear pointing elegantly out of the top. Another spearhead protracted like a hook off the side.

'Ah, Roderick, lovely to see you again; it has been far too long,' said Randle.

'Send me a scroll, and we'll meet at the Siren Inn for some whisky,' said Roderick.

'Will do,' replied Randle.

'I see you have the first-years again. Come through; you can pass,' said Roderick.

Roderick cheerfully greeted each pupil as they passed through the gate, which made a pleasant change from Eric's miserable whining.

Inside, the city was teeming with all kinds of people.

'But—what, eh?' said Charlie, scratching his head.

Charlie noticed some Romans and English knights drinking from horns, cheering and singing songs.

'TO JARV!' said the knights and Romans, toasting and laughing.

'You wait until mediaeval night,' said the giant drunken knight to the Roman.

Amanda looked gobsmacked, and Tom and the other students looked amazed. Imogen just smiled.

'I don't get it,' said Charlie.' They are...'

'Yes,' said Randle, and he began to explain. 'The Great City is a unique place, constructed from the diverse magickal cultures of the world. According to the founding agreement, each nation was required to preserve the best from each period.

'It looks amazing,' said an excited Charlie!

'People choose which era they feel more comfortable living in and enjoy the best from that time. Most trading and work exist in the centre, where the world comes together. Randle explained that they bring the best of each culture and, importantly, magickal knowledge.

'Impressive!' exclaimed Amanda.

'Still, when it is all done, they go home to live in parts of the city known as Quarters, though different from the Elemental Quarters. The Quarters comprise the Greeks, Romans, Chinese, Egyptians, Native Americans, English, Japanese, and more,' said Randle excitedly. 'All countries take turns guarding the critical areas and leading the council in the centre. This part is based on ancient Greece, the founders of democracy.'

'It sounds complicated!' said Tom.

'The Great Council is responsible for forming and dissolving laws and ensuring power is shared amongst the ruling royal houses. However, each royal house manages its internal affairs. This system has been in place for centuries and has proven effective, resulting in a peaceful society.'

'So is this why people are dressed differently, because they live in a place that, well, a time where people wore those types of clothes?' asked Amanda.

'Well, yes and no. When you visit the mediaeval part of the English Quarter, you'll step into a stunning representation of that period rather than just stepping back in time. You can move to a different Quarter if you choose to. For example, the Mordens recently moved into the Renaissance sector. It's remarkable how everyone dresses in a way that makes them feel comfortable. Dressing comfortably is key to feeling confident and empowered. At the Orberon, Vikings and knights represented different periods but worked together. Here, you can see Romans and English knights; in the future, you may see Greeks, Tudors, etc. It is a fascinating reality, a place like no other in the world!'

The students were captivated by Randle's explanations.

Whilst walking, they encountered people from different eras trading, drinking, and laughing. It was a breathtaking sight.

They were on the outskirts of the central political centre, which had a confusing mixture of architecture, yet it all fit together.

'What's that?' said Tom, pointing to a colossal grey circular brick building in the middle of a large market square.

'That's the Witches' Coven. They are a mystery even to the magick world, though no one interferes as they do nothing wrong. They chose to remain secret, so it is respected.'

Charlie and his friends walked around, spotting all kinds of buildings and people.

'Ah yes, there is the museum! Objects from hundreds of thousands of years ago are kept and preserved. Here, the Half Prophecy will live for a while before it moves on again. It is the most intriguing historical artefact because this place wouldn't exist without it. Remember, the prophecy is also a binding contract and the key to creating this city.' Charlie, Amanda, Tom and Imogen looked at this statement with significant interest.

Charlie and the rest of the first-years explored the city in all its glory: different buildings, people, and magickal enchantments from various stalls advertising their products. One Arabian market had a young lad who fired three-dimensional holographic enchantments out of the store, promoting its products as they floated down the street. To Charlie's amazement, some charms were heading back to the store with people in tow.

'How clever!' Amanda exclaimed.

'It sure is,' said Charlie.

Witches on old broomsticks flew through the air, and people walked on magick carpets. People could lock their brooms and rugs in a multi-story magick parking area. Some scroll-porters were also put inside what looked like old-fashioned phone boxes.

You could find many streets with stores and bazaars selling food and tourist trinkets and banks with cash machines at the side; they worked by using your magick name to withdraw your money.

There were apothecaries, blacksmiths, food stores, restaurants, and almost anything you could imagine. On one of the streets, a man was making and selling magick carpets, shouting, 'Carpets, starting from fifteen grundles.'

'Fifteen grundles, for that? What a rip-off!' shouted Tom, disapproving of a worn carpet he was trying to sell.

'Hey, look,' said Amanda, 'there's a Magickal Powders Store.'

'Get your powders here. We sell rare ingredients for those special powders,' shouted the Asian Indian store seller.

After hours of looking around, Charlie and his gang received another surprise. One of the statues came alive, calling himself Napoleon and telling everyone to be on guard as they would be attacked. He was then replaced by the great mathematician Archimedes, who offered help with mathematical problems.

'They are special enchanted statues,' said Imogen. 'These statues channel the essence or spirit of the greatest historical figures. My Dad loves talking to Achilles about his conquests. Not all spirits come through, but some do. It uses some special form of er, I can't remember what the concrete is called,' said Imogen.

'Well, that is just amazing,' said Amanda.

An elegantly designed piece of parchment flew over, carrying the details of Maisie's Magickal Jewels. It said they'd been "mined from the finest mines around, perfect for wands, staffs work and home."

After receiving a message to follow the paper to a stall or keep it for later, Amanda chose to keep it. It folded itself into an envelope and lay dormant in her hand.

'Terrific,' said Amanda.

'Look at that,' said Tom.

They all turned around and saw a bright blue light circling in the sky before disappearing.

'What was that?' asked Helen.

'That was the Witches' Coven,' said Randle. 'They send out different spells into the world.'

'Why?' asked Charlie as a brilliant, beautiful green light circled and shot into the air.

'No one knows exactly, though they did help out during the Beltane festival by bringing out some sunshine when torrential rain threatened the celebrations,' said Randle appreciatively.

Charlie remembered from his history class that Beltane was the May Day festival. He enjoyed celebrating it at his old school, though it was different. In the Plainlands, many are unaware of its magical origins; even the maypole bears a mystical significance.

They looked around and around, and it seemed that the city would never end.

'I'd love to come back here,' said Charlie.

'And you will! There is much to learn here, and we'll also see the Half Prophecy when it arrives next year,' said Randle.

'When is that?' asked Charlie.

'Oh, I'm not sure. It could be around the Ostara spring equinox celebration or the next Beltane festival.'

'When is Ostara?' Charlie asked Randle.

'It is on March 20th.'

'I can't wait for it,' said Charlie.

'OK, FIRST-YEARS, GATHER ROUND,' shouted Randle to get their attention.

It took them a few minutes to gather. The change in pitch indicated that Randle was uncomfortable raising his voice.

'There will be plenty of opportunities to explore the shops, the centre, and the museum. However, we will quickly explore one of the Quarters' sections. Follow me,' said Randle.

The group walked westwards, taking about twenty minutes to get there.

They walked along a dusty pathway until they reached another large wall and gate. This time, there was another guard: he was Roman.

'Greetings, Randle,' said the guard.

'Greetings, Brutus,' said Randle. 'I see the Romans have taken over the guard.'

'Yes. I see you have the young ones again; this must be the fifteenth year in a row now?'

'Has it been fifteen years? I lose track, you know.'

'That's Junii Brutus—Magickal Knight and Champion of the Roman Orberon. He's a great warrior!' said Tom.

'Cool, I never realised they had their league,' said Charlie.

'Oh yes, communities and schools have their own. There is a showdown of Champions at the end.'

'I bet that's a sight,' said Charlie.

'One of the best,' said Tom.

It just dawned on Charlie that he had just entered the most fantastic world ever, and it was significantly better than the one he had joined at school. After all, that was impressive enough.

Brutus stood up massively and nearly as tall as Sedrick.

'Wow, he's bigger in real life,' said David.

Randle and Brutus discussed the upcoming tournament, and after a few minutes, the guard let them pass.

'Good luck, first-years,' said Brutus, waving his large hand and giving them a typical Roman salute.

As they passed the gate, they entered a mediaeval-looking England.

A castle was at the top of the hill, with a town beneath it. Unlike some Plainland mediaeval towns, which lived in squalor, this place was spotless and looked immaculate. Though it seemed more natural, they had a shining edge to everything, almost like a faerie tale.

Randle waved his hand at someone in the distance, and the couple waved back.

'Who's that?' Amanda asked.

'Ah, that is Mr and Mrs Bimble; they run the local orphanage. A lovely couple taking on all those children,' he said approvingly.

'That's a nice thing to do,' said Amanda.

'It certainly is. For some reason, the orphans he cares for have experienced severe trauma, which has affected their magick,' said Randle.

'Really?' Imogen seemed surprised. 'How?'

'Well, those who have suffered trauma either struggle to do magick or can't do any magick at all.'

'That's horrible,' said Amanda.

'Indeed! So, they take it upon themselves to educate and train them as best they can. I'm told that some become completely healed and then lead normal lives. It has happened in other orphanages, but these are the most damaged,' said Randle solemnly.

Charlie and some pupils looked at them and waved, and the couple waved back. A few children were outside helping in the garden. They looked at the first-years and waved.

Moments later, they were taken inside, with Mrs Bimble gently carrying the youngest.

They looked around the village and stopped in a local Inn to eat and drink before departing for another Quarter.

The city was vast, and exploring everything would take weeks or months. It didn't matter, as they were part of the magick world and had all the time to explore.

'Is everything this nice in the magick world?' asked Charlie. 'Well, apart from those poor souls, I mean.'

'Well, a good portion of it certainly is,' said Randle. 'Some elect not to get involved with the mainstream of society. They are called Squirms.'

'That doesn't sound nice,' said Amanda disapprovingly. Helen agreed with her.

'That is because they aren't very nice people. They are quite an angry crowd who involve themselves with all kinds of craftiness. Some go and live there because they have no one or have run away from home. They are taken in and soon taught how to go about life in a less honourable way. Squirms live in all sectors and communities but have areas where normal folk dare not tread. We must have the knight guards to ensure they don't get out of hand.'

After finishing their hog roast and non-alcoholic strawberry mead, they moved to the Roman Quarter. It was as spectacular and fascinating as the medieval city. Beautifully constructed out of marble, with gold embedded in the structures, it also had a magical shine.

Some folk paid respects to the gods at small temples scattered around the place.

Some performed magick rituals in the open, and bright colours emanated from their beautifully crafted staffs and wands—it was amazing to see how magick and everyday life came together naturally.

Exploring the towns is all they had time for. The others would have to wait. However, there was one more thing that Randle had promised to show them in the Great City before they headed back. Like everything else that Randle had pledged to, it wouldn't disappoint.

Back in the centre of the Great City, they headed in the opposite direction from which they had walked whilst the Witches' Tower had fallen quiet of spell-working.

They walked down a few side streets past shops where a Victorian man bought meat from an African seller.

Charlie found it hard to process what he saw, but he found it intriguing.

Charlie was quite thirsty. He cracked open a can of *Percy Thirst-Quencher* that turned a cola-type colour.

The temperature changed wherever they went, so they continually changed various clothing items to match the changing climate.

The centre of the Great City was chilly, with fresh, clear skies. Nevertheless, they could smell and hear different aromas and sounds wherever they went.

Enchantments were everywhere, either stationary or floating around, trying to draw customers in with their latest offers.

'I know where we are heading,' Imogen smiled.

'Where?' Tom asked.

'You'll see,' she said teasingly.

Turning another corner came into view, a brilliant sight.

'WOW,' said Tom.

'What is it?' Charlie asked.

'That is the Orberon's main arena, the largest in the Magicklands,' said Tom excitedly.

'Yeah, I've been here quite a few times with my dad,' said Imogen.

'You're so lucky,' said Tom.

Randle accompanied them to the arena entrance, which was similar to the Coliseum in Italy but much more extensive.

They passed a Musketeer guard who, coincidently, was called Athos from the stories and recognised by Charlie and Amanda.

Entering a side tunnel, they reached the seating area of the arena.

Charlie's mouth dropped open when he saw the Romans, Greeks, English, Scottish, French, Egyptians, Dutch, Scandinavians and many more combatants working out and training together; it was a warrior's dream.

'This is just practice,' said Imogen.

'This is flippin' brilliant,' said Charlie, as did most first-years.

'You see, over the centuries, warriors came together to learn different styles and techniques. It is quite amazing,' said Randle.

They just sat there transfixed. As Romans instructed Vikings, the English knight taught the Japanese samurai that the combinations were endless, and they looked highly skilled.

An hour passed as they observed the training, and the students were allowed to go and collect autographs.

On the way home, there were exciting conversations about the flume rail. Completely exhausted by their experience, most fell asleep on the flume.

David was sleepwalking, or, to be accurate, *sleep fighting*, much to the amusement of the ones who stayed awake, who teased him as he waved an imaginary sword.

It was done, and the day had finished more than satisfactorily for them all. It was a powerful experience that would remain with Charlie for a long time.

CHAPTER NINETEEN

SAMHAIN

The week had gone swiftly, and now all eyes were set on the primary weekend event: Samhain—the witches' New Year. Many magickal practitioners now adopt and celebrate this custom, which, as Charlie had previously read in the Plainlands, became known as Halloween.

The meaning of Halloween has been vastly misinterpreted, and it's been used to inject fear into Plainlanders. The Plainers see it as a time when only nasty ghosts, ghouls and demons come out to scare everybody. Watching terrifying films about monstrous beings with blood and gore reinforces the energy of fear. This is about as inaccurate a description of the festival as it gets.

Mage Brimstone-Greenback explained in the History of Magick class that Samhain was a critical and powerful time for most magick folk. It is when the veil between those who have been and those who remain is at its closest. In other words, the worlds between spirit and the living are at their thinnest. So, in some cases, it is possible to see those who have died, such as your guardians, relatives, friends, and pets. It is why it is also known as the Festival of the Dead.

He further explained that it was a time to honour and pay respects to our ancestors, a point White Eagle emphasised during another session. He also said it was a time of "reflection, contemplation and honour." He also said the spirit world is as much alive as this one. However, a celebration will be held afterwards, as it is the Magickal New Year.

Students were given a plain black robe with a red silk lining and a long hood to show respect for the occasion. They were also required to bring either their staff, wand or both. Finally, to honour the dead, everyone was supposed to get a photo of someone who had passed to the spirit realms. Charlie and his friends didn't know any close family members or friends who had passed on, so there was no need to take one.

The ritual was to take place at the Orberon as it was big enough to include everyone.

The evening arrived quickly. It was cold, and the stars watched as Charlie, Amanda, Tom, and Imogen donned their new robes and hoods and spoke.

'This is great—loving these robes,' said Charlie.

'Yes, it makes you feel all mysterious,' said Amanda.

'We need to head off soon,' said Tom, lifting his staff, pretending to be Cosmolos.

'But it's early,' said Imogen.

'I know, but I want to get a seat at the bottom so I can see,' said Tom enthusiastically.

'But it's freezing,' Imogen responded.

'It will be OK in the Orberon,' Tom reposted.

'I think we'll be fine,' said Charlie, defending Tom. 'Besides, I've never seen anything like this, so I want to get a good seat.'

'Oh, OK,' said Imogen, conceding.

'Don't worry, Imogen,' said Tom. 'I love Samhain. I hear they've had to adapt the ceremony as they do something new.'

Charlie felt the excitement, and he wanted to be there.

They had a quick drink and gathered what they needed for the ceremony.

There was an icy chill in the air, but there was no frost; you could almost feel the presence of the ancestors.

They walked past the courtyard and headed towards the Orberon.

The un-potted plants that had insulted them over the term had migrated to the greenhouse. Charlie found this amusing as he saw them leave with scarves around their necks, with little suitcases clutched to their little stick-like hands made from the roots.

A parade of tall torch posts lit the ground, fuelled by the tiny firedrakes that graced the magick world so readily. The torches' heat provided comfort from the cold, which Imogen particularly enjoyed.

Most students planned to arrive early; some had already entered the arena. The theatre had a new addition: four chimney towers at four corners.

The evening possessed a power, bringing about an extraordinary atmosphere. No one dared speak.

Charlie took one more look at the sky, impressed by the lack of pollution in the atmosphere. The stars looked like small moons everywhere, and you could see the natural range of colours that emanated from them so grandly.

As the students stepped into the arena, one could sense the excitement! To their surprise, the stadium was approximately a quarter full, with plenty of time to spare.

A sea of black robes looked down from the seats. It was an incredible sight that would usually look threatening, but for the words of Hegarty, who loved to wear traditional witch clothing.

She explained that wearing black was not evil as some Plainlanders had portrayed it as.

'Bar the stars, space is black,' she said. 'Is that evil? Nonsense, pure nonsense,' she uttered under her breath whilst getting angry. 'Yes, black is used by magick folk who follow the light and dark ways. What's different is the person underneath. There is a majesty in black, a power, an aura; it is like silk,' she said with eyes gleaming.

It wouldn't be long until the stadium was filled. Many had brought pictures of family, friends and pets. Everyone looked around at each other, observing.

Many teachers, including Cosmolos and Astrophos, didn't usually wear traditional witch clothing and did so out of respect.

Cosmolos tapped his staff on the ground three times for the few muttering, and all went quiet.

'Welcome!' boomed Cosmolos. 'We have a special evening for you, a different ceremony. It has the blessing of all the High Priestesses of the Coven of Witches from the Great City.'

The few conversations in the stadium fell silent as Hecate struck her staff on the floor three times. Hecate, Cosmolos,

White Eagle, Artuk Ra, Archimedes, Guildus Grey and Sedrick all stood in and around the centre altar table.

The centre table contained various objects, including four candles, an athame, a wand, a chalice, a cauldron and a book.

Incense burned impressively, providing a mist that added to the ritual's mystery.

Several pots containing different-coloured powders were also used to empower the ritual.

Hegarty picked up a besom, a witch's broom, and made sweeping gestures, uttering some words as she went around.

On the upward sweep stroke of the broom, it shuddered, and thunderous sparks could be seen and heard escaping from the bottom, generating a wave of energy that distorted the atmosphere.

The crowd shivered as the tide receded and rose—the temperature suddenly dropped.

A terrible phantom screech could be heard, and then a murky white apparition flew out of the stadium, making several people jump out of their skin.

Silence fell once more in the arena, anticipating what was coming next.

White Eagle approached the table, picked up a pot filled with a green salt-like substance, and hurled the powder outward as he walked around the arena in a deiseal (clockwise) direction. As he did so, an earthly smell was apparent.

On completion of the circle, there was a zip and crack—some previously unseen mischievous energy shot through the arena's top, flying into the sky.

Artuk Ra was absent but arrived in time for the ritual.

He approached the altar and took a container of red powder. Like White Eagle, he walked deiseal and threw the powder, causing a giant wave of fire to expand outwards.

Many students panicked, jumping out of their seats as the fire hurtled towards them. Remarkably, the fire passed through them, causing no harm, and they were relieved to see it head upwards and out of the stadium.

Cosmolos was next. He picked up a container filled with yellow powder, followed the same procedure, and threw it outward, causing the powder to transform into a strong wind.

The wind was visible this time, making the pupils' hair and robes flutter as they left the stadium. As it went, it created a haunting sound that echoed throughout the area.

Archimedes was the last. He took some blue powder and threw it outwards, which then turned into ocean water. The water passed through and around everyone, yet miraculously left everyone dry, flowing upwards and out of the stadium.

Sedrick stepped forward, holding a long, thin sword that looked different from his fighting weapon. It was a ceremonial sword with a star embedded in the centre of the handle and several engravings marked down its blade.

He raised the blade above his head, extended it eastward, muttered Swedish words, and circled three times clockwise.

A powerful, invisible energy filled the arena, making everyone feel weightless. The power was paradoxical, as it had a calming effect and made the students feel energetic.

One by one, the housemasters approached each corner to summon the energy of each quarter.

Cosmolos started in the east.

'Guardian of the north watchtower, Lord Aldebaran, King Paralda, sylphs, zephyrs, gargoyles and pegasus. We summon you to come forward to guard our circle and witness our rites.'
Hail and welcome!'

The entire arena replied, 'Hail and welcome.'

The tower at the top of the stadium suddenly sprang to life, similar to the school's central east tower.

As it reached its peak, it made a thunderous sound, and Charlie could see everything he had summoned in the almost liquid air.

Artuk Raa went to the South Corner and said:

Guardian of the South Watchtower, Lord Regulus, King Djinn, Ra, dragons, Alsvidr, Arvakar and salamanders. We summon you to guard our circle and witness our rites.

Hail and welcome!'

Again, the arena responded with, 'Hail and welcome.'

As soon as the words were spoken, the tower burst into flames, burning ferociously and proudly, displaying its power.

Next, Archimedes walked forward to the west corner and said:

'Guardian of the West Watchtower, Lord Antares, King Necksa, Poseidon, Neptune, nymphs, tritons and merfolk.

We Summon you forward to witness our rites and guard our circle.
Hail and welcome!'

'Hail and welcome,' the students and teachers responded.

Suddenly, the tower came alive as the water enveloped it, gushing outwards majestically.

Last was White Eagle, who said a few words in Native American before saying,

'Guardian of the North, Lord Fomalhaut, King Ghob, dwarves, elves, gnomes and faeries. We summon you to guard our circle and witness our rites.
Hail and welcome!'

Everyone responded the same again.

This time, the tower burst into soil, vines and branches; the stadium vibrated as they wrapped tightly around the watch tower.

After the fourth quarter was summoned, a magical event occurred—the elements combined to form a giant pentagram that pulsated with power and provided the ultimate protection.

Hecate then went in front of the altar and said:

'I call upon the source of all things,
The great spirit of all, the ether and universal power to which all have been created. We call on you to witness our rites and guard our circle.
Hail and welcome!'

'Hail and welcome,' they all repeated.

As she did this, a glowing orb appeared around the stadium, encompassing everything and binding the elemental forces, working together as one.

Charlie realised that magick had much to offer and was a great ritual similar to the one in the forest. Suddenly, voices could be heard humming, and the sound reverberated all around, gradually getting louder.

Mage Siddhartha emerged from one of the entrances, where the Orberon sporting contestants were preparing to compete. Dozens of Buddhists, chanting profoundly and powerfully, followed him.

As they sang their mystical song, all the photos everyone had brought with them lifted and levitated towards the arena's floor near the centre altar table. Everyone was amazed.

'This is amazing! Superb!' said another student.

As the pictures floated down like snowflakes, more chanting could be heard.

White Eagle, who had previously left the arena, returned with dozens of his tribe members. They were singing a beautiful and unique Native American song, which harmonised with the Buddhist chanting.

It was a lovely moment of unity and respect between the two cultures.

The chanting subsided, and Hecate spoke.

'Welcome to this most sacred and revered festival in the Magickal calendar. It is a time for reflection and honouring those who had come before but are always here with us, watching, guarding, encouraging, and guiding us; may they never be forgotten. Blessed Be—So mote it be.'

'SO MOTE IT BE,' repeated the crowd.

The chanting progressively got louder again, and everyone shut their eyes, their minds transported by the mesmerising tones.

Charlie closed his eyes. He was amazingly relaxed and drifting to what seemed to be a far-off place. He felt comforted as he'd never felt before, though the air was becoming chilled and tingly.

Minutes had passed, and Charlie was in a tranquil place. He heard a voice: 'Charlie.' His heart kicked-started, beating quickly; he dared not open his eyes. ' Your name, Charlie, use it,' said the voice.

Charlie couldn't contain himself, and he opened his eyes. In a flash, something vanished.

Was that the shadowy thing? He asked himself. He concluded it couldn't be as there was some green and silver to it—he was confused. First, a shadow was following him, but now, this other entity existed.

Charlie closed his eyes but couldn't get back into a relaxed state.

As time passed, the chanting naturally subsided, gently bringing them out of their trance-like state.

Typically, some had gone to sleep and were snoring. David was one of them, and Tom had unwittingly decided to join him.

After some encouragement, the ones who had fallen asleep woke up.

The teachers and housemasters who worked the ritual reversed the summoning spells by respectfully saying 'Hail and farewell' to all they had called. Sedrick then went widdershins (counter-clockwise) with the sword pointing forward and slightly downward. The stadium returned to its normal state.

'Now go and enjoy your party,' said Hecate. 'Feast, celebrate and come midnight—a Happy Witch's New Year to you all.'

'HAPPY NEW YEAR, HEADMISTRESS,' they all shouted.

Charlie leads Amanda, Tom, and Imogen down a passageway to tell them about his experience.

'You're kidding,' said Tom.

'I'm not,' said Charlie.

'Not again,' said Amanda.

'Use your name for what?' quizzed Imogen.

'I have no idea,' replied Charlie.

'Well, as long as it doesn't mean getting into trouble again and me rescuing you,' said Amanda.

'Do you think it means my or magickal name?' asked Charlie. I suppose I'll find out at some point.'

'HEY, CHARLIE!' shouted a voice.

Charlie's head instantly turned. It was Emmanuel and Bruce.

'Hey guys,' Charlie chirped.

'Hey Bruce,' said Amanda.

'Hello again,' said Emmanuel to Imogen.

They spent a few samutes discussing the ceremony, the Great City and many other things.

'Hey, come and look at this,' Bruce said after disappearing into the stadium.

They all hurried back in, and the room had magically transformed into a disco.

The first live performance was by Duran Duran—he couldn't believe it. It was his mum's and Charlie's favourite group, but they were popular with everyone. "The Reflex..." sounded out.

'I didn't know they were magick,' he said.

There were two stalls where people served food and drinks to the ravenous students.

Charlie laughed at the memory of his old school's end-of-term party, even though this one was much larger.

In the centre of the room, an unusual disco ball floated above. It emitted a light that produced various colours and shapes. Some of the light danced in time with the music before fading away.

The lights swirled around the students, shining brilliantly in different intensities and hues. Charlie was captivated by the sight and was convinced he saw colours that had never existed before.

The night was amazing; everyone enjoyed eating, drinking, and dancing.

Winston was on duty that night. He spent some time removing magical powder enchantments thrown at other children. It included Bruce, who created a powder that caused people to dance frantically mid-air and another that made them dance like a slow-motion monkey, who stooped over.

Other powders included stink bombs of every nasty smell, including *Goblin Breath* and *Bog Monster Dung*.

It was close to midnight, and the party was still in full swing. Charlie and his friends went out for a breath of fresh air, and the night was about to take another eventful twist.

'Five, four, three, two, one—Happy New Year to all!' A loud voice echoed from inside, followed by a roar.

Fireworks illuminated the sky with unique patterns and shapes as everyone exchanged hugs and handshakes.

Charlie was hugging Imogen when he noticed a shadowy figure.

'Look,' said Charlie, "it's back!" he exclaimed excitedly, 'the shadowy thing.'

'Just when I thought the evening was going so well,' said Tom.

'Please don't follow,' begged Amanda, but it was too late. Charlie took off like a racehorse from the starting gate. Amanda, Tom, and Imogen gave chase.

'Charlie, wait!' yelled Amanda.

They went back up the hill toward the school, then suddenly changed direction, heading past the Earth tunnel, the Fire block, and along the wooded area toward the Door of Mystery.

Charlie stopped. He panted, catching his breath, and the others turned up moments later.

'You can't be serious,' said Imogen. 'Remember what happened the *last time*.'

'Yes, I do,' Charlie said, 'though it's different this time...I feel it!'

'If you don't watch it, you'll be feeling the inside of that room. You could even be killed,' said Tom dramatically.

'Aye, how is it different?' quizzed Amanda.

'I don't know,' he said, 'but we are supposed to be here! Remember, I saw the other half of the prophecy,' said Charlie.

'You mean, you thought you saw the Half Prophecy,' said Tom bluntly. 'It could have been a trick of the mind.'

'I know, but everything that has happened has led to this point. It has got to mean something,' said Charlie.

'Well, what are you going to do? There aren't any spells or powders that work to keep the room open. What are you going to do that is different?' asked Tom.

'I'm not sure...there has to be a solution to entering,' said Charlie.

'Mages, wizards and most magick folks have tried, and you're telling me that you can get into the room safely?' said Imogen, trying to be realistic.

'Well, no one else has had a shadowy thing showing them the way to here. No one else has seen the Half Prophecy,' said Charlie defensively.

'Or so you think?' said Amanda.

'It could be a trick. The shadowy thing could be some enchantment sent to trick you,' said Imogen.

'I'd thought of that, though it can't be. I first saw it in my bedroom in my old house. It was there before I knew anything about magick or the magick world, for that matter. Why would someone do such a thing?' Charlie asked.

No one could answer. Charlie was convinced he had to be here and wasn't about to leave.

The door stood silent, as it had before. The leaves on the trees had fallen, and their remnants lay on the floor beneath them.

Charlie started pacing around, trying to think what to do, when he suddenly noticed something on the floor that glimmered slightly before the intersection of the pathway. Charlie approached.

'Where are you going?' said Amanda, concerned.

'Wait...I can see something,' Charlie said.

As he approached, the shimmering object became clear: tiny rocks arranged in a circle that said, *"Remember before you enter."*

'Remember what?' asked Imogen, who stood behind him.

'I don't know,' said Charlie.

They all tried to think about what Charlie was supposed to remember. Imogen smiled and said, 'I think I know what you're supposed to remember.'

'Really?' said Tom.

'Remember what happened tonight at the ritual. The message you got about your name,' said Imogen.

'That's right,' said Tom, getting excited.

'You could be right,' said Amanda. 'I'd completely forgotten about it.'

Charlie also smiled as the hairs on his neck stood up.

Charlie confidently strode towards the mysterious door and, without hesitation, activated it.

The door clunked with strange sounds and illuminated with a bright light from within.

'Wow, it seems brighter than before!' exclaimed Imogen.

Charlie took a deep breath and said his name—nothing happened. He then used his magickal name. With a clunk and a bang, everything went still.

Charlie's heart pounded frantically. Imogen and Tom grabbed Amanda's chair, breathing quickly, wondering what would happen next.

Charlie took another deep breath and walked a few more feet until he stood before the door. He placed his hand on the rounded handle and slowly pulled it down.

Charlie was ready to leap onto the post like last time, just in case it decided to suck him in.

Slowly, the door opened. Charlie stood stunned, not because the room didn't spin, but at what he saw: The Half Prophecy on a lectern upon a pulpit.

'Look!' said Charlie. 'I was right. Come and have a look,' he said excitedly.

Amanda, Tom and Imogen came quickly to observe.

'I don't believe it!' said Tom, his mouth aghast.

'I never thought this...' Imogen paused, completely transfixed by what she saw. 'My dad has told me all kinds of stories about this place. I can't believe it.'

'Aye! What does this mean?' said Amanda.

'I don't know, but it is the most important discovery. It is supposed to tell us what will happen,' said Charlie.

'Let's get it quick before the room changes its mind and starts spinning again,' said Tom.

Tom began to walk forward when Imogen suddenly grabbed him.

'Ah, what are you doing?' said Tom aggressively.

'Think about it,' said Imogen. 'Enchanted objects that use magickal names are for that person only. Why is this any different?' she said logically.

'She's right,' said Amanda. 'This is for you, Charlie,' she concluded comprehensively.

'Yes, this is for you, Charlie. For whatever reason, you have to enter. It wants you to go in!' said Imogen.

Charlie agreed to take on a task and readied himself for it.

He gazed at the Half Prophecy, which was neatly rolled up and had a glowing golden counterpart. However, the prophecy looked incomplete, like a phantom limb. It was placed fifty yards away in a strange-looking room resembling old mediaeval ruins.

Charlie took a deep breath, took another step forward, and shouted, 'Help!

'Oh, no! Charlie!' called Amanda.

The entire floor had disappeared, leaving a giant chasm. Charlie had fallen through, holding on for dear life on the top of what looked like a never-ending stalagmite several feet below them.

'Charlie...hold *on*...,' said Tom.

'I had thought of that, but it's slippery. Hurry! Do something!' Imogen and Tom looked at Amanda to see if her wheelchair could do anything.

'Sorry, I don't think this can do anything,' she said regretfully.

'Hurry, please, *I'm slipping*,' said Charlie desperately. Charlie couldn't cling on any further and let go.

Amanda instinctively grabbed her Purplewood wand and said, 'Venio Charlie.' Charlie froze mid-air, but he still wasn't coming back up. 'I'm not sure how long I can keep him,' she said, sounding strained.

Tom held up his staff and said, 'Venio, Charlie.' Charlie began to rise, though he still struggled.

'Venio, Charlie,' screamed Imogen. Suddenly, a golden cloud had formed underneath him, lifting him out of the bottomless pit.

As he reached the top, he flew out and landed before them. They were all in shock, shaking and sweating.

'Are you OK?' asked Tom gently.

'That was close,' he said, restoring his composure. 'I'm alive,' he said.

'Don't you ever...' said Amanda.

'I didn't know that was going to happen,' he said defensively.

'Whoever put that in there has gone to great lengths to protect it,' said Imogen.

'You are right,' said Charlie.

'We just need to figure out what to do next,' exclaimed Imogen.

'Figure out?!' exclaimed Tom. 'You must be crazy if you want to go back there.'

'Don't you see?' he exclaimed, 'It wants to be found!' Charlie's eyes gleamed with fierce determination as he contemplated the mystery at hand.

He was convinced that the elusive prophecy was eagerly waiting to be recovered, and he would stop at nothing to unravel its secrets.

With a furrowed brow and a steely gaze, he pondered how to get to the root of the problem. He thought there had to be a way and was determined to find it.

Before closing the door, they all attempted a summoning charm to retrieve the Half Prophecy, but with no luck.

Charlie looked at it again, shook his head, and closed the door.

All four returned to the Duran Duran concert, which was still in progress. They sang out loud, "Wild Boys!" and Charlie laughed, feeling like a wild boy himself.

They all had a drink, though the mood had changed.

Afterwards, they spent hours discussing the night, including the mysterious golden cloud that suddenly appeared below him.

The mystery was set to continue.

CHAPTER TWENTY

YULE

After Samhain's excitement, the rest of the term remained relatively quiet. The shadowy creature did not reappear, and no more strange voices offered guidance. Charlie was disappointed as he had been eagerly learning the art of magick, but he found himself yearning for something more. He longed for the excitement that came with exploration and adventure. The thought of unravelling a mystery and discovering the unknown sent shivers down his spine. Despite his dedication to his studies, he couldn't shake the feeling that something was missing. The magick he was learning was fascinating, but he secretly craved the excitement of the unexpected, the thrill of a journey into the unknown.

Charlie was developing a delicate hand at swordsmanship, which was more than he could say about his magick. He was still lagging behind the rest of his friends, and he couldn't figure out why. Maybe he was meant to be more of a knight than a magickal person, or perhaps the fact that he was born in the Plainlands somehow disadvantaged him. *How could it, though?* he thought.

Amanda was storming ahead in spell-casting, coming from the same place as him. *Maybe magick works best for Scottish people,* he thought, trying to find some way of explaining what was happening to him. Tom was doing well, even matching Charlie with his swordsmanship. Still, Charlie's kickboxing endeavours made him more agile and intuitive with his movements. Amanda was in love with the whole magickal world. She loved the healing arts and learning about the body's energy centres and the energy field. Once or twice, she could see various colours within people's auras, but these were momentary glimpses.

Amanda also saw the same group of ghosts at the front of the school on her first day and couldn't figure out who they were. They seemed different from the spirits she had seen before, more vibrant. She also joined the knight training and found she could do more than she thought.

Imogen was a lively young character who was passionate and knowledgeable about the magick world. Due to her privileged upbringing and the countless stories of adventure her father had shared, her magickal abilities were excellent, and she could compete with anyone in knight training. Her father and growing up with two older brothers helped develop her skills.

Artuk Ra, a teacher and mage who had been absent for most of the year, finally started teaching. He always wore his favourite gold-threaded clothing and carried a long golden staff with a diamond at the top. He appeared powerful, rarely showing emotion, but his teachings showed his brilliance.

His knowledge of astrology was comparable to that of Cosmolos and Astrophos. He was also an expert in levitation and mathematics.

During his class, he showed the first-year students how the pyramids were constructed using advanced levitation techniques to move the massive bricks. He used tiny blocks to create a miniature version of a pyramid to demonstrate this. Afterwards, he effortlessly rearranged the classroom to his liking, moving all the pupils and furniture. The students were left in awe!

*

It was the end of the term, and winter had settled in. Everyone was getting ready to leave for their homes and families.

Charlie was particularly excited to see his mother, brother, and sisters. This holiday season was extra special for him as he would visit his grandfather in the Plainlands. So much had happened during the term that he had almost forgotten about the Plainlands.

Cosmolos arrived to take Charlie, Emmanuel, Amanda and Bruce back to Wondle using his magick carpet and Portus spell. Charlie and Amanda said goodbye to Tom and Imogen.

'Well, Charlie, Amanda, see you after the holidays then,' said Tom.

'Yeah, guys, I can't believe Cosmolos is taking you back... you lucky things,' said Imogen.

'Cosmolos only wants to see us all together to see how we are doing in the Magicklands,' said Charlie.

'OK, we must take the flume rail to reach the Great City,' Tom explained. I am meeting Mum, Dad, and younger

Brother Peter there. We plan to go shopping together and return to our home in the City of Elderick. I will be helping Dad in his shop throughout the Yule season. Imogen is lucky enough to live in the Great City.'

'What does your dad do?' asked Amanda.

'Oh, he's a jeweller,' said Tom. 'He's had the business for years and wants me to take over someday. I'm unsure if I want to, but there is plenty of time to decide. Dad would like to move his business to the Great City someday, though there is a lot of competition. He is excellent, and it'd be fantastic if he could open a shop there,' he said, being wishful.

'Wow, that sounds amazing!' said Amanda.

Cosmolos beckoned them as it was time to go.

After saying their goodbyes, they set off on his magick carpet. Seconds later, they arrived at their home in Wondle.

'Charlie!' shouted Victoria as she ran over and hugged him and Emmanuel.

Charlie and Emmanuel hugged their sisters, and everyone was excited about reuniting.

They spent a few days getting reacquainted.

Much to his mother's annoyance, Charlie loved his bed, expanding it and using it as a trampoline.

Charlie and Emmanuel spent hours discussing stories and demonstrating spells.

They were amazed at how good their mum was at spell-casting. Charlie was frustrated, as even his brother was very proficient at magick.

Victoria wasn't sure about their knight training lessons and thought they were dangerous. *Dangerous?* Charlie thought! She had no idea of the real danger he'd been in, and he dared not tell her about the little adventure he'd experienced.

Victoria explained how Andrew joined the Scottish Highland Knight Division of the Orberon. He showed them the many bruises he had gotten in practice and was very proud of them.

As for the Orberon, it would be a year before Charlie could enter the school league. Although Emmanuel, who was old enough, joined a team called the Warlock Bandits—they were doing quite well.

The introduction of Minnie, the Family Elemental Brownie, was a surprise. Not to mention the little elemental helpers who assisted Minnie with the chores. Charlie was happy to learn that Minnie could help the family from anywhere and made a note to call her to school. He thought it unusual not to thank a brownie, as it can be offensive.

Charlie was impressed by the elementals tending to the garden. However, Victoria explained that she was still unsure about using elementals in magickal workings. She explained that the head of school had told them to wait and not use them—"Don't run before you can walk," the headmaster would say.

The visit to Cosmolos was pleasant. He was ecstatic with how they had settled in, but it was time to return to the Plainlands.

In the Magicklands, the equivalent of Christmastime was called Yule, and it was celebrated on December 21st. Christmas adopted some older Yule traditions, including the Yule log, using red and gold decorations, and more. However, Charlie was fascinated by the festival's many other aspects.

Having made the journey back to the school, Eric eagerly awaited to take them back as it meant he could start his holiday.

Eric and the old guard knight exchanged deathly looks, grunts, and grumbles, much to Charlie and Emmanuel's amusement.

'I wonder what that is about,' said Charlie.

'No idea, but they do not like each other,' chuckled Emmanuel.

'Right, before we leave, I must warn you of something we call Dimension Lag,' said Randle.

'Dimension Lag?' said Victoria, sounding worried.

'Yes. Well, you see, 'I want to remind you that you have fully integrated and exposed yourselves to our world. I don't want to sound condescending, but our world is much more advanced in energy than the world you came from. You will notice that the Plainlands will be quite different now, and unfortunately, you will feel the difference,' Randle said with regret.

'How?' asked Charlie.

'You'll soon see,' said Randle, loosening his tie. You could tell his Plainland clothing wasn't as comfortable as his robes.

The gate opened. Eric and the guard gave each other some final scowling looks as they left, turning right.

'Get out of the way, you stupid Plainer,' said Eric, taking his frustrations onto the oncoming driver.

'What's that smell, Mummy?' asked Lucy whilst trying to cup her nose.

'That's the Plainlands,' said Randle. 'It is both the physical and mental pollution that ravages the atmosphere,' he said coldly. 'You are all used to the clean and clear air back in the Magicklands. It comes as quite of a shock, I'm afraid.'

Eric drove them back to their old house and disliked what they saw and smelled.

Many neighbours came out to see and greet them, asking questions, most of which they could not answer.

'I've got a headache,' said Charlie.

'Me too, brother,' said Emmanuel, feeling fuzzy.

Everyone was experiencing headaches, dizziness, disorientation, and balance issues. They started sneezing and having runny noses.

Randle handed them tissues and headache tablets but couldn't give them a Percy drink because magick was absent in the Plainlands.

'This is rubbish,' said Charlie.

'It certainly is,' said Emmanuel.

'I'm glad we don't have to stay here long,' said Charlie.

Having unloaded their belongings and frightened off the neighbours by saying they had flu, they headed for the front door.

As they proceeded, the air around them became increasingly oppressive, weighing down on their chests like an invisible burden. It was as if they were submerged deep underwater, struggling to breathe with every passing moment. The atmosphere was thick and suffocating, making it difficult to see or move around easily.

Charlie gazed around and felt a deep disgust and shame for living in a world that was so drab and unappealing. The area lacked vitality; it was dreary, colourless, filthy, and lifeless. The term "Plainlands" couldn't have described this region of the world better.

Feeling depressed and sad, Charlie and Emmanuel headed to their old rooms to unpack. They lay in their beds, wishing their headaches would disappear.

'I wish I could go back,' said Charlie. 'I will send a scroll; er, I mean telephone Amanda in a bit. I bet we're all feeling the same.'

'I bet,' Emmanuel replied.

Seconds later, they fell asleep to escape the torture they were feeling.

After two hours had passed, they were woken up by a knock on their door.

'Are you two OK,' asked Victoria. 'You were both snoring very loudly.'

'Just about,' said Charlie.

'Yeah, the headache's gone,' said Emmanuel.

'I'm just going to get some fish and chips as we have no food,' said Victoria.

'Mum, thanks,' said Charlie, cheering up a little.

Charlie got out of bed and headed to the bathroom.

'Yuk,' he said, seeing the green mould on the walls and the crack in the window.

Charlie disliked the bathroom even more but couldn't figure out why. So, he quickly freshened up and headed downstairs. Minutes later, Emmanuel followed.

Victoria went to the local supermarket to purchase groceries and returned with fish and chips from their favourite chip shop.

Emmanuel put the TV on, and they were all keen to discover what was happening worldwide.

'Utterly depressing,' said Victoria. 'I feel sorry for the people who have to live in this,' she snarled.

Charlie discovered that his football team had underperformed, giving their city rivals a chance to win the Division One title, though there was plenty of time to change the outcome.

'Mum,' said Charlie. 'How long do we have to stay here?' 'Well, we have to go and see your Grandfather first, then we'll see,' said Victoria.

She instinctively read Charlie's mind: he wanted to return to the magickal world. However, Charlie was willing and happy to see his beloved grandad, which was his reason for staying.

Later in the evening, Charlie's old friend, Lee, popped around. Charlie was pleased to see him but frustrated that he couldn't say anything about the school. Because of what Cosmolos had said, Charlie mostly lied or exaggerated about his school experience.

Lee mentioned his new school and was pleased not to have Mrs Harrington in any classes. He also made new friends, Leo and Marcus.

Charlie had told him how friendly Amanda, Tom and Imogen were, but he was frustrated that he couldn't explain his magickal adventures. However, he knew Lee would have been jealous if he had known he was training to be a knight.

Emmanuel and Victoria met up with old friends, which cheered them up.

The following day, the family visited their grandfather, Arthur, at the hospital. He was delighted to see them and looked much better than the last time they had seen him. However, Arthur remained grumpy and complained about the hospital staff, claiming they were conducting strange tests on him; it was just his way.

The good news was that his cheeks had returned to their original colour and that he had gained weight. Arthur told them he had been home, and the hospital had brought him back for further tests. Nevertheless, he would be discharged and allowed to return home on Christmas Day.

They had just missed Grandma Maria by half an hour, which annoyed them. Nevertheless, the encounter brought much-needed cheer to their miserable return.

They were excited to create a memorable Christmas, as the entire family would be present. Charlie's grandfather expressed pride in him and the family. He gifted Charlie a chocolate bar, money, and a warm hug.

After the visit, they all went home. Charlie was bored with the same old television programmes they put on at Christmas, so he put on his warm Dragonstone coat, scarf and gloves and went for a walk. He thought visiting the local woodland was a good idea, as it reminded him of school.

Ten minutes after leaving, Charlie arrived at the entrance to the woods. He smiled as he looked up and stepped inside, relieved that no cheeky, unpotted plants were lurking around. He felt a subtle shift in energy as he walked, though not quite like the Magicklands.

The air was fresh and crisp, and Charlie took deep breaths to fill his lungs with the regenerating, clean air. Until that moment, he had never appreciated the qualities of nature in the Plainlands.

Charlie walked through the area, recalling that elementals were not bound by the agreement made centuries ago. He hoped to see a wood elf or gnome smoking a pipe, but he had not seen anything yet. He kept his eyes peeled, hoping to catch a glimpse of one.

As Charlie walked through the woods in winter, he noticed that most of the trees had lost their leaves, making them appear naked.

Suddenly, he spotted something in the distance. Charlie couldn't believe what he was seeing. 'No, it can't be...' he muttered to himself.

Charlie quickly ran towards it, but when he got there, he found nothing. It was like a shadowy entity had appeared for a moment and then vanished into thin air. 'No, surely not during the holidays,' he said.

Charlie took a step forward and heard a crunching sound under his feet. He looked down to see what it was and was surprised to find the two halves of the Prophecy deeply etched side by side in the soil. Additionally, there were two arrows at the top pointing inward. Charlie wondered what this could mean, so he got out a pen and pad and drew the image.

Charlie sprinted home. He opened the door and slammed it shut.

'Don't slam the door!' said Charlie's mum sounding annoyed.

'Sorry! I remembered I had to phone Amanda and ran a little late.

Charlie picked up the telephone and dialled as fast as the dial would allow. Amanda answered.

'Hi Amanda, how are you?' she said chirply.

'Hey, Charlie—it's great to hear from you! Yeah, it took us a while. It was awful adjusting back. I had a headache for the whole day. Anyway, wow! Are you still there?' Charlie explained what had happened and asked Amanda if she had any ideas.

'Wow! Amazing! I have no idea, though I will think!'

'I know! I can't believe this is happening to me! I don't get it! Anyway, have you done much?'

I've met up with some of my old friends, though I'm missing Imogen and Tom,' said Amanda.

'Yeah, me too... It won't be long now, though,' said Charlie. I know, I can't wait to spend some time in the new house. I also want to explore the town,' she said.

'I know everything here seems boring now. There is too much to see and do back home. When we get back, we should meet Imogen and Tom and see whether they have any ideas about what this means,' said Charlie.

'I agree,' said Amanda.

'Hey, Charlie, I have to go. Mum has dinner on the table and is moaning for me to get off the phone. She says to say hi, as does the rest of the family.'

'Great. Say hi back, please. Take care, Amanda, and I'll see you soon—bye!'

Buoyed by his conversation with Amanda, Charlie also enjoyed his unexpected homework, which involved finding another clue to the mystery of the Half Prophecy.

The rest of the holiday went better than expected, though he'd spent longer in Eanor than Charlie would have liked.

Chapter Twenty-One

AN IMPOSSIBLE MISSION

It was time to head back to school, but Eric had problems with the coach. Someone set some engine gremlins loose under the bonnet, wreaking havoc, so he had to stay longer in the Magicklands. It took a few days to find the mischievous elementals, clear them, and make repairs. Eric was furious and requested a knight guard to protect the coach whilst he wasn't there.

Passing through the school gates felt like a rebirth when inhaling the fresh and vibrant air of the Magicklands.

Despite being winter, the atmosphere was distinct, and they would soon return to Wondle.

The delays resulted in the Stuarts only staying two nights at their home.

Charlie got out of bed the following day and looked out the window. Robert, the little garden gnome, was sitting on his deck chair, wrapped in a warm winter coat, smoking his pipe.

The garden was quiet and peaceful, and Robert enjoyed a relaxing winter afternoon. As the other elementals tended to the winter plants, he stood still, deep in thought, his eyes shutting intermittently.

It was snowing. The fields behind the house seemed to stretch forever. All blanketed in pure white snow untouched by mankind.

Charlie quickly gathered his belongings for the arrival of Cosmolos, who was eager to transport them to and from school.

Charlie, Emmanuel, Amanda, and Bruce said their goodbyes and were transported back to school by Cosmolo's staff. This time, there was no magick carpet; they stepped through a portal.

About a hundred students had witnessed the group's arrival. *Why would such a prominent Mage do such a thing,* they thought? You could only imagine the gossip that followed.

It took Charlie and his friends a short time to unpack. When Charlie looked around his room, he realised it was quite a mess.

He reached for his staff and said the following incantation:

'I summon the elemental brownie named Minnie to come forth and help me. Please assist me.' Within a flash, the elemental appeared with one of her helpers before him.

'Hello, Minnie. It's nice to see you again. As you can see, I need some help.'

'Hello, Charlie. No problem. I'm glad to be of assistance,' said Minnie. Charlie stopped short of saying thank you to avoid offending her.

He then pulled out a delicious pastry with butter and sugar topping and placed it on the side. Minnie's eyes widened and shined appreciatively.

'OK, Charlie, I know what needs to be done,' said Minnie. Without warning, Minnie vanished into thin air.

Then, a familiar whooshing sound came—it was a scroll.

Hey, Charlie, Tom here; are you back? Please send me a reply.
Ta—Tom. ;o)
PS – Imogen has just arrived also.

Charlie replied instantly, and they agreed they would all meet for a snack and catch up.

Charlie arrived late at the canteen, whilst Amanda, Imogen and Tom sat laughing and discussing the holidays. Amanda told Tom and Imogen about Charlie's experience in the Plainlands.

'Hey Charlie, whatever is happening, this thing you keep seeing is very persistent,' said Imogen.

'What do you think it means?' asked Tom.

'I don't know. It was the complete scroll with two arrows pointing inwards towards the centre—very strange. Do you have any idea, guys?' said Charlie, hoping for inspiration.

'No,' said Tom and Imogen.

'Ah, but of course,' said Amanda.

'What, you know what it is?' Charlie asked.

'No, but what do we have here that could help us?'

Charlie, Tom and Imogen all looked confused.

'We have the Room of Reflection to help us,' she said.

'Of course!' shouted Charlie, leaping off his chair, catching the attention of everyone in the room.

'That is a fantastic idea, Amanda; I can't believe we didn't think of it before,' said Charlie.

'Yeah, I've never used the room before, though my Dad swears by it. He's thought of various fighting strategies using it,' said Imogen.

Charlie, Amanda, Tom and Imogen left for the Room of Reflection. They walked through the old corridor and entered, sitting at the designated soundproofed seating cubicles.

As they sat, the stained glass lit up. It was remarkable! It shone as if it were daytime in the middle of summer. The glowing yellow meant logic was needed to solve a practical problem.

Charlie and his friends were surrounded by potent concentrations of light, which became more intense as they closed their eyes.

They had a clear intention of what they wanted to achieve in the room, and as they did so, a sweet fragrance filled the air, helping them to relax. This was vital for Charlie, whose mind tended to be very excitable.

Please help me, he thought. Charlie decided to use Mage Siddhartha's breathing technique, which worked.

Ten minutes passed, and gentle music was playing. The soothing tones were designed to aid their thinking.

Charlie could see the image of the whole prophecy with the two arrows he'd seen on his walk in the Plainland woods. The arrows began to move backwards and forward, confusing him.

After an hour, the lights dimmed, and the sweet scent and music vanished, returning the room to its normal state.

'Well?' said Charlie. Did you get anything?

'Not really,' said Tom.

'Me neither,' said Imogen.

'I'm afraid I didn't get much either. I kept seeing it, but the image kept distorting, separating and coming back together,' said Amanda.

'Oh well, all that happened in mine were the arrows kept moving backwards and forwards, meeting in the middle,' said Charlie.

'In mine, I saw one arrow pointing inwards,' said Tom.

'My prophecy didn't make much sense either. One part kept floating away and coming back,' Imogen struggled to explain.

They went back into the common room to drink hot chocolate before bedtime. Tom particularly enjoyed this, so he had two glasses.

They continued to discuss what they'd seen, trying to make sense of it all, but couldn't. They thought it best to sleep on it, and then the answer might present itself in the morning.

The next day, Charlie woke up to Sebastian's alarm.

'Charlie, you're running late,' a voice blasted out, so Charlie jumped out of bed and rushed to the bathroom.

A cacophony of horns, shouting and screaming filled his accommodation block, signalling that everyone had overslept.

Charlie didn't have time for breakfast and headed straight toward his lessons, meeting with Amanda, Tom and Imogen.

The day's lessons went as usual, with Siddhartha teaching them meditation using the flame. Gildus' teaching style was confusing, alternating between sarcastic responses and helpful hints.

Despite his efforts, Charlie struggled with spellcasting and found the sessions tiring. Even David Moarns was getting proficient, and Helen was at the top of the class. Nevertheless, Charlie was determined to persevere in the art of spellcasting, so he made sure that he attended every lesson and society practice.

In the evening, Charlie was enjoying his knight training even more, sparring regularly with Tom.

Sedrick monitored Charlie closely and assisted him whenever he could. "I see you're doing well in the Orberon practice," he told Charlie, motivating him to train harder.

However, he needed to address the issue of improving his magick, as you had to be good at both to become a magickal knight.

Along with some theoretical aspects of knight training, Charlie enjoyed learning the knights' code of honour of loyalty, fairness, and respect. He understood you should use your skills to lead and help those who need it. "These are some of the signs of true nobility. Those nobles who can't live by these rules do not deserve such titles," said Sir Barnaby.

The weekend quickly arrived, and Charlie reunited with his brother for an early morning kickboxing sparring class, enjoying Emmanuel's company. Emmanuel was his equal, and they regularly scored points off each other. Tom couldn't attend practice because he wasn't feeling well, and

Imogen and Amanda were too tired, wanting to relax in the morning.

After enjoying the luxury of the power shower, Charlie was hungry, so he helped himself to a serving of Gobby Brisks and drank a Percy Refresher Juice.

After noticing the open door, he turned and entered the Room of Reflection. The room displayed a multispectral light show that eventually settled on a beautiful purple.

Charlie sat in the empty room, closed his eyes, and took deep breaths. He could hear his heart beating.

Charlie couldn't understand why his thoughts returned to when he saved little Tommy at his old school. They became erratic and wandered all over the place.

After ten minutes had passed, he saw something unexpected: one half of the Half Prophecy was hovering outside the Door of Mystery. Then, the scroll was replaced by a key, and the image faded. The Prophecy then appeared as a jigsaw puzzle, with a picture of an opened padlock replacing it shortly after. The padlock closed and locked. Charlie was astonished!

The vision was so vivid that Charlie felt like he was watching a film. Shivers ran down his spine, and he was initially confused. Then he proclaimed, 'I got it!!' He celebrated, thumping the air.

Tingling with excitement, he ran out of the room and up to Amanda, Imogen, and Tom's bedrooms, banging on their doors and telling them to come to his bedroom immediately. It was about the "you know what"—something he called it so that others couldn't understand.

Charlie ran to his room, pacing up and down, agitated that they weren't there. To emphasise the urgency of his request, he sent them scrolls with royal trumpet sounds played by an animated trumpeter.

Five minutes had passed, and there was a knock at the door.

'Enter,' said Charlie. The door opened. They entered, though Tom was still in his Dragonstone bathrobe, blowing his nose.

'What's the matter, Charlie?' asked Imogen.

'I've got a stinking cold,' said Tom, changing the subject.

'Oh, you should come to the healing arts class: we always need volunteers to practice,' said Amanda.

'Well?' Imogen said, bringing their attention back to why they were there.

'It's the Half Prophecy, said Charlie. 'The two pieces have to be united, but there is more,' he said.

'What do you mean?'

Charlie explained what had happened in the meditation room.

'So why the jigsaw,' quizzed Amanda.

'Well, that's obvious: a jigsaw is something you *put together* if you catch my drift.' said Charlie.

'Of course, how silly of me,' she said, half-asleep. 'So, the jigsaw represents the two halves of the Prophecy coming together. Yes! Clever!'

'The key?' asked Tom.

'Yes, it's something that opens something,' said Charlie.

'Very funny, Guildus,' reposted Tom.

'Remember what Siddhartha talked about: images are symbolic, representing something or a situation,' said Charlie.

'Yes, I get it!' cheered Imogen.

'It represents the scroll, but it's the key to getting into the room,' Charlie wisely said.

Yes! Of course! It must act as a trigger to stabilise the room; the final component to enter!' replied Imogen, enlightened.

'Yes,' said Charlie. 'I'm sure of it,' he said convincingly.

'So, the padlock means the prophecy must be locked together. It's just another way of showing you that it has to be united, or it will lock once united,' said Tom. 'Brilliant, this will be the discovery of the entire magickal world—I'm sure of it.'

'Hang on a second,' said Imogen. 'Just one small point—how on earth do we get the other half of the Half Prophecy? It is one of the most protected objects in history! My Dad is one of the knights protecting it, and, ooh, let me think, Sedrick is another. Not to mention Brutus and the many other top-class knights,' said Imogen.

That was it. Charlie's bubble had burst. Imogen was right; how on earth could they get to it?

Charlie looked deflated, Amanda shook her head, and Tom rubbed his head and blew his nose.

'There must be a way,' said Charlie.

'We could just ask the museum,' said Tom.

'Yeah, right...Hi, I was wondering if I could borrow the Half Prophecy for the afternoon. I'm sure that would go down a treat,' said Imogen sarcastically.

'OK, let's all take it in turns to be Guildus then,' said Tom, slightly irritated by her remarks.

'I think there must be a way,' said Amanda positively, 'but it will need some thinking. I mean, this has all happened for a reason, so there must be a solution to the problem,' she said, thinking logically about the situation.

They all spent some time trying to generate ideas but reached a dead end.

'I agree,' said Tom. 'Well, maybe we should use the Room of Reflection again and see what happens.'

'Great idea—after all, it is where I found the solution to the prophecy,' said Charlie. 'We're going to work this out!' he exclaimed, rousing Tom and the others.

*

Two weeks had passed, and there was still no solution.

It was Friday, and the snow showed some sign of dissipating, from five feet to four feet.

Trudging through the snowflakes, they headed to the magickal powder class. It was popular because of all the great things you could do with the powders and the eccentric and loud Professor Lambert Snuffle.

He was teaching them powders that make you move quickly, which is ideal for combat situations.

'It is important to add some Mind Quickness Powder so your mind can coordinate and get up to speed with the body. Otherwise, you might end up moving so quickly that you run into a wall or, worse, feel a sword in your gullet,' he said, laughing.

'Yeah, really funny,' said Tom, scrunching his face.

Amanda had become unusually distracted while exploring the hundreds of powders in an advanced potions book she had obtained from the drawing room. Suddenly, she came across something that could help.

'Humm, yes, it could work...but no, there is still a problem,' she muttered.

'What are you talking about?' whispered Charlie.

'Well, I think I might have an idea of how to get the Half Prophecy, I mean, the one that's going to be in the museum,' whispered excitedly.

'Really—how?' asked Charlie.

'Yes, really, but there are a couple of problems that need working out first,' she said excitedly.

'Is there something so captivating that it commands all of our attention?' bellowed Professor Snuffle.

'Sorry, sir,' said Amanda.

The professor continued discussing the importance of using the right blend of ingredients when concocting Dual and Triple-Purpose Powders: 'Otherwise, it could "spell" disaster,' he said at the top of his voice, laughing at his joke.

The final lesson ended, and they returned to their accommodation to prepare for a society spell-casting session.

'Tell me, Amanda,' said Charlie instantly.

'I can't—not yet,' she said.

'What's going off?' asked Imogen.

'Yeah,' said Tom, 'you two have been arguing since we left powders.'

'Amanda seems to have a plan regarding the, *you know what*, and she's not telling me what it is,' he said grumpily.

'Really!' said Imogen.

'I'll be impressed if you have, Amanda,' said Tom.

'I've told you, a couple of things need working out. I don't *want* to say anything, just in case I am wrong,' Amanda said defensively. 'I don't want to get people's hopes up,' she concluded.

'Well, if you tell us, we can surely put our minds and ideas together to figure it out,' said Charlie, but Amanda said nothing.

Charlie grunted, knowing he wouldn't get anything out of Amanda, but his curiosity grew. After all, what kind of plan could she possibly have in trying to obtain the Half Prophecy?

Charlie tried several times to prise the cunning plan out of her, but she didn't reveal anything.

They all returned to their rooms to prepare for the evening's spell-casting society, followed by food and a game of Wizopoly.

Charlie was pacing around the room, unable to settle, so he decided to head out again. Meanwhile, Amanda ran around like a crazed werewolf, trying to get her plan together.

Charlie heard Amanda moving around on the floor below. Then, she entered Imogen's room. Charlie waited a few moments, then went to investigate.

'But I can't,' said Imogen disbelievingly. 'He'll kill me if he finds out,' she said.

'But it's the only way,' said Amanda.

'It's a great idea, but where?' asked Imogen. 'Surely they would realise straight away?' she said.

'Humm, I see your point,' said Amanda, disappointed. 'I'll have to give it some more thought. There must be a way, there must be!' said Amanda, sounding as determined as Charlie.

Imogen started to move towards the door. Charlie panicked and ran speedily upstairs, back into his room. Tom opened his door to see all the commotion, saw nothing, and returned to his bedroom.

'What was that about?' said Charlie to himself. He was left none the wiser and even more frustrated.

During the society spellcasting practice, Charlie's thoughts were scattered across the universe to the point of being dangerous. A flying moonometer caught Felicity Phelps straight in the face. Charlie tried to send it to Tom on the other side of the room but gave her a black eye. Felicity just scowled at him while everyone else laughed.

They sat in the common room, eating sandwiches, when David came over with the main Wizopoly board.

'Here you are,' he said, beaming. 'I finally won a game,' he said happily and left.

Amanda's turn was to roll the dice and enter the game. She stayed a bit longer than usual and then emerged frowning.

'How rude was he?' she said, describing a stubborn barterer in the game. 'Relaxing in the inn was nice, but how much did he want?' she said, muttering about her Wizopoly encounter. 'By the way, I've got it—I have a brilliant plan,' she said boastfully.

CHAPTER TWENTY-TWO

HUNT FOR THE PROPHECY

Subsequent months seemed to pass quickly, but Amanda's plan couldn't have been better timed.

The special powders required the utmost accuracy, and they all helped concoct the powders for the ultimate and most daring mission.

The situation was difficult because they couldn't consult Professor Snuffle for advice. After all, he would have certainly become suspicious.

Charlie, Amanda, Tom and Imogen sat in the main canteen.

Amanda and Imogen ate healthy breakfast cereals, whilst Charlie and Tom had full English.

Charlie had gotten egg yolk on his nose, which Tom found amusing but didn't tell him about. After five minutes, Amanda pointed it out.

'Spoilsport,' Tom said.

'Thanks, Amanda,' said Charlie as Tom frowned.

'Not long now,' said Imogen. 'This had better work. I've taken a huge risk in getting this,' she said, holding a pouch with an object inside.

'I know,' said Amanda. 'I'm amazed you managed to get it,' she said, beaming.

'Yes, thanks,' said Charlie.

'I must be crazy,' said Imogen.

'I agree,' said Tom. 'Complete madness, by the way—what's the worst thing that could happen?'

'I never thought this moment would come, but the trip got delayed for a third time,' said Charlie.

'At least this has allowed us to do a little reconnaissance. Remember, timing is everything,' said Imogen.

An announcement came over the tannoy for all the first-years to meet Winston and Randle in the courtyard.

They made one final check of their equipment and then headed out.

'Hello there, first-years; glad you could make it on this magnificent day,' said Winston with his usual swagger.

'Yes, what a marvellous opportunity this will be to go and see the Half Prophecy. It is a true part of history, a rare and outstanding opportunity to see such an extraordinary artefact,' said Randle, who was more excited than anyone about the trip.

'Once you're there, you'll have an hour to spare before the rest of the students arrive,' said Winston.

'Yes!' said Charlie, shaking his fist with approval.

Fifteen minutes later, they were all on the flume, travelling toward the Great City.

Nerves of excitement abounded as they realised they were inexperienced first-year students attempting to steal the rarest magickal item, which experts had sought after for centuries.

'Are you OK, Charlie?' asked Imogen.

'Yeah, I've just got a few butterflies in my tummy,' he said. 'Don't worry; I've bought some *Percy Calm* and *Confidence* drinks, which should do the trick,' said Imogen.

'Good thinking,' said Tom, looking slightly paler than usual. 'I think I need the toilet,' he said.

Charlie closed his eyes in an attempt to meditate. Before he realised, the flume rail had arrived at the Great City.

'OK, first-years,' said Randle as they stood on the port station platform. 'Please be at the museum 30 minutes before seeing the artefact. You have two hours to explore!'

'Yes—and please don't be late; otherwise, you'll miss an opportunity of a lifetime,' said Winston as the group dispersed.

'OK, you two, you know what to do,' said Charlie to Amanda and Imogen.

'Yes, we certainly do. Good luck to both of you,' responded Imogen. They quickly drank their Percy drinks and departed hurriedly.

'Imogen hopped on the back of Amanda's chair. They rushed off to their destination at top speed in the fastest gear.

'Oi you—watch it!' yelled a passer-by as Amanda nearly knocked him over.

'Sorry,' she shouted back. Moments later, they arrived.

'Are you sure about this?' asked Amanda.

'Yes, it took a while, though he told me himself. There will be a change shortly. We must hurry before they get here,' said Imogen.

Imogen got out of her little pouch and pulled out a key. She opened a gate, and they sneaked inside, moving cautiously along a corridor and into a changing room. It was crammed full of knight armour belonging to the English mediaeval knights.

'We must hurry,' said Imogen sharply.

Amanda took out her magickal powder and applied it to the armour. Suddenly, a patter of footsteps and deep voices passed by the window on the opposite side of the room to the door.

Imogen flung herself to the ground, and Amanda hid in a corner. They were both about as nervous as they could be.

Imogen was starting to look a little like Tom did earlier.

'Have you finished?' whispered Imogen.

'Just one more, but it is the one by the window.' Unfortunately, two knights now stood discussing the Orberon outside the window.

Amanda put some powder on her hands. Then she retrieved her wand and said, 'Reverto corpus.' The powder flew off and scattered itself over the appropriate area of the armour.

'That's it!' whispered Amanda.

'Great work—let's go,' said Imogen.

Carefully, they opened the door, exited, and then closed it.

Imogen climbed on the back of Amanda's magickally adapted wheelchair, moving swiftly towards the exit.

They had walked a few yards outside when, suddenly, someone interrupted them, asking, 'Excuse me, what are you doing?'

'Hello, Sir Richard,' said Imogen.

'Oh, hello there, Imogen,' said Sir Richard.

'Have you seen my father?' asked Imogen coolly.

'No, he's in the Political Quarter, my dear. Shouldn't you be at school?' said Sir Richard, sounding suspicious.

'We're on a school visit to see the Half Prophecy at the museum,' she said.

'Oh, wonderful—I've seen it before—it is a wonderful item!' he said. 'I'm going to be on guard there very soon,' he said as the two girls looked at each other with wide eyes.

'Who is this young lady?' he asked.

'Oh, this is Amanda, my best friend,' replied Imogen.

'Hi,' said Amanda, beaming at what Imogen said.

'Hello, there! Pleased to meet you!' said Sir Richard.

'Er, OK, I'll send a scroll to my father later,' said Imogen. 'See you soon,' she said, trying to make haste.

'No problem. You sound in a hurry, so I had better not keep you any longer. This way,' said Sir Richard, escorting them out of the gate. He was oblivious to what they had done. 'Have a wonderful day,' he concluded.

Amanda sped off with Imogen still on board, heading back towards the city to rendezvous with Charlie and Tom.

*

'How do you think they have done,' asked Tom.

'Well, I hope,' said Charlie. 'Otherwise, we might get into serious trouble,' he added nervously.

Charlie huffed quietly, and Tom just let out a nervous sigh, looking at the vast building before them.

Randle would describe the museum's architecture as neoclassical. The Greco-Roman style inspires the building, though it has a brownish tinge instead of white marble.

Many steps lead up to the main entrance, and massive pillars extend along the front of the museum.

'Look, the museum is open,' said Tom.

'Do you think they will let us in?' asked Charlie.

'I don't see why not,' said Tom. 'There are other parts that are open to the public.'

Charlie and Tom walked up the steps. Looking up, they saw that the building seemed to get bigger the closer they got to it. They walked inside the central archway, and statues of ancient, powerful wizards dominated the area.

'They're big,' said Charlie, looking very impressed.

'They certainly are,' said Tom. 'That is the great wizard, Valdore. He was the one who stayed to oversee the building of the Great City. The other is Romanus Oberon. I bet you can't guess what he invented,' laughed Tom.

'Humm, now let me think,' said Charlie jokingly. 'Why is it spelled Orberon and not Oberon, like his name?

'I'm not entirely sure, but I think the first arenas were sphere-shaped. Look, Charlie,' said Tom, quickly distracted. 'The knights have arrived with the scroll inside a plain wooden casket.'

'Crikey,' said Charlie as he and Tom ran into the museum and started to look at the dwarven tapestry.

The knights marched in with the casket. It was small enough to be carried by one person.

The museum curator, who resembled a funeral director, approached them enthusiastically.

'Wonderful, wonderful—at last, it is here; follow me,' he said gleefully.

Charlie's heart stopped.

'Oh no, we didn't think,' he said. They hadn't accounted for an additional person being there.

'Oh, cripes,' said Tom. 'What are we going to do about him?' he said in a panicked tone.

'Well, we can't stop now. We'll have to blag it,' said Charlie. 'We'll be quick enough to get away from him.'

Charlie and Tom followed the knights and a curator into the museum, keeping their distance. They then walked down to some lower levels.

'Hope it's not far,' whispered Charlie to Tom.

'Yeah, it seems a bit creepy down this part,' Tom replied.

The corridor was dimly lit, with only crackling flames glowing the way. They walked past strange three-dimensional portraits of scary-looking people, ancient weaponry, and antique trinkets.

Charlie and Tom dived behind hideous-looking statues as they entered an area that suddenly lit up.

Charlie and Tom raised their heads slightly to see what was happening. One of the knights placed the casket on a magnificently crafted display.

'Let's look,' said the knight wearing golden armour, as Charlie had never seen before.

The other knight, wearing traditional silver armour with strange red markings, opened the casket.

'This is exquisite,' said the knight.

It was dark. Charlie reached into his bag, pulled something out, and opened it.

'What security enchantments are we to use?' asked one of the other knights.

'Oh, just the usual,' said the man in the golden suit.

Charlie grabbed his wand and said, 'Aktivieren.'

Within a single breath, the knights had vanished.

The curator looked confused, panicked and scared.

He was about to raise the alarm when Tom raised his hand and said, 'Reverto scorpus,' pointing at a small piece of marble on the floor, which hurtled through the air, knocking the curator out.

'Brilliant Tom—let's get it,' said Charlie. 'We've only ten minutes left.'

They grabbed the other half of the prophecy and placed it securely in Charlie's bag.

Adrenaline had taken over, and they ran up the stairs as fast as possible, straight for the museum doors.

'Hey, you, slow down!' shouted an old man with glasses. They ignored him.

They arrived at the doors and saw Winston.

'Oh no, it's Winston and Randle with half the year,' said Tom as they flung themselves behind one of the giant ancient support columns.

'You know what we've got to do,' said Charlie.

Tom opened his bag and pulled out two powder vials. They sprinkled the powders on themselves and moved as fast as lightning.

Standing on the edge of the group, Giuseppe had his hair blown around as if caught in a storm due to their speed. 'Mamma mia!' he said, whilst his friends looked somewhat flummoxed.

They arrived at the flume station within minutes, and the quickness powder had worn off, and Amanda and Imogen confronted them.

'Have you got it?' Amanda asked. Charlie just lifted his bag and smiled.

'Brilliant,' said Imogen.

'There were a few scares, but we did it,' said Tom.

That very second, the Dragonstone flume arrived carrying the second-years.

They sneaked on, narrowly avoiding Emmanuel and Bruce, who exited the second carriage.

With a whip and crack, the flume disappeared, and they were off, heading back to school.

'I don't believe it,' said Charlie. 'I can't believe it worked. We'll be in more trouble if scroll doesn't work,' he said, fully realising the consequence of their actions.

CHAPTER TWENTY-THREE

NO TURNING BACK!

Pandemonium gripped the Great City. Knights from all nations were on patrol, searching and checking the city. Each quarter was on high alert and lockdown.

The knights guarding the prophecy were dazed and confused but joined the hunt. The governors of the Political Quarter were vexed and angry at what had happened. The curator was in floods of tears because the theft had occurred in his museum. Lord Balfour was particularly concerned and sent his investigation team. Even Cosmolos was requested to join the search using his powerful magickal abilities to help track down the thieves.

Nothing like this had ever happened in the Great City, hence all the shock and outcry. It was as if, at that moment, the light that encompassed the magickal world went dim, and a strange fear gripped the lands.

Charlie, Amanda, Tom, and Imogen returned to campus.

They hid in Charlie's room, jumping at every noise before sipping a *Percy Camomile Special* drink to calm their nerves.

Tom asked Charlie to turn on the TV, so Charlie obliged. He pressed 123 on the strange-looking control, and Magickal World News (MWN) came on.

'Reporting live from outside the museum is Graham Golden, an award-winning news journalist and popular personality.'

'Well, it still isn't looking good. The knights are embarrassed and refuse to comment, but the curator said this in a report earlier.'

'Why, why, would somebody do such a thing? It is a national treasure. Please, please return it, and you will be treated fairly. If not, may Zeus have mercy on you!'

'On the advice of Cosmolos, the High Inquisitor, Philbus has been drafted to lead the investigation. The likes of an inquisitor haven't been used since those dreadful murders several years ago. This is what he had to say earlier.'

'I am deeply saddened at what has happened. However, it is my duty to find the culprits who have done this. If you surrender the artefact today, nothing more will happen. If you don't, the inquisitorial team will unleash wrath upon you; it won't be pleasant.'

Tom turned off the TV, and they all gulped.

'This is serious,' said Imogen. 'I've heard of Philbus before; my Dad mentioned him. He is not a nice man at all.'

'Why would Cosmolos use or know such a man?' Charlie asked.

'I don't know, but he was around when the murders happened years ago. Dad never told the whole story.'

Charlie appeared worried that a friendly mage would associate with Philbus. However, he was glad he remained silent, saying nothing to him about the prophecy.

'What shall we do?' Amanda said in a shaky voice.

'Well, we've come this far. We'll have to see it through; there is no turning back,' said Charlie.

'Let us hope Philbus doesn't catch up with us,' said Tom.

The afternoon had passed quickly, and it was nearly dark.

Charlie looked out of the window and observed the sun had set.

'Right, guys, it's time. We must go now before it is too late,' said Charlie, sounding prophetic.

The news then reported that schoolchildren were seen running out of the museum.

It was a matter of time before they discovered what had happened and caught up with them.

Charlie opened his door quietly, listening for other students. Some doors could be heard shutting, and the TVs in most rooms were on with the news on full blast.

Tiptoeing out of the building, they scrambled towards the Door of Mystery, avoiding several teachers and pupils.

Charlie clung tightly to his bag.

They entered the small woodland until the frightening door faced them. Charlie and his friends walked cautiously towards it.

They crossed the threshold. The door began making its usual groaning and clanging noise, which seemed to get more frightening each time they visited.

Charlie said his magickal name, and a massive thud stopped their hearts; their anxiety was apparent.

A thunderous crack shouted at them from the sky, making them all scream. Lightning filled the heavens. The rain began to pour, and the winds picked up rapidly.

'Hurry, Charlie,' said Imogen.

Charlie entered the room and saw the prophecy gleaming before him, just as it had before. He then opened his bag and took out the other half of it.

Magickal energy filled the sky with glowing orbs as Philbus arrived.

Charlie held out the prophecy in his hands and stepped into the room. The chasm that nearly swallowed him previously did not appear, much to everyone's relief.

Charlie walked forward, followed by Amanda, Tom and Imogen. As Tom moved forward, he suddenly found himself trapped by an invisible force field.

'We can't come in. We're stuck,' said Tom, outshouting the storm.

'Charlie, use the powder!' shouted Amanda.

Charlie sprinkled some golden powder from a velvet pouch on the prophecy.

Suddenly, the room transformed into a long walkway, and Charlie couldn't hear anyone.

The landing had twisted and turned, with levels and pathways branching off in various directions. Corridors were located in each of the four corners of this massive and impressive enclosure.

The interior of the building was filled with mind-boggling structures featuring staircases that seemed to defy the laws of physics. The stairs folded and contorted, appearing almost impossible to navigate, with steps above and below.

The entire scene resembled a piece of art from the Futurism movement.

'I can do without this,' said Charlie, wishing there weren't more complications.

Exploring an unfamiliar room, Charlie suddenly noticed a faint glow emanating from the top left corner.

Excited by this discovery, he stepped forward and looked up at the light. However, he soon realised that he could not reach it.

Frustrated, he shouted, 'How am I supposed to get up there?' To his surprise, the light shifted to another part of the room, specifically to the middle right area.

Charlie attempted to walk towards it, but the light kept moving, leading him on a wild goose chase around the room. No matter how hard he tried, he could not catch up with it.

Charlie's frustration mounted as he chased the elusive light. It was as if Philbus had set up a cruel game to torment him. Every time Charlie thought he was getting closer to the light, it would shift to another part of the room, leading him to a dead end.

Despite his best efforts, Charlie returned to where he started, feeling defeated and discouraged. The glowing light was still there, taunting him with its elusive movements.

'I need some help,' said Charlie out of frustration. Immediately, the shadow creature appeared out of nowhere and stood ten feet away from him. It looked at him, staring intensely.

Charlie was having flashbacks to the first day he saw the school. He remembered the doorway that shouldn't have been there when he was in Hecate's office.

Then he thought of what Cosmolos had said, a spell to send them into the magick world.

Tingling went down his spine when he remembered it—but was he good enough to use it?

Armed with his staff, Charlie lifted it as Cosmolos did and roared, 'Apocalypton!' The prophecy began to glow. Its light filled the room instantly, transforming it into something more recognisable.

He was now outside another room. As he began to enter, he felt a paralysing sensation even more potent than the one he had experienced after the trip to Sherwood Forest.

Charlie shrieked in pain beyond toleration.

He felt sick and stumbled into the room, trying to reach the other half of the prophecy.

The temperature in the room plummeted suddenly, sending a shiver down Charlie's spine.

The silence was broken by an ear-piercing shriek that seemed to resonate within the walls.

Before he could gather his thoughts, he saw phantom-like apparitions, their dark cloaks flowing behind them in a macabre dance.

Their robes' black and blood-red fabric seemed to absorb all light, casting an eerie glow around them.

They floated towards him, their eyes fixed in a menacing stare.

They all landed and surrounded Charlie. Their eyes lacked any compassion, and a suffocating stench emanated from them. They had a translucent look but were otherwise human in appearance.

Charlie wished he wasn't there.

As one of the creatures approached him, it held up a twisted, evil-looking staff and cast a sinister spell.

Charlie then rolled in immense pain before sliding into profound paralysis.

Charlie saw one of the creatures move to pick up the prophecy, and it received a violent shock. Simultaneously, the prophecy was catapulted closer to its other half. The creature was furious and sent a shock spell through Charlie.

During his initial class, Charlie recalled Mage Siddhartha's advice: "Relax and don't put too much effort." He took a deep breath to calm his mind, and surprisingly, his paralysis didn't seem as severe. However, he was still unable to move.

Loosely gripping his staff, he opened his left eye and breathed calmly.

The creature was about to use a summoning spell when, with one last effort, Charlie whispered, 'Reverto scorpus.'

His visualisation was more precise than he'd ever seen before, and the prophecy flew to its counterpart.

Two creatures flew after it, but it was too late; the parchment landed, united once more.

As Charlie watched, a faint glimmer caught his attention from the corner of his eye. Gradually, the glimmer grew and began to take shape.

In the background, a silvery-white light began to form and grow brighter with each passing moment.

It was then he noticed a figure emerging from within the light.

As the luminosity faded, a tall man in white robes emerged. He exuded a commanding presence, radiating power.

His long white hair cascaded down his back, and a large beard adorned his face. His deep green eyes bore into Charlie with an intensity that seemed to see right through him.

Charlie couldn't help but feel awe and wonder at his appearance. It was as if he had come from another world yet seemed so familiar.

As Charlie gazed upon him, he couldn't help but wonder who he was.

The phantom creatures' deathly faces raced towards the man.

The wizard spoke with unwavering confidence, 'Evoco globulum lucis!' Instantly, a colossal white and silver sphere appeared over their right shoulder, and sparks erupted from it.

The sphere eagerly awaited its master's command, trembling with energy and power.

Foul black energy zipped towards the wizard to kill him, but he sent out some golden magick that ate up the dark mass.

A battle then commenced.

All the creatures were flying, sending foul energies toward the wizard. One of them vanished in mid-air. Seconds later, it appeared behind the wizard, holding some hellish dagger, and then went to stab him.

The ball of light that sat above him was suddenly alerted. Beams of energy reached out and grabbed the creature, shaking it violently and sending shocks through it. The entity screamed and managed to escape the orb's grip.

Another dark creature released vicious etheric entities to eat a magician's energy field. The magician cringed, then instantly sent a powerful jet of water and an electric charge through his staff, which automatically sent them scurrying back.

The entities then gathered, circling the wizard faster and faster. When he shouted, 'THURISAZ!', another mass of black energy surrounded him like a blanket of death.

A light circled the magician. Combined with the silver-white ball, it dispersed the energy like a nuclear blast. The light cut through the death blanket and forcefully flung the creatures back, slamming them against the sides of the room.

The creatures' attention was now focused on Charlie. One of the entities used a magickal summoning beam to pull him towards them, making him squeal in agony.

Then Charlie's arms were flung above his head whilst his legs were forcefully pulled downwards.

Every bone stretched, cracked and elongated like cruel torture from a bygone age.

Immediately, the wizard used a counterspell, pulling Charlie towards him. He then sent a silver-coloured energy burst to surround and protect Charlie whilst instantaneously repelling the dark creatures.

Without warning, the entities turned around and flew in the opposite direction, obliterating the door and disappearing into the night.

The wizard shook his head, looking disappointed, and then went to Charlie.

He leaned forward and touched his forehead with a finger—Charlie began to return to normal.

Charlie stretched to compose himself and stood up.

'Thank you, sir,' he said.

A kindly smile replaced the severe expression, and the man replied, 'No problem. Let us leave this place. ' They then proceeded to walk outside.

'Charlie!' shouted Imogen, Tom and Amanda.

Sedrick, Cosmolos, Hecate, Philbus and his inquisitorial lieutenants surrounded them.

'He's mine,' said Philbus, sending some chains flying towards Charlie.

Sedrick moves to protect Charlie when the wizard sends a blast of gold energy, destroying the chains and sending Philbus flying.

He was fuming and was about to attack back.

'Wait, Philbus,' said Cosmolos, stroking his beard.

'This boy is under my protection,' said the wizard.

'The boy is a thief,' said one of the knights.

'He most certainly is not. He bravely returned one brother to its sister,' said the man.

He showed them the prophecy, and they were united once more. The tear that existed between the two scrolls had disappeared.

'Who are you?' said Imogen nervously.

'My name...is Lord Gideon Mortus. Just call me Gideon,' he said coolly as stunned faces stared back at him.

CHAPTER TWENTY-FOUR
END OF YEAR

Charlie was fast asleep in his quarters after the night's shock, entirely drained by the experience, whilst Amanda, Tom, and Imogen were all sitting in Imogen's room. It was decorated with Orberon posters and pink bedding, which amused Tom because they were very different styles.

They couldn't get over what had happened, though they were happy that Gideon intervened on their behalf.

Gideon and Cosmolos went around the school, placing additional protection using ancient symbols magickally embedded into various rocks, trees and the earth. These were necessary, as the phantom-like creatures left were the Lordos, the closest of the Dark Keepers to Zordemon, who might be tempted to return to the school. Their Phantom-like appearance was due to a time drain drawing on their life force. However, they would now be able to regenerate into their human form.

Philbus, unhappy at Gideon's interference, left the school grounds and returned to the Great City, uttering curses that he was denied the enjoyment of an inquisition.

Hecate wasn't sure what to make of it, so she opened a vintage brandy to steady her nerves. Randle was also visibly shaken after being sent flying by the outbound Lordos, indulged in a tot of whisky.

Unfortunately, reporter Graham Golden, who had sneaked onto the school grounds following Philbus, Cosmolos and everyone else who had descended onto the school, captured some of the events.

By the morning, everyone would know of the great wizard's return, and it would certainly send shockwaves throughout the Magicklands.

Many questions would now be asked, and Gideon would soon have to go to the Political Quarter to explain what had happened.

At least Gideon could now answer some of the greatest magickal riddles, including what happened during that famous battle with Zordemon. What does the other half of the prophecy reveal? Why had he been cooped up behind the perfectly preserved door? Why were the Lordos in there with him? What consequences would this have on the magick world that had moved on uninterrupted for nearly a millennia? What of Charlie? Why was he so important in all this? Why did he receive the guidance and clues that led to this?

Gideon had much to adjust to after missing centuries, but it only seemed like a few weeks. He kept a low profile, avoiding everyone he wanted to. Some said he was seen with Cosmolos, but there was no way of finding the truth.

The next day, Charlie woke up with a splitting headache, and dozens of scrolls had fallen onto the carpet.

'Charlie,' said a voice quietly through the door.

'Enter,' said Charlie, and the door opened. Amanda, Tom and Imogen ran in.

'Are you OK?' asked Amanda.

'Yeah, I guess,' said Charlie. 'I have a bit of a headache, though.'

'I bet,' said Tom. 'What happened?'

Charlie explained everything in the Door of Mystery, including the battle and how Gideon saved him. He also clarified to Tom and Amanda the sensations he had experienced.

Imogen and Tom were shocked, while Amanda looked saddened that Charlie had gone through this process again.

Charlie found a positive; he performed a spell more than competently, which cheered him up.

'Are you going to tell him?' said Imogen.

'Tell me what?' Charlie said.

Tom turned on the television and went to the news station.

His face and Gideon's were splattered across the news before his eyes. A clip of Philbus being sent flying was looped, showing every conceivable angle of his confrontation with the great wizard. It was even projected out of the TV in 3D for extra emphasis.

'I bet he'll be happy,' said Tom, laughing at Philbus being humiliated live on TV.

'Yeah, I'm sure he'll keep his copy at home,' laughed Charlie.

Charlie wasn't sure what to make of it.

'Turn it up,' said Imogen. The report started.

'Well, as if the shock of the theft of the Half Prophecy by school children under the watchful eyes of the 'so-called' magickal knights wasn't enough, the return of Lord Gideon Mortus was undoubtedly the icing on the cake for the day. Some question whether it is him; after all, he supposedly died nearly a thousand years ago. Reports by some of the children who were awake at the time saw "strange things" flying over the school. However, these can't be substantiated. The question remains: What is the meaning of all this? What is the story behind this Plainlander magician in all this? I'm sure the truth will come out over time—back to you, Gloria.'

'Thank you, Graham....' Charlie turned off the TV.

'Well, you've made TV,' said Amanda, 'everyone certainly knows who you are now.'

Charlie ignored his mail and got ready. They all went outside to the main canteen when Winston came over and said, 'You four need to go to the headmistress's office to answer questions.'

They all looked worried as they accompanied Winston to see Hecate.

There seemed to be no let-up about the prophecy, but questions were bound to happen.

'We're going to get expelled,' said Tom.

'Crikey, do you think?' said Amanda.

'He could be right. After all, we did some pretty danger-ous things, not to mention stealing,' said Imogen.

'You're right,' said Charlie, and not for the first time.

Charlie looked dejected. *Surely they weren't going to suspend me? What were they going to do? Banish me to the Plainlands?* He didn't like this line of thinking.

Minutes later, they arrived at the headmistress' office.

Winston knocked at the door.

'Enter,' she said authoritatively. The door opened, and they all went inside.

Standing behind the desk was Hecate, with Cosmolos, Astrophos, Lord Balfour, Sir Sedrick, Sir Anton Shine—Head of the Magickal Knights section of the English Quarter, and Randle.

All these top officials staring at them was overwhelming, though Charlie was getting used to this.

'Can you pour us some tea,' she said to Randle.

They sat quietly, hardly breathing.

Hecate walked around the front of the desk and spoke.

'Last night saw a momentous event happen—something that seemed unbelievable—even for the Magickal world. After witnessing several strange events, we have seen the unity of the prophecy and the return of a remarkable wizard from our past. The world as we know it is about to change, and unknown forces are let loose. Many will embrace the change, and others will fear and fight it. Whatever happens, unravelling these strange mysteries and why the Fates have guided you to do such extraordinary things will take time. Ordinarily, you would be suspended without question for participating in highly illegal activities. However, on the one hand, you have shown cunning and ability way beyond your years. On the other, you have shown reckless behaviour that endangers the lives of yourselves and others. Honestly, I'm unsure whether to thank you or discipline you all. However, after an emergency meeting, we agreed that you should stay. But as an example to others, you will all face detention, be banned from attending society work, and a curfew will be put in place for two weeks beginning in the next academic year. There is another condition,' she said as Sir Anton Shine approached the front desk.

'Well, well. I never thought I'd see the day my best knights would be hoodwinked in such a fashion—and by children. Maybe I should recruit you into security—but first, I'll cut straight to the chase—how did you do it? Bear in mind that a less-than-honest answer or no answer will see you expelled from the school, and other punishments will be handed out. Well then—tell me,' he said commandingly.

'Well, sir,' said Amanda. 'We figured the prophecy needed to be brought together, and the one in the museum was crucial to stabilising the Door of Mystery. There was no option but to try and steal the other half. We knew the prophecy was going to the museum, so this was our chance.'

Imogen explained how she stole the key from her father and entered the guard changing area.

'So, what did you do then?' said Shine.

'Amanda sprinkled some teleportation powder on the armour.'

'Really, top-grade armour is quite impenetrable to basic spell work, including powders,' said Shine.

'Yes, said Amanda, 'but at the opening of the Orberon, Imogen saw one of the knights use some quickness powder to speed towards his opponent. She pointed it out, so I knew it could be used. The knight had a small opening in his armour where the powders could be thrown! It meant that any powder could be used on the inside. All the protection work is done outside to prevent anything piercing the armour,' explained Amanda.

'Quite brilliant,' exclaimed Shine.

'But why didn't the knights teleport as soon as they put on the armour?' Shine quizzed.

'Well, that was a problem. I came across a book, *Advanced Powder Making*, which said that the powder could be activated using a spell command,' she said.

'Amazing,' said Shine. 'OK, but where did you teleport them to? My knights could swear that they were there in the museum. They knew something was up when the curator vanished and then reappeared unconscious on the ground,' he said with a confused look.

'This was a massive problem, but my favourite part of the spell-working. If the knights had teleported elsewhere, they could have easily made their way back, raising the alarm, so we had to send them somewhere that would seem familiar. They teleported to the Wizopoly board,' she said. 'It has an identical replica of all the key places, road properties, etc. The new version is more detailed and realistic. The powder had about a ten-minute delay, so when it finished, they would teleport back to the same place.'

'That is incredible thinking, such cunning! So, it wasn't that the curator disappeared; the knights had disappeared and never knew it. So when they reappeared, it was like the curator had suddenly appeared again.'

'Yes,' said Tom. 'We didn't think the curator or anyone else would be there, so I used a sending spell to throw an object to knock him out. Sorry about that,' he said apologetically but proudly.

'Once we had the prophecy, we used some quickness powder. When we got outside the museum, we escaped without anyone seeing us, but we were seen running on the inside.'

'Well, that is the most incredible plan I've ever heard. Of course, we must make various security adjustments, but I take my helmet off to you all.'

Cosmolos quizzed them about the Door of Mystery. Charlie explained what had happened, although heads' turned when he said the room only went still when he used his magickal name and that he was the only one who could enter. This was why all his friends were on the outside.

However, Charlie purposely withheld the shadowy entity's help because he didn't want to reveal everything to his teachers.

In the meantime, the teachers and some political officers decided to remove information about the Lordos not to panic the public. Still, they knew the information would have to come out eventually.

Cosmolos twisted and stroked his beard reflectively, then walked away. He knew Charlie would tell him more but didn't want to tell the others. The meeting lasted over an hour, and then they left.

The hours passed quickly. Whilst he was out, Minnie and her helpers cleaned the rest of the room and helped with the packing. Later, his friends came over to see him.

*

'Put the TV on,' said Tom. Tom grabbed the control and turned on another channel. 'Great, it's Sun Beach City, my favourite programme. Quick, put your suncream on.'

'Why on earth would I want to put tanning lotion on?' asked a confused-looking Charlie.

'So you won't get sunburnt. With some channels, you get the full experience of being there,' said Tom. Charlie looked aghast as he smelled the sea air from the TV.

Later, Charlie showered, drank some warm milk and got into bed.

He was still unable to determine who the shadowy and silver entities were or why he was so crucial, which was maddening.

Charlie eventually fell asleep, dreaming about his exciting and frightening adventure.

When daybreak came, Charlie opened his eyes and screamed, nearly jumping out of his skin. A ghost-like figure of a child reached out to him and then vanished.

'Oh no, not again! What is it now!' said Charlie, shaking his head.

As the year ended, Charlie reflected on an incredible journey that had made them a central figure in one of the greatest stories ever to grace the Magicklands. Despite lingering questions, the Half Prophecy had finally been unified with its counterpart, paving the way for the return of a great legend.

With the world on the cusp of a transformation that would change it forever, Charlie felt confident that they had played a crucial role in shaping the destiny of the Magicklands.

The adventure continues!

ABOUT THE AUTHOR

Meet James, an extraordinary author from Nottingham whose journey of personal transformation and unwavering determination has inspired countless individuals. From overcoming mild dyslexia to pursuing further education and earning a PGCE from the University of Nottingham, James has continually pushed the boundaries of his potential.

Not only is he a certified gym and fitness instructor and a skilled massage and rehab specialist, but James has also discovered his remarkable singing talent and explored his musical abilities. He showcases his unique voice range by performing in various prestigious settings.

However, a transformative idea struck James during a seemingly ordinary train ride. Despite initial doubts, he penned down the concept that would eventually lead to the creation of the captivating Dragonstone School of Magick.

This literary sensation has touched the hearts of many.

James' commitment to inspiring young people to discover their creative abilities and reach their full potential is commendable. Through the City Council's "Relishing Reads" and his "Inspire" campaign, as well as library and school tours, he has passionately encouraged children to embrace the joy of reading and writing and unlock other avenues of creative potential.

Dragonstone School of Magick and the Magicklands is a mesmerising tale that symbolises personal growth and unlocks hidden potential. It stands as a testament to James' belief in the power of self-discovery and the resilience of the human spirit. His unwavering message of empowerment continues to resonate deeply with readers of all ages.

www.ingramcontent.com/pod-product-compliance
Lightning Source LLC
Chambersburg PA
CBHW010317100726
47906CB00006B/1025